INTO THE GREY

INTO THE GREY

A Dulcie Schwartz feline mystery

Clea Simon

severn
House

This first world edition published 2016
in Great Britain and the USA by
SEVERN HOUSE PUBLISHERS LTD of
19 Cedar Road, Sutton, Surrey, England, SM2 5DA.
Trade paperback edition first published
in Great Britain and the USA 2016 by
SEVERN HOUSE PUBLISHERS LTD

British Library Cataloguing in Publication Data
A CIP catalogue record for this title is available from the British Library.

ISBN-13: 978-0-7278-8627-9 (cased)
ISBN-13: 978-1-84751-731-9 (trade paper)
ISBN-13: 978-1-78010-792-9 (e-book)

All Severn House titles are printed on acid-free paper.

Severn House Publishers support the Forest Stewardship Council™ [FSC™],
the leading international forest certification organisation.
All our titles that are printed on FSC certified paper carry the FSC logo.

MIX
Paper from
responsible sources
FSC   FSC® C013056

Typeset by Palimpsest Book Production Ltd.,
Falkirk, Stirlingshire, Scotland.
Printed and bound in Great Britain by
TJ International, Padstow, Cornwall.

For Jon

ONE

'I could kill Roland Fenderby.'

As soon as the words were out of her mouth, Dulcie regretted them. 'I'm being hyperbolic, of course.' She looked around the small office, suddenly aware of the silence that greeted her words – and of the three people staring at her. Surely they would understand that her nasty outburst had not been literal, or even especially heartfelt, but rather the product of a particularly frustrating meeting.

The three faces that had turned toward her as she had stormed into the office did not, in fact, show the horror that her expostulation could have caused. Instead, they revealed varying levels of sympathy and amusement.

'Oh, dear!' Nancy, the departmental secretary, was the first to respond, with her usual motherly concern. The other two – fellow students, albeit undergrads – exchanged knowing glances as Dulcie felt the color climbing to her cheeks.

'I feared something untoward might happen.' Nancy had already risen from behind her desk. 'Would you like some more coffee, Dulcie?'

'Thanks, Nancy.' Dulcie let the plump older woman fill her travel mug. But even the rich brew – the best coffee in the university – couldn't assuage her mood. 'It wasn't – I shouldn't be so . . .' She caught herself. It was, and she was. Taking another sip, she tried to explain. 'It's just that Fenderby is such a toad. He even looks like one, except that no self-respecting amphibian would sport a comb-over like that.' Dulcie warmed to her subject. 'He's like a bloated Thorpe.'

'Dulcie!' Nancy's aggrieved tone stopped her short. Dulcie had forgotten that the secretary, for her own unfathomable reasons, had a *tendresse* for Martin Thorpe, the acting head of the department and her own thesis adviser.

'I'm sorry, Nancy.' Dulcie apologized as the secretary scooped out the beans for a fresh pot. 'I guess I'm angry with

Mr Thorpe, as well. He could have vetoed Fenderby's request to be on my thesis committee.'

'Maybe,' a musical voice chimed in. 'But it isn't exactly fair to focus on his appearance like that. You know he's had health issues, and I believe he's been trying to lose weight.'

Dulcie looked up, surprised. Alyson Beaumont was an unlikely champion for the offending academic. The undergraduate was one of the few Dulcie was advising this spring. A junior, Alyson was trying to decide on a topic for her own dissertation, and Dulcie had been spending extra time with her. As was fitting with the romance novel name and the soft, melodious voice that had issued the gentle reprimand, Alyson was quite lovely, with a cloud of golden blonde hair and eyes of clear grey. She was so beautiful, in fact, that Dulcie's friend Trista had labeled her 'trouble' when they'd met a few weeks earlier. And although Dulcie had chided her friend on her lack of sisterly sentiment – she hadn't wanted to call Trista sexist, exactly – she had to confess, the undergrad's protest startled her.

'I do. I'm sorry.' Dulcie admitted. Sometimes graciousness was the best policy, and everyone in the department knew that Roland Fenderby was prone to a stomach disorder that undoubtedly contributed to his pale and puffy appearance. 'But handsome is as handsome does, and you can't get me to say he's being fair.'

'What – what happened?' The fourth party in the small office, which functioned as the de facto gathering place for students in English and American Literatures and Language – chimed in, in a quavering voice Dulcie had gotten used to over the past few years. Because of his stutter, Tom Walls tended not to speak in public, but his concern for Dulcie had obviously won out.

'It's probably nothing.' Dulcie gave the thin young man a smile. She suspected Tom of having a crush on her, given the way he looked at her, and credited this with giving him the power to overcome his habitual shyness. 'Only, I felt he was being a bit unfair in his review of my latest chapter.'

It was worse than that. Far worse, but Dulcie didn't want to cause concern. Besides, she was a little embarrassed by her outburst, especially since her own student had witnessed it.

Dulcie was supposed to be helping Alyson with her undergraduate thesis, not instructing her in the horrors of life as a doctoral candidate. Then again, she mused, maybe it was just as well that the pretty younger woman learned the truth.

'Professor Fenderby has been added to my thesis committee,' she explained, trying to keep her voice level. 'At Martin Thorpe's request.'

Nancy had stepped out of the office, the empty coffee pot in hand. Still, Dulcie didn't need to elaborate. Winding up their junior years, both the undergrads should know by now that graduate students could form their own thesis committee – inviting senior scholars to read and advise them on their dissertation, guiding them through the process. Only this spring, just as Dulcie was finally completing the three-hundred-page opus that was the apex of her graduate career, Thorpe had brought Fenderby in. Her adviser had said it was to round out the committee. On paper, it made sense. Roland Fenderby specialized in nineteenth-century American political tracts, and Dulcie had linked her dissertation subject, the anonymous author of the underappreciated Gothic novel *The Ravages of Umbria*, to some political writings that had been published in Philadelphia at the very start of that century. But Dulcie suspected the reasons were more venal.

For starters, the move was sudden and a bit late in the process. Dulcie's dissertation was nearly done. More to the point, Martin Thorpe had been the acting head of the department for two years now, and the administration had still not named a permanent replacement for the long-vacant seat. Putting Fenderby on her committee was a way for Thorpe to cozy up to another tenured professor, and maybe win some support for his own bid.

'But–but . . .' Tom struggled to put his thoughts into words, his own frustration showing on his face.

'I'm sure Mr Thorpe had his reasons.' Nancy had returned with a pot full of water. 'After all, as I understand it, the committee is supposed to point out weak spots in your dissertation before you submit it. That way you can polish it up before your defense. Make it . . .' She paused to pour the water into the coffeemaker.

'Bulletproof?' Tom offered.

'Exactly.' Nancy didn't look up.

'Well, I understand the principle.' For the sake of peace, Dulcie wouldn't talk about Thorpe. Not with Nancy there. 'But the way I feel right now? Fenderby better be the one with the ability to withstand deadly violence.'

TWO

'Chris, you don't get it.' Dulcie had called her boyfriend as soon as she'd left, dialing as she strode into the Square. The white clapboard house that served as the departmental headquarters usually felt cozy, but today it was claustrophobic. Plus, Dulcie had to admit, the extra coffee had pushed her over the edge. She needed to walk, as well as to air. And while Chris, a graduate student in applied math, didn't face the same kind of pressures she did – quantitative work being somewhat less open to arbitrary criticism – he had been at the university long enough to understand the politics. Or so she had thought.

'No, I didn't get to argue.' Her raised voice was drawing stares. Chris's usual calm was tipping over to nonchalance, and pushing Dulcie to the opposite end of the spectrum. 'His criticism was written,' she explained. 'I mean, I will get to respond, but . . .'

She took a breath. The meeting had started off peaceful enough, Dulcie explained once again, doing her best to keep her own cool. At this point, as her boyfriend knew, she was meeting with Thorpe almost weekly to keep him in the loop about her progress – and to begin to prepare for the dreaded defense. After five years, Dulcie finally could see the end of her studies – and, while she didn't mention it now, the end to the life she'd shared with Chris.

Knowing that things would change – they had to, since she'd be looking for a job and he'd still be working on his degree – had made her feel a little better about missing the final deadline for the spring Commencement this month. Still, she was pretty sure she could finish up in the fall. And though it would feel odd to submit her dissertation in September, when everyone else was just starting the school year, she knew that would give her a bit of breathing room to figure out what to do next. Breathing room for her and Chris to consider their future together, either here or in another university town. Or, Dulcie thought with dread, commuting between cities as each pursued tenure.

That future had been weighing on Dulcie when Thorpe had called her. After all, she was nearing the end of her dissertation. As she reminded her boyfriend, over the last few weeks, she'd been putting the final touches on this penultimate chapter – a chapter she had intended to submit to *Studies in Pre-Modern Fiction*, the most prestigious journal in her field. She even had a title: 'Gender Issues in the Concept of Pre-Modern Authorship, a Discussion of Boundaries and Grey Areas'. It would be the last article before she submitted her dissertation, and the best, she told him. Or so she had thought.

'"The author's research seems a tad shallow."' Thorpe had read the note to her, partly, Dulcie suspected, so he wouldn't have to look her in the eyes. 'I'm afraid Professor Fenderby goes on a bit here,' he'd said. '"Either the candidate misunderstands the materials or she thinks such a flip handling will suffice to blind the committee to the gaping holes in her scholarship. We recommend that the candidate abandon this later material and focus more closely on the area she does seem to understand."'

Her adviser had looked up then, blinking. 'I'm sorry, Ms Schwartz. I did warn you, you know.'

'But—' Dulcie felt like someone had punched her in the stomach. 'But you agreed that I had reason to expand my topic. That I had made my case that the new manuscript – a manuscript I discovered – belonged in my thesis.' She paused to gather her thoughts. Yes, she was remembering correctly. 'You said you were convinced.'

'Yes, yes.' He nodded, apparently in agreement. 'I was, but perhaps that was my error.' He handed her the critique, brows knit over his watery eyes. 'You can be quite a forceful person, you know.'

'Well, you can be.' Chris's voice broke into Dulcie's recollection. From the laughter in his voice, she could tell he wasn't taking her seriously. A computer geek, he did tend to be of a more even temperament, a trait she usually admired. 'And you have broadened your topic quite a bit.'

'But the work led me there, Chris.' Dulcie had stopped walking. Equanimity was one thing, but if her own boyfriend couldn't understand the work she'd put in . . . 'You know I've done my research.'

'I know that, and you know that.' Chris sounded conciliatory now, his deep voice warm and calm. 'And even Thorpe knows that. You just have to convince this guy, too. I mean, he probably hasn't seen the papers you're working from – you only started that section over the winter, right? Maybe he hasn't read your other articles on the new stuff either.'

'Maybe.' Dulcie wanted to believe Chris was right. He was smart, and she knew he loved her. 'He's supposed to have read the rest of the dissertation, but maybe he's been sick again. This is the first chapter he's even commented on.'

'There you go, Dulce.' Chris's confidence rang out. 'He wasn't feeling well and, besides, he's a tenured professor. He can't sign on and not say anything, right? Maybe you can make a few changes and then he'll calm down. It's not like he's got an axe to grind.'

'No,' Dulcie agreed. Chris's optimism had jollied her into a marginally better mood. Marginally. 'If anyone's going to be grinding an axe around here, it's going to be me.'

'You mean to take this guy out?' Chris was chuckling again.

'If I have to, Chris Sorenson.' Dulcie started walking again. Academic politics were one thing, but she had a deadline to make. 'But only if you'll act as my alibi when they find Fenderby, bludgeoned to death with one of his own books.'

THREE

After she'd stuffed the offending note into her bag, Dulcie did her best to put the humiliating criticism out of her mind as she made her way to the Yard. Fenderby was a bother, but she would deal. With luck, he'd be taken ill again – suffering from one of those mysterious spells that seemed more appropriate to a nineteenth-century heroine than a contemporary academic. That wasn't a charitable thought, she realized with a twinge of guilt . . . and something resembling anxiety. Her mother, still a proud member of the counterculture, would have called her on it, citing the 'rule of three' that would have negative wishes rebounding three-fold back on their source. But surely she could be excused this time, Dulcie thought. Her research time was precious, and she had already lost too much of it in that stupid meeting. She didn't want to waste any more of it worrying.

The day helped. Spring had finally, belatedly, come to Cambridge, with a balmy freshness that reminded Dulcie more of her childhood in the woods of the Pacific Northwest than of a New England city. Maybe it was the moisture in the air, a welcome change after the dryness of too many overheated university buildings. Maybe it was the touch of color – new green leaves now joining the crocuses and daffodils along the sidewalk – but Dulcie found she couldn't hold a grudge for long.

Or maybe, she realized, as she walked through the brick gate that marked the campus boundary, it was because she finally had a clear vision of her future. Despite Fenderby's criticism, neither she nor Thorpe had any intention of delaying her thesis. As per university policy, she had filed all the necessary paperwork. All she had to do now was finish the actual writing. And no interloper, no matter how curmudgeonly, was going to stop her.

If all went well, she decided as she trotted up the stone steps of the library, she would put Fenderby's ridiculous complaint to rest this very day. So he didn't think her research had validity. She'd incorporate a few more citations, noting the specific documents she had already combed over so carefully. Rather than cut anything out, she would add references – quotes, even – until not even the fussiest of critics could question her conclusions. All she had to do was go over the original material again. And that would be a pleasure.

'Good morning, Will.' Dulcie had been waiting in line to check in when the white-haired guard had waved her over.

'Morning, Miss.' He held the access gate open, and with a twinge of guilt – she was clearly not disabled – Dulcie passed through. Such courtesies came with being a recognized regular at the library, and today of all days she was grateful for the privilege. Without looking back at the undergrads still queued up, she sprinted through the library's palatial lobby. All during the elevator ride down to the library's lowest level, she fidgeted, eager to get to work. But once she stood at the entrance of the Mildon Collection, the exclusive library-within-a-library where so many rare treasures were housed, she forced herself to calm down.

'Good morning, Mr Griddlehaus,' she paused to take a breath. 'And how are you this morning?' Thomas Griddlehaus, the director of the collection, was both a dear friend and a bit old-fashioned. Although she had come to know something of his own wild history, Dulcie automatically reverted to a slightly formal – or, rather, courtly – behavior around him. Much, she reasoned, as one would with any other small, sensitive underground creature with whom one had developed a trusting but respectful relationship.

'Well, I'm – I'm well, Ms Schwartz.' With a brief nod, the librarian ducked out of sight only to emerge with a ledger, which he placed, open, on the counter. 'I hope you've been enjoying this brilliant weather.'

'I have.' Dulcie signed in with a flourish and then scanned the previous entries, mostly the chicken scratch of people more used to keyboards than pens. They were scarce and did not include her student Alyson. They also, she noticed, were all dated from the week prior. 'Are you only opening now?'

'I was – we were – delayed.' Griddlehaus looked down. Not to check her signature, Dulcie was sure, but embarrassed, perhaps because of the unusual admission. The Mildon always opened right after the main library was unlocked, at ten.

'Is everything all right?' Her voice fell to a near whisper. 'Is your health . . .' Griddlehaus was decades her senior, but not, she would have thought, likely to fall victim to the predations of age. Still, her recent discussion of Fenderby had made her conscious of health and aging. If anything were to happen to the gentle man . . .

'No, no, please.' He looked up, blinking, his delicate white hands raised in protest at the idea. 'I am quite well, thank you. No, it was a bureaucratic matter that delayed me. Had you come by earlier?'

'No, I was – I had a meeting with Thorpe.' Dulcie felt a wave of relief. Relief, followed by anxiety. Having already lost at least an hour, she was ready to get to work. 'May I?'

'Oh, of course.' The librarian stepped aside, and Dulcie marched past him – only wavering when she came to the spare white reading area. There, most scholars would take a seat at the empty table, donning gloves from the box in the table's center and waiting for Griddlehaus or one of his few employees to fetch the books, manuscripts, or other documents that they had requested. But Dulcie had become such a regular and faithful scholar that recently she had become accustomed to proceeding into the storage area itself. Still, it was irregular and so she waited.

'May I?' she decided to ask, turning back toward her mousy friend. 'I need Box 978 again, I'm afraid.'

She smiled at her own request. Only last week, she had told Griddlehaus that she was done with this particular set of documents – fragments, really, kept in protective covering. As much as she loved re-reading the story they told, a thrilling Gothic adventure that had been lost to time, and as important as she felt the text to be – its depiction of relations between the sexes was really quite revolutionary – she had, she'd thought, moved on. With Griddlehaus's help, she had pieced together as much of the lost novel as she could. And while she hoped in the future to find more of the forgotten work – and maybe even finish its story – Dulcie had put it aside, focusing instead on the complex job of formatting her footnotes and tidying up her writing in order to submit this chapter to the scholarly journal.

But Griddlehaus didn't smile back. In fact, his wide eyes – unnaturally large behind his oversized glasses – blinked rapidly, as if holding back tears.

'Mr Griddlehaus!' Dulcie's voice rose in alarm, decorum forgotten. 'What is it?' She kicked herself. She had known something was bothering her friend, only she'd been too caught up in her own concerns to follow up. 'Please, sit. Tell me.'

He let himself be maneuvered over to the table, where he perched on the edge of one of the white chairs. Dulcie did the same, anxiety mounting as she waited.

'I had thought you were finished.' He pulled a handkerchief from his pocket and dabbed at his eyes. 'I was so hoping that it, well . . . that it might not have come up then.'

'What might not have come up?' Dulcie fought to keep her voice even.

A sigh bigger than the man himself, and Griddlehaus slumped into his seat.

'Mr Griddlehaus?' She couldn't keep the worry from her voice.

'I'm sorry, Dulcie.' He blinked up at her, and she felt herself go cold. The librarian never used her first name. 'I had no choice. I hope you understand. Professor Fenderby is a tenured professor and sits on the Mildon's advisory committee.'

'I didn't know that,' Dulcie whispered. Her mouth had gone dry.

'He's very rarely active, because of his, well, his issues.' Griddlehaus put the handkerchief away. The ability to clarify – even if vaguely – seemed to soothe him. 'However, when he summoned me and told me that Box 978 was to be sequestered, well, I had no choice.'

'Sequestered?' Box 978 was the acid-free container where the manuscript fragments were stored. It was the librarian's choice of verb that was confusing Dulcie. 'But why?'

Another sigh, not quite as big. 'He said the work was too important to be handled lightly. That it should be reserved for serious scholars only, under his jurisdiction. He was quite upset about it being in circulation. I told him that other scholars were using it. That it was central to your dissertation. And – I'm sorry, Dulcie – I'm afraid he implied . . . he called you a dilettante.'

Griddlehaus had not wanted her to leave. He'd begged her to stay, in fact, reminding her of all the other pages in the collection. 'Please, Ms Schwartz, I'm sure this will pass,' he'd said. 'Let me get you Box 803. You haven't gone through half of those pages yet.'

'No, I haven't,' she had agreed, her mind still reeling. 'But I've read enough to know that they aren't important. *As* important,' she added, sensitive to the gentle librarian's feelings. 'It's those manuscript pages I needed to see. Fenderby was the one who called my scholarship into question.'

None of it was making any sense.

'Surely, you have sufficient documentation?' Once he'd unburdened himself, Griddlehaus had recovered and now stood, worrying over Dulcie. 'You've been taking such excellent notes.'

'I guess.' She shook her head, confused. 'I don't have much more of the recovered text in my notes, but I could reference the box and envelope numbers. Only . . .' It was baffling. 'Why would he pull my material, especially when he said I hadn't done enough work?'

'Maybe he wants you to focus on something else?' Her friend suggested, his voice tentative. 'And he believes that he's doing you a service?'

That was when she'd realized she had to talk to Fenderby. Clearly, there had been some confusion. He was on her committee: he had to want her to succeed. If she could only explain to him *why* those pages were so important.

'Please, Ms Schwartz,' Griddlehaus had protested when she had made her intent known. 'I think you may be too upset right now.' Griddlehaus wouldn't lay hands on her, but he had stood before her, as if to physically block her.

'I am upset.' Dulcie couldn't deny that. 'But I need to clear this up.'

He hadn't been able to argue with that. He had even allowed her to use her phone to call Fenderby, against all library policy. When she had listened to his voicemail for a second time – he wouldn't have office hours till later that day – she had made her decision.

'I'm going to his house,' she said. 'He lives in one of those new townhouses just outside the Square.'

That was when Griddlehaus had really protested. 'Ms Schwartz, please,' he'd said. 'Intruding on an academic's private life . . .'

'What do you think he's done to me?' Dulcie's nerves were frayed. 'Besides, I think he wants me to beg. I bet this was his plan all along.'

'Oh, dear.' Griddlehaus blinked and bit his lip as she retrieved her bag and turned to go. 'Please, Ms Schwartz,' he said. 'Oh, dear.'

FOUR

*T*he Storm wail'd with unremitting Fury, tossing the poor Barque upon the Waves till she no longer knew Sea from Sky. Indeed, all seemed in Darkness as the Wind howl'd unabated. 'Twas all she could do to keep the Candle lit against the Night, and by its sputtering and guttered Light she penned what well could be her Final . . . her Final . . .

'Bother!' Dulcie sputtered as she stormed across the Yard, ignoring both the early blossoms and the startled expressions of those she passed in her fury. 'Her final who cares?' The words burst out of her, releasing, as they did, the forgotten word. 'Final Passage, indeed.'

Some of her anger was at herself. Although Dulcie could nearly recite by heart the content of those last pages – most of them, anyway – she knew that wouldn't suffice. The pages, which told of the heroine's 'storm-toss'd' voyage from England to America, had filled in a vital early part of the novel. They had also, she suspected, echoed the author's own travels and travails, fleeing a restrictive, if not abusive, relationship in search of autonomy. And while Dulcie had referred to the pages in her latest chapter for their metaphorical content – it was patently clear that the author was using her heroine's voyage to illustrate the movement of literary and political freedom from the Old World to the New – she had neglected to copy the text out fully.

She hadn't thought more detailed citations would be necessary. The chapter had been ready to send off, until Fenderby had put his two cents in. But even if she could work around his criticism, Dulcie had private reasons for wanting further access to this part of the manuscript. A secret suspicion that she barely dared articulate to herself about the anonymous author – a dream that she had been afraid to examine too closely, lest it dissipate. Which, she acknowledged, was one reason she was so angry not only with the annoying professor but with herself.

'That doesn't make what he did right!' The words burst from her mouth, scaring a squirrel, who dashed up a tree, and two undergrads, who looked as though they might like to follow. 'Bother!'

'*Now, now.*'

Dulcie stopped short. That voice – calm and warm – had apparently come from right behind her, a gentle murmur in her ear. She knew better than to turn, however, and simply froze in place.

'*Only kittens rush about so heedlessly, Dulcie.*' The voice was accompanied by a velvety touch, as if a furry face was nuzzling against her ear, softening the reprimand. '*Unconcerned with the connection . . .*'

The voice faded as a boisterous trio walked by lugging instrument cases. The cases outlined trombone, a trumpet, and – strikingly – a tuba. A brass band, Dulcie thought. The kind of music a cat would most certainly avoid.

'Mr Grey?' She kept her own voice low. She didn't see a

cat, and certainly the average cat wouldn't talk. But there was something about that voice . . .

'*Between predator.*' The voice picked up where it had left off. '*And prey,*' he said, as Dulcie got a sharp image of a cat – a long-haired grey – waiting by a crack for a mouse to appear. A mouse, Dulcie was suddenly aware, that might be quivering with fear behind that baseboard.

'*Only kittens.*'

With that, the voice fell silent. The visitation had ended. Although Dulcie couldn't have explained how exactly she knew that he had left, she felt her shoulders slump. Mr Grey – the spirit of her late, great pet – still came to her, especially when she was in trouble. But he seemed to manifest less often in recent months, as if his visits were winding up along with her studies. And although his presence was comforting – more comforting, she had to admit, than her boyfriend's latest call – his advice was, as usual, enigmatic and not immediately useful. Instead of providing solace along with the soft brush of his whiskers, in the time-honored feline manner, it was almost as if he had become another of her proctors, trying to teach her. Prepare her for being on her own . . . No, she couldn't think of that.

Besides, it wasn't as if he was telling her anything new. Yes, she had gotten upset, but she understood about working for the long haul. She hadn't done five years of thesis research hoping for a quick reward. And surely the wise grey spirit she remembered so fondly would want her to try to right the wrong done to her. To correct – she amended her own thoughts – a situation that had become misinterpreted. Surely even the placid feline philosopher wouldn't expect her to sit back and take this. If, as she feared, Mr Grey was fading from her life, surely it was because he trusted her to handle her own affairs. Wasn't it?

A skittering sound made her turn, thoughts of that frightened rodent fresh in her mind. But it was only that squirrel, once again attempting his descent from a nearby oak. He froze as Dulcie craned toward him, and for a moment their eyes locked.

'It's OK.' Dulcie said, hoping her tone if not her words would reassure the nervous creature. 'I'm not a predator. Not a cat, anyway.' She smiled at the idea, the rule of three echoing through her consciousness. Maybe there was something to her mother's ethos after all. First, do no harm. Or, at any rate, focus on your own work. And with that, Dulcie realized, she needed to continue with her errand. If the feline spirit intended her to do otherwise, he should have made his intentions a little less opaque.

While she was mulling this over, she had reached her destination and took a moment to look around. To a newcomer, the townhouses might have looked like they fit in. Grey clapboard, like the departmental headquarters, with neat trimming picked out in glossy black, the three-story buildings resembled classic triple-deckers. They even sported bay windows opening on to their pocket-sized front yards, as if someone had heard about Cambridgeport and tried to reproduce it with a more modern design. Maybe it was this quaint perfection – the granite steps leading up to each stoop, the shiny fixings on the shutters – that made them stand out. Maybe it was simply that Dulcie had lived here long enough to remember the rundown buildings where classmates could afford to rent, which the new development had replaced. But that kind of thinking was antithetical to the live-and-let-live philosophy Dulcie had espoused only moments before, and so, conjuring up the image of her mother – and, more importantly, of the great grey cat she still loved – Dulcie filed that thought away and approached the building.

'Fenderby/Wrigley.' Dulcie found the buzzer minutes later. Although the spiffy end unit had the right number, she had hesitated until she had seen the discreet label, the names inscribed in an understated script. A riotous garden – with daffodils already budding, lilies of the valley beginning to unfurl, and some kind of creeper making its way up the trellis – hadn't seemed quite right for the home of the sickly professor. Her resolve had been shaken slightly by Mr Grey's visitation. Was she the kitten or maybe, she wondered, the mouse? Now she wavered a bit more.

Fenderby as a singular burden – a smarmy authority figure who was throwing his considerable weight around – she was ready to face. Fenderby as a part of a couple . . . that was a different matter. Dulcie had forgotten that the balding academic had a spouse – wife or girlfriend, she wasn't sure. She had to be responsible for the garden, but unlike most of the faculty, he never seemed to refer to her, or to bring her around to any of the sherries or other parties designed to bond the department.

'Probably doesn't want us to see him as human.' Dulcie worked up her nerve. 'Probably thinks we're too far beneath him.'

She rang the bell, hoping to get the professor himself and not anyone who might humanize him.

'Hello?' The query that emerged from a small speaker – female, hesitant – dashed that hope. It also reminded Dulcie that she had indeed met Fenderby's significant other.

'Mrs Wrigley?' A girlish name popped into Dulcie's mind, along with a memory of a faded woman of indeterminate age dressed in some kind of outdated paisley outfit. It had been the Harvest Moon festival, an annual party that had morphed from a post-mid-term break into one of the grander events of the fall semester. Patty or Peri or, no, Polly – yes, that was it – Polly Wrigley Fenderby had seemed quite taken with the theme, going on about her own undergraduate days. 'Polly Wrigley?'

'Fenderby,' the voice corrected her, and Dulcie rushed to explain.

'I'm sorry. We've met,' she said. 'This is Dulcie Schwartz. I'm looking for Professor Fenderby.' She paused. Silence. 'Is he here?'

Another pause, and then the building's door buzzed. Dulcie grabbed at it. Either Polly Fenderby had gone to get her mate, or she had misunderstood. Either way, Dulcie was beginning to regret ever coming to the academic's home.

'Hello?' Dulcie called up the stairs. The building retained the tall, narrow outlines of the triple-decker it had replaced, and she stood now in a small foyer. 'Anyone there?'

In for a penny, in for a pound. She climbed to the first landing. There, at the end of the hall, a door stood slightly ajar. 'Hello?' Dulcie rapped softly as she called. 'It's Dulcie.'

'Come in.' The voice didn't sound much more animated than it had through the intercom. If anything, it was flatter and, despite the words, not very welcoming. Still, she'd come this far. Dulcie pushed the door open and stepped inside.

'Hello?' Dulcie looked around to see a woman, standing back from the door as if waiting for Dulcie to make the first move. Any doubt Dulcie might have had about who had let her in was dispelled – this was the woman who had accompanied Fenderby to that party, and even on this gorgeous spring day, she was as drab as Dulcie remembered. Her hair, a reddish brown dulled with grey, was pulled back into a ponytail, the paisley skirt replaced by orange corduroy overalls that only emphasized how much the woman wearing them had faded. But clearly they hadn't been worn for fashion, clashing oddly as they did with the green thermal top she had on underneath. It was a leafy hue picked up by the stains on her knees, as well as the gloves she was holding. Polly Fenderby was responsible for the garden out front. And likely one out back, thought Dulcie, which would explain not only her appearance but also the delay at the door.

'I'm sorry to have disturbed you.' Dulcie looked around the landing. Sure enough, it seemed to be given over to horticulture, with packages of seeds and a small spade lying on a low cabinet. Several young daffodils – they looked small, anyway – lay on a sheet of newspaper. 'Were you planting?'

'These are trash.' The woman rolled up the paper, crushing the young sprouts. 'Invasive species.'

'Oh, I'm sorry.' Dulcie didn't understand the animosity in the woman's tone. Then again, she wasn't a gardener. 'It looks like you've got quite a green thumb.'

'It's a serious interest, you know.' With her arms crossed over the overalls bib, the faded, dirty woman looked like a stunted flower herself, leaves folding in on themselves. Or, perhaps, she was an unhappy plant, recoiling from the first blush of spring. It should have been an amusing image, the colors playfully bright. But as Dulcie stood there, the woman's scowl deepened, furrowing her brows.

'Of course.' Dulcie's reply was reflexive, as if she'd disturbed the cat. Maybe it was the brows, but she almost

expected a hiss. At any rate, she decided that any further
pleasantries would be useless. 'I was looking for Professor
Fenderby?'

'I heard you.' The same flat voice. 'You're his student, the
one working in the Mildon.'

'I am.' It wasn't a question, but Dulcie felt compelled to
respond. At least the woman wasn't hissing at her. 'I was
hoping to speak with him?'

'He's not here.' The intent was the same. 'He's probably in
his office.'

'You could have said that when I rang.' Dulcie was confused.
She took a step back, reaching behind her for the door. 'I'm
sorry to have bothered you.'

'You didn't bother me,' said the woman. 'I'm glad you came
by, no matter what your excuse.'

'My excuse?' Dulcie took another step back. She was
beginning to be frightened.

'Yes, your excuse. But I'm grateful,' the woman continued.
'You see, I wanted to see you for myself. Like you wanted to
see his home. See what you have been trying to destroy.'

FIVE

D ulcie tried to respond. She opened her mouth.
Attempted to form words. But nothing came and so
it was with another series of confused apologies – 'I'm
sorry, really. I shouldn't have come' – that she retreated out
the door and flew down the steps. It wasn't until she was
halfway back to the Yard that she stopped running. When the
events of the day hit her, she felt suddenly overwhelmingly
exhausted.

'Mr Grey?' She looked up at a sky that was still the same
deep blue as it had been an hour before and at trees with the
same hopeful green buds. 'Can you explain – any of this?'

A half block up, a new coffee shop had put benches out
front in anticipation of the milder weather, and Dulcie made

her way over to collapse in the nearest one. 'Is this what you were warning me about?'

There was no response, forcing Dulcie to draw her own conclusions. The woman had to be ill, she decided. That was the only explanation. And Dulcie had disturbed her at home, obviously aggravating a pre-existing condition. No wonder Professor Fenderby didn't take her around much – and Mr Grey had cautioned her. If only she had listened. Instead, she'd gone off like, well, like Esmé. The tuxedo cat might no longer technically be a kitten, but the way she careened around the apartment she shared with her two humans was as heedless and energetic. And, to be honest, often as destructive. No wonder Mr Grey had tried to stop her. She should have heeded his advice.

Well, she was being still now. And as thoughtful as her older pet might wish. In fact, sitting here, on this beautiful day, Dulcie even found her anger with the professor subsiding. It was a misunderstanding; that was all. Fenderby had clearly talked about her work, and his wife had misinterpreted his concern as something more serious. He probably thought he was doing Dulcie a favor by removing a temptation to stray further from her original topic. Maybe this was something he had gotten accustomed to doing because his own wife was unbalanced. And maybe his temper or his manners weren't what they should be because of his living situation. For all she knew, stress could be behind the professor's ongoing health problems, too.

Dulcie's own family was far from balanced. Her mother, despite her Philadelphia Main Line upbringing, had declared herself a free spirit – moving herself and her only daughter through various alternative living situations before settling in the commune where Dulcie spent the latter half of her childhood. That commune, to which Lucy – as Dulcie called her, once her custodial parent rejected the 'patriarchal authority of the parental institution' – had moved them both when Dulcie was eight, hadn't been a bad place to grow up. Dulcie loved the quiet of the woods, and there was a library close enough for her to indulge her other passion. But its offbeat inhabitants had also encouraged Lucy to believe in her so-called psychic powers with occasionally disastrous results.

At least Lucy had been there, Dulcie recalled. Her father had taken off years before in the search for some ineffable sense of self. He did write occasionally, but Dulcie had no idea if her own letters back – addressed to post restante – ever arrived at his yurt in northern India. No, Dulcie understood unconventional families. And she could cut Fenderby some slack, if only he restored her privileges at the Mildon.

They simply needed to talk.

'Is that what you meant, Mr Grey?' Even as she voiced the question, Dulcie felt confident of the answer. Even in the beginning, soon after his mortal death when his appearances were more than a comfort – they were a veritable life saver – her feline protector had never answered her in obvious ways. In fact, the oblique nature of his communications had on occasion made her doubt she was hearing her beloved pet at all.

After all, during his lifetime, Mr Grey had not spoken with her. Not, that is, beyond the usual mews and gestures of tail and ears by which any feline makes himself understood. But over the past two years since his death – what Lucy would call his departure from this plane – Dulcie believed she was beginning to understand the complex nature of her spectral visitor. He had first appeared to her nearly two years ago, when she was sharing a summer sublet with a particularly obnoxious roommate. He'd been gone for several months by then, not that she'd stopped missing him. And when he had appeared on her stoop one evening, she'd been surprised – but pleasantly so. She'd recognized him right away: those tufted ears, the proud, wideset whiskers that shone against his pearl-grey fur. He had appeared to warn her – *'Don't go inside, Dulcie'* – the voice she now associated with him had come through clearly, but in her delight and surprise, she had ignored his warning, to her dismay.

These days, he continued to guide her, often with a caution about future events that he seemed to have some knowledge of. His warnings were rarely as clear as that first one, however, and were often as cryptic as one would expect a cat to be. In addition, he never manifested to more than one sense at a time. For example, if she heard his voice – the low, warm rumble that reminded her so much of his purr – she couldn't see him, and to seek his sleek grey form would end the conversation. If she felt his presence, as when he'd jump on to the bed late at night and begin the rhythmic kneading she remembered so well, she couldn't talk to him. And if she asked him a direct question, well, she was usually disappointed.

Even as her words faded into the balmy air, Dulcie felt herself relaxing. She certainly still treasured Mr Grey's company. However, she took it as a vote of confidence that maybe she no longer needed him quite so much to steer her path through life. Like Esmé, the young cat who now shared her and Chris's apartment, Dulcie was growing up.

'That doesn't mean I don't want you around,' she was quick to say, as a sharp-eyed sparrow tilted his head toward her. Mr Grey, she was convinced, sometimes used other animals as his emissaries, and that bird had a quizzical look. 'Or are you just hoping I have some crumbs?' She craned around. The coffee house was known for its scones, and it was hitting her now that she hadn't had breakfast. With all the turmoil of the morning, she hadn't felt hungry. Now the combination of caffeine and roiling emotions was making itself felt.

'Hang on, little fellow.' It was the work of a moment to purchase a snack – the iced lemon scone the last of the morning's leavings, except for a tired-looking focaccia that appeared to have been chewed. Dulcie had bagged the scone herself and left two dollars on the counter. Tipping was unnecessary, she decided, if the barrista didn't even look up from her phone. Two minutes later, and Dulcie was on the bench again, crumbling a corner of the scone for the little bird and several of his colleagues, who seemed to take such offerings as their due.

'So you agree, don't you?' Dulcie ate the rest herself, licking the sweet-tart icing from her fingertips. 'I should just assume Fenderby meant well. He's clearly under pressure at home. And that's all added up to what must be a misunderstanding.'

Now that she'd eaten, Dulcie felt a ton better. But she still had to do something about the situation at the Mildon. If she didn't, then she would have to cut most of that last chapter. And while she certainly had enough material already written

so that her dissertation wouldn't be lacking, this last bit hit
the note she wanted. Not a summary, as might be usual, but
a way of looking forward – an appraisal of where the author
had gone after *The Ravages of Umbria*. Besides, with its
particular focus on the political writings of an author most
distinguished for her fiction, it would be perfect for the article
she had planned. *Studies in Pre-Modern Fiction* adored inter-
stitial analyses, and Dulcie had to admit that at times she could
be a bit, well, not limited, but perhaps overly disciplined in
her thinking.

'Maybe that's it.' Dulcie sat up, scattering the remainder of
the scone to the happy flock. 'Maybe Fenderby doesn't understand cross-genre research.' She didn't like to think of the
university as that hidebound, but it was always a possibility.
And so with that thought in mind, Dulcie tossed the bag and
headed back toward campus. Fenderby's office hours didn't
start for another thirty minutes yet. But she'd be there the
moment he opened his door, ready to make her case.

With a bounce in her step, Dulcie made her way back to the
library. Maybe, she mused, she could clear this up and go right
back to work. Fenderby's office, after all, was only two levels
up from the Mildon. She'd passed it before, his name made out
in gold letters on the frosted window of an actual door, so much
more private than the carrels assigned to graduate students.
Rumor had it, Fenderby even had a window, although on Lower
Two, that probably meant a ceiling-high slit just big enough to
let in the noise of passers-by.

No matter. With a cheery greeting to the security guard and
a wave of her ID, Dulcie was once again waiting for the
elevator, and then bounding through the stacks, the tall metal
shelves filled with books. Only her respect for her surroundings kept her from breaking into song. Not that anyone seemed
to be studying. The carrels she passed were empty. The overhead lights – set to be motion sensitive to conserve energy
– only flipped on as she passed. And, over by Fenderby's
office, a cart, loaded with books to be re-filed, sat, abandoned
and ignored. A day as fine as this one was not likely to draw
many into the depths.

'Professor Fenderby?' The door, with its marbled glass, was

closed when Dulcie approached, but it wasn't latched and, instead, stood slightly ajar. Dulcie leaned in, putting her face close to the slim opening. 'Are you in yet?'

No response. An index card, tacked rather indecorously to the door frame, indicated that, in fact, the professor's office hours would not begin until noon. Dulcie had, of course, turned her phone off before entering the library, but now she powered it up. Twenty to. She turned it back off with a sigh. Twenty minutes. No wonder Fenderby wasn't answering. Most likely, he was reading or desperately trying to finish up some project of his own before he had to deal with students.

Dulcie knew well enough how time-consuming teaching could be, and how it distracted one from research. This semester, she had managed to shed all but two sections, one for English 10 and one a seminar, and mentoring duties for all but two students, and only one – the lovely Alyson – was working on a thesis, if in a somewhat desultory manner, which made her an easy, if uninspiring, charge. Still, between grading mid-terms and weekly meetings, Dulcie had found her days eaten up, her nights consumed with papers that were not her own. Out of respect, she wouldn't do the same to a fellow academic, no matter how he had treated her.

Ten minutes passed. Dulcie was sitting on the floor by then, her back against the wall. It would have helped if Fenderby's office were in a part of the library where she could do some work. Before slumping to the floor, she had tried to find something to read, pulling a journal on mid-century semiotics and then another on chaos theory as applied to linguistics from the cart. Neither held her interest. Neither, she realized, even belonged in this section, with its focus on nineteenth-century politics. As well trained as she was, Dulcie resisted the urge to reshelve the two volumes. Books got lost that way, hopelessly misfiled through the best intentions. And so she had returned both to the cart, leaving them as evidence of her failed – she wouldn't use the word 'dilettantish' – browsing. The clerk returning them wouldn't know how quickly they had been discarded.

Ten of. Dulcie was tempted to duck out, just for those remaining minutes. One floor down was her carrel, as well as the books that she had made her own over the last five years. *The Ravages of Umbria,* the fragments of it that had survived, could be found there in several editions. Although parts of it were lost to time, Dulcie still found the Gothic tale of a smart and resourceful young woman thrilling. In fact, the adventures of Hermetria, as the protagonist was named, often inspired Dulcie. Unlike Hermetria, Dulcie never had to deal with a mad monk or an unfaithful attendant. But she had her own struggles. Add in that one of Dulcie's more recent discoveries, pages she believed came from a lost, later novel by the same author, introduced a mysterious stranger dressed in grey, and Dulcie found even more reason to relate to the work. Even re-reading the best-known fragments gave her ideas sometimes. At the very least, they gave her pleasure.

But she shouldn't leave. Dulcie knew too well what office hours could be like. The way her luck was running, she'd step away only to come back to a line of anxious undergrads, all holding some form or an unfinished paper that needed saving. No, she'd wait.

Still, that door wasn't closed. With a deep breath, Dulcie resolved to act. Standing, she knocked gently on the glass, careful not to touch even the black outlines of the gilt letters.

'Professor Fenderby?' she called again. Surely, at five of noon, he could at least acknowledge her.

Nothing, not even a rustle to betray a presence inside, and another thought hit her. Maybe, after all, the professor wasn't here. Maybe he was out having lunch, or working in another part of the library. In which case, maybe he didn't know his door was open. Over spring break, the library had been victimized by a gang of well-organized thieves. Since their arrest, Dulcie would have thought everyone alerted to the dangers of leaving doors unsecured. But although routines had changed for a while – with IDs required and bags rigorously searched – before the month was out, she and other regulars were being waved through again, so it made sense that a professor would revert to long-held habits. The university mentality bred complacency, especially among old-timers, who may have forgotten that not everyone lived the life of the mind. She thought of old Will, at the front desk, who always waved her in. Surely, that was different. He knew her, or at least recognized her as a regular. It wasn't like she wanted to wait in line.

'Professor Fenderby,' she called louder, pushing thoughts of her own privilege aside. 'Your door is ajar.'

No answer. What's more, Dulcie got no sense of movement inside – not even the quiet sounds of someone avoiding a visitor. What she did get was a flash of green – light from that inside window, perhaps. Or the reflection off a glossy book jacket, as bright as cat's eyes. *'Don't go in . . .'* No, that was a memory. Something that had happened years before.

'Professor?' She put her hand on the door, resting it on the wood beside the glass. If it was, in fact, somehow secured, then no harm would be done. If not, she could peek inside and then pull it firmly shut. Unlike the absent-minded academic, she would make sure it was latched.

'It's me, Dulcie Schwartz.' She made one last attempt at introducing herself, shaking off the image of her late, great cat, before giving the door a gentle shove.

'Professor?'

But Professor Fenderby did not answer her. Not even as Dulcie gasped and tumbled backward, knocking two oversize journals off that loaded book cart as she fell. For Professor Roland Fenderby was unaware of the graduate student who gasped for the breath to call out for help. Unaware of the struggling scholar whose work he had torpedoed and who now stared at his still form, lying on the floor of his office, among the scattered papers and clutter of the day. Unaware of the new form of horror his bloated body aroused, as he lay there, cold and still and apparently very dead.

SIX

Screaming would have been the appropriate response. When Dulcie opened her mouth, however, she found herself struck mute. Some of it was surprise – of the many options she had considered, finding Roland Fenderby prone on the floor was not one of them. Some of it was her ingrained training. No matter what the provocation, one simply did not scream in a library.

Instead, Dulcie emitted a soft squeak, rather like what Esmé would produce. The sound, however, did suffice to break her out of her stupor.

'Professor Fenderby?' Once she found her voice, even in its current breathless form, Dulcie realized that she needed to act – and that her initial impression might have been incorrect. 'Are you – all right?'

It was a ludicrous question. What she really meant was, 'Are you still alive?' However, those words refused to form in her mouth, and so Dulcie followed up her own query by stepping into the cluttered office and gingerly reaching for the professor's shoulder. 'Professor?'

With a sound like a sigh and yet somehow most disturbingly not, his head fell back, exposing the gaping wound at his temple. It was an odd sight – red and clotting – set off further by the white and crumpled papers that lay beneath. Most were printed: 'ENG 101,' she read. 'METAPHOR AND THE USE,' the rest of the title obscured by 'CHARACTER DEVELOPMENT IN THE SUCCESSIVE WORKS OF,' the sheet overlaying it. Another, a small handwritten scrap, lay on top that. 'Your little blossom,' Dulcie read in a daze, noting the graceful cursive as much as the blood spatter that marked it. There was something poignant about it: perhaps the personal touch, the old-fashioned script. Amid the surrounding clutter – more typed pages, an old plate, and a twist of ribbon as if from a long-ago birthday present – it seemed set apart from the damage. The awful, bloody damage. As Dulcie watched, the color seemed to spread, the slight movement perhaps shifting the balance of paper and fluids. Behind her, in the stacks, a timer clicked. A light switched off, leaving her in shadow. And that was when Dulcie jumped back and ran out the door.

'Help. Help!' She pushed the cart out of the way and stumbled, once more. If there were any students on the floor, she didn't see them. Scrambling to her feet, she could barely breathe, let alone call, and so she made a beeline for the elevator. For the surface. Even once she reached the main entrance, Dulcie found it hard to get the words out. Found it hard to stay steady, even, as she grasped the edge of the guard's desk and gasped for the breath to articulate the thoughts crowding her head. 'Fenderby,' she managed at last. 'Level Two. Dead,' she said at last. And then the great entrance hall started spinning and people were shouting, and then she was done with it all.

'Ms Schwartz?' A familiar voice was calling to her. A soft touch, like the pad of a cat's paw, was patting her cheek, and Dulcie opened her eyes to see a pair of oversized glasses staring down at her.

'Mr Griddlehaus!' She started to sit up, but other hands held her shoulders. 'What's happening?' She turned and realized she was lying on the floor. Behind her, a clerk whose name escaped her had his hands on her shoulders. Behind him, she could see her friend Ruby from circulation, her round face creased with concern.

'You blacked out,' the librarian said, his voice soft with concern. 'Please, maybe you should lie still until the EMTs get here.'

'EMTs!' She struggled to sit up as memory returned, pulling free of the hands on her shoulders. 'Professor Fenderby – he's hurt. He's . . .'

She swallowed, her mouth suddenly dry. But there was no need to say more. The faces watching her were all nodding.

'We know,' said Griddlehaus, as Ruby reached forward to take her hand.

'Oh!' Ruby pulled back, and Dulcie looked down. Her hand was covered with rusty smears. Sticky, too. A wave of dizziness crept over her, and she turned away, licking dry lips. 'My bag,' she said, determined to focus elsewhere. 'Where's my bag?'

'You're . . .' Griddlehaus turned around to look as Dulcie stood, careful to hold her bloodied hands away from her body.

'I hope I didn't leave it . . .' The idea of going back down to Fenderby's office made her sway.

'Careful there, Miss.' A young uniformed cop grabbed her

upper arms, steadying her as she clambered to her feet. 'Maybe you should sit back down.'

'No.' The panic was wearing off, leaving Dulcie irritable. 'I need my bag. It has my computer and all my work.'

'It's safe,' the officer said. 'You dropped it.'

'You have my bag?' She turned to really look at him now. His age, she guessed – mid-twenties – but a good five inches taller and certainly a lot less soft around the middle; he didn't look happy under her scrutiny. He didn't look away, either.

'Please, Miss.' His voice was calm and deep. 'I'll have someone fetch it. But may we have a look through it? Why don't you sit, Miss?'

That last was to Ruby, who was pushing a rolling chair toward Dulcie.

'Come on, Dulcie,' she said. 'We don't want you to keel over again.'

'OK,' said Dulcie. She was talking to Ruby, but the young cop nodded and walked away.

More to comply with her friend's wishes than because she thought it necessary, Dulcie sat. Griddlehaus was still standing before her, wringing his hands. The motion made her suddenly very conscious of her own.

'Ruby?' She looked up at her friend. 'Do you still have those wet wipes?'

'Sure thing.' Ruby turned toward her desk, only to be interrupted by the young cop.

'Hang on, please.' They stood, frozen, while he went off to speak with an older man in an ill-fitting suit jacket. When he turned back, he nodded. 'You're OK.'

'Sheesh.' Two minutes later, Dulcie was scrubbing at her cuticles. On the damp surface of the wipe, the sticky brown had turned an alarming red and so she focused instead on cleaning. 'Now I know how Esmé feels,' she said, and was rewarded by a smile.

'Now you're sounding like yourself again.' Ruby had pulled a second chair up and sat, facing her friend. Griddlehaus still stood, his drawn face eloquent.

'Please, Mr Griddlehaus.' Dulcie looked up at him,

concerned. 'I'm fine. And Professor Fenderby, well . . . it has to have been an accident.'

'I don't know, Dulce.' Ruby leaned in. 'You haven't seen all the cops coming in.'

Dulcie looked up at the mousy librarian for confirmation – and was struck by a sudden hopeful thought. 'Mr Griddlehaus,' she asked, her voice tentative. 'Do you think this means that I can see those pages now? I mean, I feel awful about Professor Fenderby, but surely his proscription can no longer be valid.'

'I don't know, Ms Schwartz.' Surely, those weren't tears making his eyes so large. 'I'm afraid we may have to wait until all this—' He gestured, making Dulcie aware of the hubbub around them. 'Until this matter is cleared.'

'Bother,' Dulcie muttered. 'And I guess they've got other things to worry about than getting me my bag back.' She caught herself as if hearing how she sounded for the first time. 'I'm sorry,' she said. 'I know the library gives me all sorts of leeway. But . . . maybe?'

She looked up at Ruby. Her friend worked up here, in circulation, where everybody knew her. Plus, perhaps because of her position here or perhaps because of her size, she emanated a gentle authority. 'Ruby, do you think that you could ask?'

'I'll try. You know I'd do anything for you, Dulcie.' With a smile that looked a little forced to Dulcie, her friend stood and made her way over to the nearest grouping of police.

'I can't believe this is happening.' She turned toward Griddlehaus, as he sat in the vacant seat. Before he could respond, Ruby was rushing back.

'You're not getting your bag back anytime soon.' The smile was gone. 'I gather you gave them permission to search it?'

Dulcie shook her head, confused.

'Well, they seem to think you did,' Ruby said with a sniff. 'They've handed it off to one of their so-called experts. They tried to shoo me away, but I heard them talking about a search. They're saying that Fenderby's – that it looked intentional, Dulcie. They're looking for a weapon.'

SEVEN

'I can't believe you said you wanted to kill him.' Trista's voice wasn't helping Dulcie's headache. 'I mean, you specifically said you wanted to bludgeon him, right? Over his comments?'

Dulcie didn't nod. Instead, she grunted what she hoped sounded like assent and lay back on the sofa. Her friend had called her soon after she'd gotten home, having already heard the news. Now as she lay back on the sofa, a cold compress over her eyes, she began to wish she hadn't picked up.

'They can't take that seriously as motive, though.' Trista seemed quite happy to carry on the conversation by herself. 'Not with everything that bastard has done.'

'I don't know, Tris,' Dulcie managed to reply. She could hear Esmé bounding around the other room, apparently in hot pursuit of prey. A toy, she hoped, rather than anything living. 'I mean, I'd have to have been pretty stupid . . .'

She let the sentence trail off. The officer who had questioned her had gone over every second of her morning up until that fateful encounter. By the time he had spoken to her, he seemed to have already heard about her outburst in the department office. She'd told him the rest, about going to the Mildon and then to Fenderby's apartment. No, she didn't have a receipt from the coffee house, but surely if questioned the clerk would remember that someone had bought the last iced lemon scone shortly before noon. Maybe they could check her bags for crumbs, while they were at it.

'Where was that detective you know?' Trista's voice broke into her recollection. 'Big guy, looks like a pile of rocks?'

'Rogovoy.' Dulcie had wondered the same thing. It wasn't that she expected special treatment. A criminal investigation wasn't a library. But she had helped the university police before and the ogre-like detective did know her. 'He's on assignment, someone said. Some special task force.'

'They should call him back!' Trista's affronted tone finally roused Dulcie to sit up.

'I'm sure this will all blow over,' she said, with more conviction than she felt. 'It's just really bad timing. And with those pages being sequestered and my bag . . . Oh, Trista, I was getting so close.'

'I know, Dulce.' Trista did. She'd nearly lost it finishing her own thesis, and even though she complained often and loudly about life as a post-doc fellow, Dulcie knew her friend would never minimize the last desperate struggle to finish a dissertation. 'Believe me. And Fenderby, well, I can't think of anyone who will miss him.'

'Tris . . .' Tempted as she was to agree with her friend, Dulcie had a flash of a rundown woman holding a trowel. 'He was married.'

'She'll be better off.'

That was harsh, even for Trista. 'I think I've got to go,' said Dulcie. 'My head . . .'

'Sure, hon.' Her friend sounded distracted, or maybe that was regret speaking. 'I'm sorry. I shouldn't have gone on. You wouldn't want to go out tonight, would you?'

'No, thanks.' Dulcie almost smiled. Trista was only being loyal. 'Chris will be home soon, and he's getting takeout.'

'You're in good hands, then. Mary Chung's, I hope.' Trista might not ever be the homebody that Dulcie was, but she appreciated good dumplings.

'Better be,' Dulcie answered. For the first time since mid-morning, she began to feel hungry. As if she'd been eavesdropping, her cat came bouncing into the living room and jumped onto the sofa beside Dulcie. 'Esmé's here. I swear, she knows when I'm talking about food.'

'You better take care of her, then,' Trista said. 'And I should get going.'

'Have fun.' Dulcie reached to pull the chubby black and white cat into her arms.

'I will,' said her friend. 'And I'll report back.' Dulcie waited, stroking her pet's sleek black back. Something in Trista's voice told her that her friend had more on her mind.

'Hasn't it occurred to you that the police know an awful

lot about how you spent your morning?' Trista said after a moment's pause. 'Don't you want to know who's talking?'

And with that, Dulcie wasn't hungry any more.

'Trista's a troublemaker.' Chris's take was straightforward. 'And she's getting worse. I can't believe she said that about that poor professor.'

'She was only defending me, Chris. She knows how his criticism upset me.' Dulcie felt honor bound to speak up for her buddy, even as she silently acknowledged the truth in Chris's words.

'She's become really touchy about everything.' Her boyfriend, unloading the paper bags he'd brought in, didn't see the pained expression on Dulcie's face. 'Jerry's not the kind to complain, but I've been with him when she calls.'

'Good thing nobody's eavesdropping on us.' Dulcie kept her voice neutral at the mention of Trista's longtime boyfriend, but mentally she tried to remember the last time she'd seen them together. Her own sweetheart's arrival had started to dissolve the knot in the pit of her stomach. The fragrant containers spread around them had helped too. She really didn't want to think about squabbling couples or romance gone sour. 'You got moo shi, too?'

'Yeah, I wasn't sure what you'd be in the mood for.' He grabbed a dumpling, depositing another on Dulcie's plate. 'So I got everything. But saying that his wife would be better off?'

'Chris, please.' Dulcie thought back to her odd encounter. 'She's a sad woman, and this is going to be awful for her.'

He shut up then, and they ate in silence for a few minutes. Esmé, who'd had her own dinner, curled in Dulcie's lap. It wasn't until the dumplings were gone that Dulcie brought up the incident again.

'Don't you think it's weird?' She reached for the rice.

'That Trista's blaming the victim?' He'd softened the edge in his voice, but Dulcie still heard it.

'No,' she answered, hoping she sounded definitive. 'That they're keeping my bag.'

'I think it's protocol,' Chris said, as if it were the answer. Maybe, thought Dulcie, that was because he was an applied math scholar, so to him it was. 'I mean, you were the one to report the crime—'

'I found him, Chris.' As much as she wanted comfort, she wasn't going to let him soft-pedal the situation. 'I pushed open the door and found him lying there.'

'Yes, and you were heard making outlandish threats earlier in the day.' He seemed to sense that arguing would do more harm than good. 'And so I'm sure there's a certain amount of data they have to gather.'

'Data.' She scooped more rice into her bowl. 'There were only three people in the office that morning. Nancy, Alyson, and Tom—'

'That you know of,' Chris interrupted. 'You were in that tiny side room, right? You don't know if any other students were coming in or out of the building. And, besides,' he said, before she could break in. 'That doesn't mean anything. Nancy is a law-abiding type. She may have felt compelled to report what you said.'

'I can't believe that.' Dulcie shook her head. 'Why would she?'

'Because the police asked?' Chris sounded so reasonable, Dulcie found it hard to argue. At least for now she was home, safe and warm.

EIGHT

'*T was all she could do to keep the Candle lit against the Night, and by its guttered Light she penned what well could be her final Resolve, her words the Chain that would bind forever as they reveal'd that which she kept hidden. Outside, the Thunder crack'd, the Fury of the Tempest too fierce for one lone traveler to bear. The Ship would founder, it would Fail, so too her Secret would be carried down beneath the Mountainous waves . . .*

Dulcie woke, breathless, her heart pounding. Whether because of that horror she'd witnessed the day before, or the spicy dumplings which had seemed like an appropriate comfort after, she had tossed and turned until even Esmé had given up, jumping to the floor with an annoyed grunt sometime before dawn.

Dulcie had managed to get back to sleep, as the bedroom she shared with Chris began to lighten. But it hadn't been an easy rest, and a few hours later, bleary-eyed, she had shuffled into the kitchen to find her boyfriend already gone. And although he'd left a cheery note by her mug, suggesting that perhaps she might want to take the morning easy, the idea of being alone – even alone with Esmé – didn't particularly appeal.

Instead, she shuffled off to campus, hoping for something akin to normalcy, or at least a mug of Nancy's good coffee. Trista, who had beaten her to the departmental office, seemed to have had an equally bad night. In fact, from the way she bundled Dulcie off into a corner, Dulcie wondered if she'd been to sleep at all. There was a frantic edge to her friend, one that no amount of Nancy's coffee could explain.

'We've got to get on this, Dulcie.' Trista's blue eyes looked particularly intense, although not, her friend was glad to note, bloodshot. 'We can't waste any time.'

'But, Trista?' Dulcie blinked up at her blonde friend. Trista had been a loyal support, but first thing in the morning, with a voice to match her multiple piercings, she could be a bit abrasive. 'May we have coffee first?' Nancy did make the best coffee.

'I don't know.' Trista looked over her shoulder to where the departmental secretary sat, sorting through a pile of paperwork. 'I still haven't ruled her out.'

'Trista.' That did it. Dulcie marched by her friend. If she couldn't trust Nancy Pruitt, she may as well give up. 'Good morning,' she called over to the plump older woman.

'Oh, good morning!' Nancy was up from her seat in a moment. 'Dulcie, how are you?'

Her approach might not have been as practical as Trista's but it was a good deal warmer. Right now, that's what Dulcie wanted, and as she fixed herself a mug of the good dark brew, she found herself smiling back at the grey-haired secretary.

'I'm OK. Thanks.' She paused, unsure of how to ask. 'Has there been any news?'

'About poor Professor Fenderby?' Her kind face pinched up. 'No, I'm sorry. But the police have already been in. They wanted his files.' Her voice dropped to a whisper. 'Two of them are up with Mr Thorpe now.'

'But surely . . .' Dulcie paused, the memory of what she had found obscuring any other thought. 'If someone . . . if it wasn't an accident,' she managed to form the words. 'Then it must have been a stranger. Someone ill or crazed.'

Nancy was shaking her head, her mouth set in a grim line. 'I know that would be preferable, dear, but it's unlikely. As I'm sure you're aware, access to the library is limited, and this did appear to happen in an office in the stacks. No, I'm afraid the implication is that poor Professor Fenderby was targeted, and that the perpetrator was a member of the university community.'

Suddenly, the coffee turned to acid in her stomach, and Dulcie had to fight a bout of queasiness. 'Thanks,' she managed to gasp out, as she retreated to the building's main sitting area and sank onto a tattered sofa.

'News?' Trista gestured toward the secretary with a tilt of her head.

'The police.' Dulcie put the mug down on the side table, her hands shaking too much to hold it. 'They're upstairs.'

'Good.' Her friend surprised her. 'Maybe they'll get to the bottom of this.'

'But you said . . . I said . . .' The queasiness had passed, leaving a sense of unease.

'Look, you didn't do it, right?' Trista's eyes were a striking blue. They held Dulcie's own until she nodded assent. 'So the quicker they find out what happened, the better. What I want to know is who is bad-mouthing you.'

'Someone's bad-mouthing me?' Dulcie let herself be pulled upright.

'Yeah, I talked to that cop. The young one?' Dulcie nodded, vaguely recalling a muscular young man around their age. 'He didn't want to say anything, but I made out like I was worried about myself, and he said I shouldn't be. He said that a witness saw a woman – a redhead – rushing out around eleven, apparently distraught. That's what they're following up on. That's an hour before you say you got there. Right around the time he was killed.'

'A redhead?' Dulcie felt like her brain must be frozen. Trista, however, didn't seem to mind that her friend was parroting her words. 'At eleven?'

'Uh huh. Now come on.' Trista took her hand.

'Wait, you got a cop to talk to you?' Dulcie paused, the inanity of her own question hitting her. Trista knew how to flirt. That she could get a young man to confide was no surprise. 'What did you find out? What's going on?'

'I've got an idea.' Trista was pulling her back toward the campus. 'Call it a hunch.'

'I'm not going to the library.' Dulcie found the strength to pull back. 'If that's what you think . . .'

'The library?' Trista turned back to look at her, one pierced brow raised. 'Why would we go there? No, we're going to the women's center.'

Trista was walking so quickly that Dulcie didn't have the breath to question her any further. Besides, it was a bit of a relief to be led – particularly to someplace as non-threatening as the center. The basement suite might not look like much; the stairs that led down were marked only by a small sign, white letters on a red background. But Dulcie knew that nobody was likely to accuse her there. The women's center served several functions on campus – meeting place, resource library, and the source of the second-best coffee on campus. But basically it existed to help women who needed either sympathy or support. Right now, Dulcie felt like she could use both.

'I'd like to talk to someone about Roland Fenderby.' Trista addressed the student volunteer who seemed to be the only person present. She was an undergrad, Dulcie thought, remembering her bouncy dark curls from a seminar on Shelley. 'About cases filed against him.'

'Excuse me?' The student had been shelving books and turned to address Trista. Seeing Dulcie, she smiled. 'Ms Schwartz!'

'Nola.' Dulcie grinned back, partly with relief at having dredged up the name. 'How are you?'

'I'm good.' The dark-haired girl looked around. 'I'm a psych major now.'

There didn't seem to be a response to that. From what Dulcie had remembered, she figured it was probably just as well that the sophomore was no longer focused on literature. And besides, Trista was getting impatient.

'Do you think you can help us?' Trista had softened her voice a bit, but Dulcie could hear the impatience in it. 'I'd like to talk to someone about Roland Fenderby.'

'I don't know if I can,' Nola replied, shaking her head. 'Those files are confidential.'

Trista looked like she was about to say something. Dulcie reached out and put her hand on her friend's arm. 'That's fine,' she said. 'We're sorry to bother you.'

Now it was her turn to lead her friend out. Once they'd emerged in the spring morning, Dulcie turned to Trista.

'What was that about?'

'Proof.' Trista leaned in, a sly grin on her face.

Dulcie shook her head, confused.

'I knew that masher was up to no good. A redhead leaving his office? Fenderby had a reputation as a creep, and we just got confirmation.' Trista was clearly pleased with herself. 'That girl said there was a file on him. It's just as I suspected. Fenderby pushed some girl too far.'

NINE

It wasn't that she didn't appreciate Trista's efforts. Her friend's concern, if not her methods, said a lot about the years they'd known each other. But Dulcie didn't want to get more involved in this than she already was, a position she tried to explain as they walked.

'You weren't there, Tris,' she said. The two were crossing the Yard, and Dulcie was trying to steer her buddy toward the river. Despite Dulcie's early start, it was getting near time for her section. 'You didn't see him.'

'No, but you did. And you were angry enough at him so that everyone knew you threatened him.' Her friend made her case sound like the voice of reason. 'And everyone knows the cops are lazy.'

That stopped her. 'Detective Rogovoy isn't,' she said. 'In fact, I think he prefers it if I don't get involved in these things.' In the past, Dulcie had gotten a little too interested in some of the misdeeds around campus – she didn't like to call them crimes. But even as she protested, she found herself wondering. As recently as spring break, she had managed to clear the name of a fellow scholar – a poor fellow who had been hounded for years by a corrupt cop.

'You don't think anyone is out to frame me.' She stopped walking, her voice getting tight. 'Do you?'

Trista's shrug wasn't very reassuring. 'Someone killed Fenderby,' she said. 'And I bet whoever it is would rather not be caught.'

Any hope that teaching would offer a respite to the whole mess was dashed when Dulcie walked into her section. All twelve of her students were there – a rare enough occurrence on a bright spring day – but the silence that fell as she walked into the room signaled that they had more on their minds than *The Castle of Otranto*.

'Good morning.' Twelve sets of eyes, all wide open, regarded her. 'Shall we start by discussing the reading?'

'Is it true, Ms Schwartz?' Sonia, a junior, asked in hushed tones.

Dulcie paused for thought. This was what her mother would call a message from the universe. 'You may have heard that I made an unfortunate discovery yesterday,' she began. 'And that Professor Fenderby is dead. But that doesn't mean—'

'You didn't do it, did you?' Louis, who never asked questions, opened his mouth for the first time all semester.

Before she could respond, another voice chimed in. 'Did you see anybody? Was it gruesome?'

She looked from one side of the table to the other. 'Excuse

me, are we scholars or are we ghouls?' As soon as the words were out of her mouth, she realized her mistake.

'It's just like one of your Gothic novels,' Mariela piped up. 'A dead body, a beautiful heroine in distress. All you need is a ghost!'

Dulcie could feel herself blushing. It was nice to be called beautiful, albeit in distress. But there was no way they could know that the part about the ghost was true.

'Please, people.' It was hopeless. Although her students finally stopped their questions, once they realized she was not going to respond, getting them to focus on the work at hand was impossible. In all fairness, *Otranto* was tough going. Overwritten and preposterous, it really epitomized all that could go wrong with the Gothic genre. Isabella running away from Manfred, everyone hiding in either an underground church or a cave . . . all of it kicked off when some weird giant helmet falls on Isabella's intended, crushing him to death. Rather like . . .

'Ms Schwartz?' The voice, softer than the others, roused her from her thoughts. 'Are you all right?'

'Yes, thank you.' She forced her face into what she hoped looked like a grin, swallowing down the wave of nausea that had suddenly come upon her. 'I was just wishing that we could read one of the works I prefer. Something like *The Ravages of Umbria.*'

'That's your dissertation topic, right?' Dawn, a quiet girl, smiled up at her.

'That's what it started with, anyway.' She looked around. 'You know it?'

'My old roommate, Alyson Beaumont, was telling me about it, about how promising it was,' Dawn explained. 'She said her mentor was really enthusiastic about it and super helpful.'

'I'm so glad.' Dulcie could feel her color deepening. 'Super helpful' was even better than 'beautiful'. Besides, it was encouraging. Alyson had often seemed uninterested, and Dulcie hadn't realized that her tutee had gone so far as to read the book – the fragment of a book – that was at the center of her own academic career. 'Has anybody here read *The Ravages of Umbria*?'

She was about to embark on a description. Surely, once she explained about the conflict between the two main characters – the noble Hermetria and her duplicitous companion Demetria – they'd be intrigued. Yes, *The Ravages* used the Gothic conventions of a maiden under duress, with a mad monk and a knight who might or might not simply be out for her lost fortune. But it was so much more. Particularly those passages that describe her flight from her own ancestral home, a castle set high on a mountainous peak. And the eerie, but seemingly benevolent, grey stranger who comes to her aid. Only as she gathered her thoughts, a hand shot up at the far end of the table.

'Lonnie?' This was great. Lonnie was clearly taking the course as a distribution requirement, and Dulcie had been hard pressed to find anything that would interest the bored gov major. 'You've read it?'

'Well, no, Ms Schwartz.' He leaned forward in his chair. 'But will it be on the final?'

Rarely had Dulcie been so relieved to hear the tolling of the Memorial Church bell. Her students, on the other hand, hesitated, and it wasn't until she reached for her phone that they began to file out.

'See you next week,' she called, as she waited for the message to load. She had felt guilty leaving the device on during a lesson, but Trista had insisted. Besides, she was hoping that Detective Rogovoy would return her call. Surely, he would come back from his task force for a murder.

This wasn't him, however. But it was good news. Officer Newbright, the young cop Trista had flirted with, had sent a brief note: her bag was no longer necessary and could be picked up at the library's front desk. With a sigh of relief, Dulcie followed her students out of the conference room.

'Ms Schwartz?' She should have known. Four of them were waiting outside, including Dawn, the quiet junior.

'I'm sorry.' She was, but discipline was important, too. Besides, they probably just wanted to grill her more about Fenderby. 'I really have to go. Please come see me at my office hours.'

*   *   *

Relief, Dulcie decided, was the dominant emotion she felt as she trotted over to the library. Life would never be the same, of course. And she thought it likely that she'd never want to return to Level Two again. But at least she was getting her bag back. She could return to work.

'Dulcie Schwartz,' she announced herself to the clerk at the front desk. 'You have my bag?'

'Dulcie!' Ruby, waving, was making her way over, as quickly as a woman of her size could. 'There you are.'

'Ruby.' Dulcie turned toward her, relief washing through her. She'd feared having to deal with the police again. That young cop might have been nice enough, but the police didn't belong here – not even Detective Rogovoy. And the idea that someone might be trying to cast suspicion on her . . . 'I guess my bag has been released.'

'Of course it has.' She turned from Dulcie to the clerk. 'It's at the guard station. Would you?'

While they waited, Ruby took Dulcie's hands. 'How are you? I didn't get to ask. That must have been horrible.'

'Thanks.' Her friend's concern warmed her. 'It was pretty horrible. Especially because, you know, he and I – we had our differences.'

She nodding, rolling her eyes back in exaggerated assent. 'You and every other female on campus.'

'He didn't . . .' She looked at Ruby, afraid to finish her question.

'I'm not his type,' she said, her voice dripping with an acid tone that Dulcie had never heard her use before. She looked at her friend. Ruby was big, queen-size at least. And a dark-skinned African American.

'Malleable,' said Ruby, answering the unspoken question. 'I'm not the type to be easily cowed, especially by a bully like Fenderby. Though he had other ways of showing how he felt about us "little people".'

Dulcie noted the air quotes about the last two words and tamped down what she feared might be a size-ist response. 'I don't doubt it,' she said, looking up at her friend. 'He was hardly respectful to me.'

'Disrespectful is the least of it.'

'So it's true?' Dulcie caught herself. 'I mean, I guess there were some complaints?'

Ruby grimaced. 'Not enough, if you ask me. The university has got to become more proactive about harassment. I mean, I understand innocent until proven guilty and the need for an investigation, but that man got away with—' She stopped herself, both of them suddenly aware of what she was going to say.

'Surely, even with all the bureaucracy, that wouldn't be . . .' Dulcie stumbled, unsure how to put her thoughts into words. 'I mean, if he was that bad, surely somebody would have filed a complaint. And not . . .'

Her friend shrugged. 'I'd like to think so, but you hear things. I *do* know that none of us here liked him much.' She paused. Dulcie didn't dare ask. 'Word was that the latest complaint against Fenderby was dismissed for lack of evidence. I heard it was classic "he said, she said", although why any pretty undergrad would even bother making up stuff about such a gross lech as that is beyond my pay grade. What's worse, I heard she was bound by some sort of confidentiality agreement. Because the case was dismissed, she can't even talk about it, lest she ruin his reputation or something.'

'How awful.' Dulcie understood the principle. The application, however, seemed flawed at best. 'That poor girl. Still, they can't think that she – whoever she is . . .'

'I don't know,' her friend said, before turning toward Dulcie. 'So, he didn't bother you in that way, did he?'

'No.' She thought of the overweight, sweating man and shuddered. 'He was just— Did I tell you he was added to my committee?'

Her friend grimaced. 'I wonder whose idea that was?'

'Thorpe, I think.' Dulcie kept her voice down.

'Wonder what Fenderby had over Thorpe?' Ruby's voice had also gone soft.

Dulcie shook her head. She'd made her peace with her adviser, and the university gossip mill was always at work. 'For me, it's the opposite question,' she said. 'I can't imagine why Fenderby would have wanted to work with me, when he thought so little of my scholarship.'

Before she could go any further with that idea, though, the other clerk showed up with her bag.

'Thanks.' Dulcie beamed with sincere gratitude and, pulling off the paper tag with her name on it, lifted the flap that covered its main compartment. Her laptop, her yellow legal pad, the print-out of Fenderby's awful letter. Even her pencil case – everything seemed to be in its proper place. By the time she checked the outer pocket and found her roll of laundry quarters intact, she realized she was breathing more easily than she had all day.

'I wonder what they were looking for, anyway?' She flipped the top closed, buckling it for good measure. Only then did she realize that the clerk had been standing there all along, and that both he and Ruby had been watching her go through her belongings.

'Didn't you hear?' Ruby and the clerk exchanged glances. 'We've been told to look for a large, hardbound volume of at least five hundred pages – ten pounds, that would be. They might think we're cloistered here, but it doesn't take a forensics expert to figure it out. They're still looking for the murder weapon.'

TEN

'**K**illed by a book.' Dulcie was talking to the cat, but she might as well have been addressing herself. She'd gone home after retrieving her bag. Somehow the idea of working at her carrel, down in the depths of the library, had lost its appeal. Even though she would be on a different floor – Level Two was off limits while the police conducted their investigation – her accustomed study area just seemed too, well, grim today. Besides, she reasoned, she and Chris had a perfectly lovely apartment.

'I wonder which title?' The problem wasn't the apartment. Dulcie had set up her laptop on the kitchen table. The window before her let in the bright April sun, and the straight-backed chair wasn't as conducive to napping as their old sofa. Still, she was having trouble concentrating. And when Esmé jumped to the tabletop, Dulcie gave in to her curiosity.

'And could the harassment complaint have been behind it?' An image of Roland Fenderby, not as she'd last seen him but as he had been in life – sweaty and pale – made her shudder. In response, she reached for the little cat, pulling her on to her lap. 'That would be horrible,' she said, rubbing the furry white belly. 'But would it drive someone to kill?'

'Depends.' With a flick of her tail and a soft mew, Esmé answered – and then grabbed Dulcie's hand. *'I'd get all bitey.'*

Dulcie carefully removed her hand before the overstimulated feline began to act on her thoughts. Once she'd accepted that she heard Mr Grey's voice, it hadn't surprised her much when Esmé started talking too. At times, she still wondered if she really heard her cat's voice, or if she was simply projecting or, perhaps, mad. The voice fit Dulcie's impression of the little tuxedo so perfectly. Impertinent and feminine, with a bit of the edge that Dulcie understood. For most of her life, she'd been the smallest one in any gathering, too.

'I don't think anyone would dare touch you in a way that was unwelcome. I'm talking about some poor human student.' Dulcie wasn't sure why she was arguing with the cat, however civilly. It was a fight she was unlikely to win.

'Just saying . . .' Esmé clambered back onto the table, from where she gauged the distance to the floor. *'We are who we are.'*

The cat landed with a thump, leaving Dulcie to consider. In some ways, what Esmé had said backed up Ruby's comments. If Fenderby had acted improperly once, he probably had done so at other times – and maybe he'd finally tried his tricks on the wrong person. Or, Dulcie mused, watching her cat strut out of the room, proud tail high, someone hadn't been content with filing a complaint. The confidentiality agreement had been put in place to protect the accused. The police were probably talking to the young woman who had filed the complaint now.

'Poor girl.' With a shudder, Dulcie turned back to her keyboard. She'd had enough experience of Fenderby so that her sympathy was automatically with that nameless young woman. But the police were on the case. She had her own work to do, and for better or worse, one of her biggest obstacles had been removed. If only she knew for sure that her name had been taken off the list of suspects.

Shaking off the feeling that she was shadowed by a less friendly specter, Dulcie opened the file that contained her most recent chapter. Before Fenderby's critique, she had thought it ready to go. Now, well, she might as well give it another read. What had Tom said? To 'bullet-proof' it?

Disgusting phrase. Only a man . . . no, that was beneath her. Besides, Tom was the nicest sort of man. His admiration for her had been apparent, when he'd taken her seminar last semester. Despite his obvious shyness, he'd sat up front, his concentration total. He'd made a similar effort in the small group discussions on characterization and allegory and always focused so carefully on his classmates when they spoke. It was true, he never lost his stammer or the hot flush that would color his cheeks when he struggled with a word. But his valor in the face of such an impediment only made Dulcie like him more. He and Alyson had been the stars of that small group, the pretty blonde engaged in a way that now, only six months later, Dulcie found hard to remember.

'*If we take into consideration the assumed gender of the author . . .*'

Dulcie's own writing stopped her. It was true that nobody knew whether the author of *The Ravages of Umbria* was male or female. She had come close to uncovering the author's identity, but at this point in her thesis she had just about given up on finding anything definitive. However, she had found so many clues to the author's gender that she ought to make this sentence stronger.

'*Taking into consideration the likely gender of the author . . .*'

There, that was better. After all, it wasn't simply *The Ravages*. In the course of her research, Dulcie had linked the unnamed author to several political tracts – all of which lamented the laws that bound women to their families, particularly to unhappy marriages. And her major discovery, apparently fragments of a later novel, clearly dealt with this theme, with a heroine who flees an abusive man, seeking only to establish her independence.

'. . . one sees the unconscious effect of bias, like a dark moon whose gravity distorts the orbit of a planet.'

Dulcie sighed, discouraged. Maybe that was a bit much. Where had she gotten that anyway? As the screen went dark again, she remembered. It had been in one of her student conferences. She'd been trying to explain how, even without knowing much about the author, the reader could infer a lot.

'That's how astrophysicists know to look for a black hole,' her student had said.

Alyson. Of course. Dulcie remembered now. It had been just after spring break, the season still more a wish than a reality, and they'd been meeting in her office. Unlike senior faculty, Dulcie had to share her office. Usually she didn't mind. She and Lloyd not only got on well, they shared a certain dogged temperament. They were also pretty good about staying out of each other's way, the overstuffed basement room not really being conducive to study when one or the other was having meetings.

Only on this occasion, Lloyd had been present. Mid-terms had descended like a late blizzard, and between panicked students and last-minute papers, both of them were working all out. Which would have been fine, except that when Alyson had said that about astrophysicists, Lloyd had snorted. Quite audibly.

'Really?' Dulcie had tried to cover, and distract her student. 'Black holes?'

'Yes, it's also how they're looking for dark matter.'

Another snort. Dulcie winced. Alyson was more direct.

'Excuse me?' She had turned to Dulcie's office mate. 'Do you have a problem?'

'Me? No.' Lloyd wasn't the confrontational type. He couldn't hide the grin on his face, though.

'I used to date a professor of astrophysics, you know.' She turned back to Dulcie. 'I do know what I'm talking about.'

'I believe you,' said Dulcie. Whether or not the science was true, she'd been taken by the imagery. 'And I like the idea of proving the existence of something by its effect on others.'

Lloyd had excused himself soon after. To his credit, when he'd returned, he'd brought donuts, and the incident was soon forgotten. But Dulcie thought of it now – not in terms of her office mate's rudeness: they'd both been under pressure and she'd long ago forgiven that. But in terms of her student. Alyson had expressed interest in the topic. More interest than in anything else, recently. In January she had even indicated that she might want to do her thesis on something related to bias – in her own way, following Dulcie's lead. And for that reason, not because the undergrad had seemed to have insight into the late Professor Fenderby, Dulcie thought maybe it was time they have a chat.

She could hear Esmé charging around the apartment as she went in search of her phone. For a small creature, Esmé made an amazing amount of noise. Then again, Dulcie reminded herself, females have been taught to be silent for too long.

'Alyson?' The little device had begun to vibrate as she picked it up, and if her student had a simultaneous urge to speak to her, Dulcie was too well versed in seeming accidents to downplay this.

'That's the name!' Or not. Dulcie recognized the voice of her mother, as well as her usual habit of starting a conversation in the middle.

'Hi, Lucy.' Dulcie took the phone over to the sofa, determined not to mention her recent thoughts about her mother's Wiccan beliefs. Lucy would see more there than the obvious – that Lucy was undoubtedly missing her only child. 'What's up?'

'Alyson,' her mother said. 'Who is she?'

Dulcie took a deep breath. Sometimes she worried that her mother was getting flakier with age. Then she'd remind herself that Lucy had been like this for as long as she could remember. 'She's one of my students, Lucy. I was reading something and thinking that I should call her. She . . .' There was too much to explain. 'She might have some insight into something I'm researching.'

'She might.' Her mother sounded doubtful. Lucy tended to see magic in what Dulcie would call coincidence. Magic that Dulcie didn't put too much credence in. 'But you should be careful, Dulcie, about trusting these hunches of yours.'

Dulcie bit back her response. It was coincidence, nothing more.

'In fact,' Lucy continued, 'the name Alyson comes from the aristocracy. Very patriarchal. I knew an Alyson once who—' Her mother broke off. If it were anyone else on the line, Dulcie would think she had thought better of what she'd been about to say. With Lucy, however, Dulcie assumed a distraction. Her mother had the concentration of, well, Esmé. Sure enough, although Lucy had apparently put her hand over the receiver, Dulcie could hear someone calling.

'Never mind,' her mother said a moment later. 'Anyway, dear, I wanted to talk to you because your chi needs strengthening. I had a dream about it, and it was all very clear. Something about too much time around books.'

Dulcie's complaint was interrupted before she could enunciate a complete word.

'Please,' her mother cut her off. 'Don't thank me yet. I'll do what I can at our next circle. But, Dulcie, you need to be among people, too, you know. Real, live people, with good energy.'

'Thanks, Lucy.' Dulcie suppressed a shiver. There was no way her mother could know what was going on. That her words had brought up what Trista had uncovered. How exactly had Trista gotten that information, anyway? Her multiply pierced friend had always been a flirt, but she'd become more frantic in recent months. Not what Lucy would call 'good energy', Dulcie was pretty sure.

'And that Alyson?' Lucy had continued to talk. 'You should tell her to be careful, too. The patriarchy has a way of eating its own.'

'I'll tell her,' promised Dulcie. 'In fact, I'll call her as soon as we get off the phone.'

'Don't put it off too long.' Her mother had adopted her stern voice. 'There's so much blocked energy around you, clogging your aura. I mean, what with that horrible murder and all.'

'Murder?' Dulcie sat up. Lucy's visions tended to be much more vague and usually incorrect. 'You "saw" about the murder?'

'Of course I did,' her mother snapped back. 'It's all over the news. "Professor Bludgeoned in Campus Library." And now I've got to run, darling!' In the distance, Dulcie could hear voices calling her mother's name. 'Toodle-oo!'

'Toodle-oo?' Dulcie turned to find Esmé staring up at her. For once the little cat had nothing to say.

Shaking her head as if to clear it of the cobwebs, Dulcie took the phone back to the kitchen to call her student.

'Alyson?' The undergrad picked up on the first ring. 'It's Dulcie, Dulcie Schwartz. I was wondering if you had a moment.'

Dulcie had her screen open in front of her, but even as she scrolled back down to that one line, she felt a flash of regret. Calling a student for help with her own work might be selfish. Might even, it occurred to her, be inappropriate.

'Oh, hi.' The delay said it all. Alyson might have picked up right away, but she wasn't thrilled about talking to her tutor. 'Can you tell me what this is about?'

'I'm sorry.' Dulcie could have kicked herself. 'I shouldn't have called.'

The silence only confirmed her suspicion.

'Please, just tell me if I'm out of line.' There was nothing to do now, Dulcie thought, but to carry on. She'd reached that bit of text and so, with a deep breath, she continued. 'Only, do you remember when we were talking about gender roles a few weeks ago? About, well, the effects of sexism?'

'Yes.' Alyson drew out the word. 'I think so.'

She didn't. Dulcie could hear it in her voice. Why else would she sound so tentative? It hadn't been that important a conversation, except for the ideas it had sparked in Dulcie's mind. Still, maybe she could refresh the undergrad's memory. She'd already interrupted her day.

'I'm going over some of my own work and something has come up with those pages we were discussing. I probably shouldn't even be asking you about this, but I've been hoping to submit this chapter and, well, you seemed to have such a fresh take on the work.'

'No, no, it's fine,' Alyson answered, her voice sounding

normal again. 'In fact, I'd enjoy talking about work. Things have been so weird, you know?'

'Tell me about it.' Dulcie felt a surge of sisterly warmth. 'Hey, have you had lunch yet? Maybe we could meet at Lala's and go over my notes.'

'That would be wonderful.' Yes, whatever bother she had caused her student was forgotten. 'I really could use the distraction.'

Dulcie was about to respond – she wouldn't have called a meeting with any of her tutors a distraction – but then she remembered what Lucy had said. Maybe it was simply time for both of them to step away from their studies and to socialize, like normal people do.

ELEVEN

'**N**ow?' Esmé's mew, half question, half complaint, made Dulcie pause. Yes, she had intended to work in the apartment.

'Lunch with Alyson will jump-start my thinking,' Dulcie explained, as she packed her bag. 'Besides, I'll be helping her with her work too.'

The little cat stared at her person, ears out flat making her look like a disgruntled owl.

'It's only lunch, Esmé.' Dulcie felt the weight of that cool green glare. 'A girl's got to eat.'

'*Huh.*' Turning her black back on Dulcie, Esmé walked off in a huff, tail held high.

Silently promising to spend more quality time with her pet, Dulcie slipped out of the apartment. Being able to understand her cat's thoughts had its definite advantages, but the downside was that it was very hard to live up to feline expectations.

'You don't blame me for going out. Do you?' Dulcie addressed the budding branches that waved over her as she walked. The breeze was picking up, but Dulcie liked to think there was something friendly in the gesture. A benediction, or maybe a celestial stroking of her metaphorically ruffled fur. 'I mean, it's not like I'm consorting with the enemy or something.'

The day had grown warm enough that the breeze was welcome, but Dulcie felt a chill as she walked. Why had she said that, about an enemy? Surely, whatever had happened to Roland Fenderby had nothing to do with her. The horrible discovery had been bad timing, she was certain. In fact, the whole thing would probably prove to be an awful accident. Tragic, certainly. But not malicious. Who would want—?

Dulcie stopped in her tracks, heedless of the pedestrian traffic. 'Watch it, lady!' a large man in a dark suit grumbled as he ducked around her, bringing her back to the present. To what Trista had told her, and Ruby too. Yes, there was someone who might want Fenderby dead. Someone whom the regular channels of justice had disappointed.

It didn't matter. Dulcie continued walking. This was not her concern. Simply because she had had the unfortunate timing to discover . . . to discover what had happened, she told herself, dismissing from her thoughts the memory that threatened to overwhelm her. Simply because she, too, was a young woman. One whose voice, too often, was not heard – or adequately respected – on campus. A scholar studying an author who also wrote of harassment and abuse, and whose work hinted at a flight from her homeland, simply to escape a man.

Like Fenderby?

'I said, *watch it!*' This time it had been the man in the suit who had stopped short. Or stopped, at any rate, while Dulcie, preoccupied, had walked into him. He was standing on the corner but turned to glare at her. His tie looked uncomfortable in this weather. Too tight, which had to explain the red flush climbing his neck to his face.

'It says "walk".' Dulcie pointed to the signal. The flush climbed higher as he glared. 'Excuse me.' Dulcie veered to the right to pass and tried to ignore his muttered imprecations. Women had to put up with so much in the city. It did not necessarily make one into a murderer.

'Alyson!' Her student had made it to Lala's before her, and

stood outside, leaning against the glass front, pretty face turned up toward the sun. 'I hope you haven't been waiting long.'

'Just got here,' the younger woman said, stepping forward from the wall. 'It was kind of nice to have a moment to myself.'

'Oh.' A wave of unease swept over Dulcie. She shouldn't be bothering her students. Not for her own selfish reasons. 'If you're busy, maybe we shouldn't . . .' She left the sentence unfinished.

'Nonsense.' The undergrad waved her off. 'It's just what with everything going on.' She shook her head as the lunchtime crowd surged around them.

'I know. I'm sorry.' Dulcie didn't ask for any further explanation, especially not out here on the busy sidewalk. Not when her favorite restaurant beckoned. As if on cue, the door swung open, releasing the scent of coriander and onion. Maybe Lucy was right, Dulcie thought, and she did need more company. At least, both she and her student needed sustenance. 'Shall we?'

Ten minutes later, they were settled at a back table, and Dulcie was growing impatient. 'I recommend the three-bean burger,' she said, trying to keep her voice level. 'Or the split pea soup. But you really can't go wrong with anything on the menu.'

'I'm just . . .' Alyson had her face in the menu. Dulcie and the waiter exchanged glances. 'The soup, then. It's not too creamy, is it?'

'No cream,' said the waiter, reaching for her menu. 'Vegan. And the three-bean.' This was to Dulcie, who had ordered as soon as the young man – one of the proprietor's nephews – had appeared.

'I can't believe you haven't been here before.' Now that they'd ordered, Dulcie felt her mood leveling out. Hunger made her impatient, if not downright cranky, and the younger woman's obvious distraction had her second-guessing the lunch invite. 'Not only is the food great, it's one of the most afford-able places in the Square.'

Alyson smiled at that and gave a little shrug. 'I guess I'll be coming here more often then,' she said.

By the time their food had arrived, Dulcie was sure she'd

made a convert. Ten minutes after that, Dulcie's conviction faded. Her own burger might be nearly gone, but Alyson had barely tasted the rich potage in front of her. It wasn't immersion in their conversation that was holding her up, either.

'I did say that about gender roles. Didn't I?' Alyson dragged her spoon through the soup bowl before her.

'Yes, you did.' Dulcie regarded her with concern. 'I found it most insightful. But maybe this isn't a good time?'

'I'm sorry I'm so flustered.' Alyson brushed a graceful fall of honey-colored locks back. Her face, Dulcie could now see, looked tired, her eyes rimmed with red. 'I thought lunch would be a good idea, but . . .'

She shook her head, words obviously failing her.

'It's the – tragedy.' Dulcie chose the word carefully. 'It's got everyone on edge.'

Alyson nodded. 'It's just been horrible.' Her voice fell to whisper.

'Did you know him?' Dulcie kept her own voice soft. The other woman nodded. 'I'm sorry.'

'Don't be.' Alyson looked up. 'It's not—' She bit off the word. Shook her head. 'The police just would not let me go,' she said finally.

'What?' Dulcie started. She couldn't help it. And as if hearing her own words, Alyson dropped the spoon. It fell out of the bowl, hitting the table with a clatter.

'Miss?' Their waiter had a dish cloth out. Replacing her spoon, he wiped up the spatter. Alyson, her hand over her mouth, seemed barely to notice.

'Alyson.' As soon as the waiter had retreated, Dulcie leaned forward, reaching for the other woman's arm. 'What did you mean? They were questioning you?'

'Yeah,' Alyson whispered and let Dulcie take her hand. Despite the day, the soup, it felt cool to Dulcie. Unresisting. 'They called me in. I told them what I knew. That I had maybe seen someone. You know, there. By his office. That morning.'

'Oh!' Dulcie sat back, startled, the full import of what she was hearing registering. 'That was you!'

'No, I—' Alyson shook her head, confused. 'What do you mean?'

'I heard that someone said a redhead was there.' Dulcie struggled to remember exactly what Trista had said. 'Someone who looked like me.'

'You? No.' Alyson appeared to be as distraught as Dulcie. 'Not you.'

'But why—' Dulcie paused. There were so many questions. 'I mean, I *was* there. But after. And when I left, nobody was around. I'm sure of it.'

'I'm so sorry, Dulcie.' Alyson's voice caught, as if on a sob. 'I never meant to drag you into this. She looked so much like you.'

'What do you mean?' An awful suspicion began to grow in the back of Dulcie's mind.

'Just that she could be your younger sister or something. You don't have a sister, do you?'

'No.' Dulcie spoke softly, the suspicion taking form. 'I'm an only child.' She stopped herself before she said more, turning instead to a question. 'Why?'

'It's—' Alyson's voice grew breathy, her eyes wide. 'It had to be that awful woman. The one who accused Fenderby of – well, of harassing her and all sorts of awful things. It has to be.'

'Wait, a redhead, *the* redhead you saw . . .' Dulcie didn't want to believe it. It couldn't be . . . this had to be wrong. 'You can't – you don't know.'

'She was obsessed with him. She threw herself at him, but he rejected her.' Alyson wasn't listening. She began to speak faster, her voice growing louder. 'She went out of her way to destroy his character, poor man. And then, when she couldn't do that, she must have killed him.'

TWELVE

'What are you talking about?' Dulcie's voice ratcheted up to the point where other diners turned to stare. She quickly quieted, leaning in to ask, 'How can you say that?'

'About that redhead?' Alyson's eyes were wide. 'Because I know!'

Dulcie waited. This wasn't making sense.

'Fenderby was miserable. He was literally sick about it.' Alyson kept her own voice low. 'I was in his office when he took a call about it, and I saw. He started swallowing antacids like they were candy. You know how he got.' She shook her head. 'He ended up telling me all about it. I know he wasn't your favorite person, but even you would have felt bad for him, Dulcie.'

Dulcie bit her lip. Alyson was a generous soul. And her defense of Fenderby, as misguided as it might be, had sparked an idea in Dulcie's mind.

'I doubt it,' was all she could muster in response. Not if what she suspected was true.

'It had to be.' Alyson was nodding, a far-off look in her eyes. 'When I saw her running off, I wondered. But now it makes perfect sense.'

There was little Dulcie could say in response besides repeating her earlier protests, and by then even Lala's famous hot sauce couldn't make her cooling burger appetizing again. Alyson, however, seemed to have regained her appetite after unburdening herself and dug in, her spoon soon scraping the bottom of the wide soup bowl.

'Wow, that was good.' She finally sat back, beaming. 'Thanks for bringing me here.'

Dulcie tried to return her student's smile, but the effort felt forced. 'My pleasure.' Speaking felt difficult.

'What's the matter?' She looked up, startled. Lala herself was standing over her, looking down at Dulcie's plate as if it were a personal affront. Then she turned to Dulcie herself. 'Are you OK?'

'I'm fine,' Dulcie replied. She wasn't, but right now the proprietor's mothering was more than she could take. 'Lala, this is my student, Alyson.'

The undergrad extended her hand, but the namesake chef had already scooped up both plates. Nodding at the newcomer, she turned back to Dulcie. 'I'll make you up a doggie bag.'

'Lala doesn't take no for an answer,' Dulcie explained, once the big woman was gone.

'I gather.' Alyson leaned in. 'But why was she looking at me that way?'

'What do you mean?' Dulcie had never been so tired.

'Like, well, she knew something bad about me.'

'I'm sure it's nothing.' The effort to smile was nearly beyond her. 'She was just upset that I didn't finish.'

'Here you go.' Lala was back, a white paper bag in hand. As Dulcie took it, she could feel the weight of the Styrofoam container inside. It was heavier than a quarter of a leftover burger.

'Thanks.' She could feel her face thawing under the other woman's warm gaze. 'I— It's just been a weird few days.'

Lala nodded in acknowledgment. 'You seen your cousin recently?'

'Cousin?' Alyson broke in, surprise evident in her voice.

Dulcie winced. 'No, I— I should. I will, Lala.'

Another nod, and she left. Taking, Dulcie noticed, the check with her.

'I didn't know you had a cousin.' Alyson's voice had fallen to a conspiratorial whisper. 'Is she – do you think that's who I saw?'

'I really couldn't tell you.' Dulcie fumbled for her bag. Between stowing the warm package and extracting several bills for a tip, she was able to avoid the undergrad's eager gaze. 'And now I really have to run.'

She wasn't lying. Dulcie broke into a trot once she was outside the restaurant, pausing only to wait for a walk signal as she crossed Mount Auburn to head for the river. She didn't have an appointment, but then, she reassured herself, she hadn't said she did. No, Dulcie told herself, she simply had to run. If she didn't, she was going to scream.

'Please, Mr Grey.' She reached the dorm in less than five minutes. But although she had punched in the apartment number, it was the feline spirit she addressed. 'Please let her be in. And let her be—'

'Hello?' At the sound of the familiar voice Dulcie exhaled, for what felt like the first time in hours.

'Mina! It's Dulcie.' She leaned forward, resting her forehead on the cool metal of the intercom. 'May I come up?'

'Uh, sure.' The reply sounded tentative to Dulcie's ears. But that could mean anything. Surprise. Mid-terms. A bad connection. The door buzzed and Dulcie grabbed it, racing over to the elevator.

'Please don't let her be involved in this,' Dulcie whispered to the air as the elevator lurched and squeaked its way up. Unlike the aging – Dulcie preferred 'historic' – river house she had lived in as an undergrad, the Norbett Tower had all mod cons. Circa 1980, that is. 'It's too . . .' Dulcie caught herself. She'd been going to say 'Gothic'. But she meant so much more. If what she feared was the case, then the young woman whose suite she was approaching was caught up in something that not only would be horrible in real life, it would echo what she feared was their shared ancestor's past.

'Dulcie?' The young woman who had buzzed her in was standing outside her apartment door. 'What is it?'

'You're OK?' Dulcie ran over to her, holding the younger woman at arm's length before enveloping her in a hug. 'Tell me if you're OK?'

'Yeah, I'm fine.' The other girl stepped back, and Dulcie could see the rings under her eyes. Her skin, like Dulcie's, was almost translucently pale. In a month or two, they'd both be freckled. But although her hair was also touched with red, the younger woman's curls hung softer and looser, the copper burnishing a richer bronze. 'Why?'

'I—' Dulcie bit her lip. Now that she was here, she wasn't sure how to even ask. 'You know people think we look alike, right?' She smiled. It seemed wonderful to her that anyone would think she resembled this beautiful girl.

'Yeah, I know.' A faint smile lit up the younger woman's face. But the slight dimpling of her cheek only served to accentuate the tired look of her eyes. 'That's why you first suspected we were cousins, as I recall.'

'Well, that and a certain author we have in common.' Dulcie leaned in and dropped her voice to a murmur.

She had never been able to prove that she was descended from the author of *The Ravages of Umbria*. She hadn't yet definitively identified the author at all. But over her years of research, she had found many clues. Even if she discounted Lucy's crazier claims – both about their 'artistic' heritage and her own psychic ability – Dulcie knew she could trace her maternal line back to the same Philadelphia neighborhood where the author had lived. Add in the line of red-haired women – an oddly persistent trait for a supposedly recessive gene – and the clues she had received from her own spectral guardian, and she was pretty confident about her supposition. And when she'd met Mina, here on campus, a year ago, their connection had been easier to trace. The two students weren't direct cousins – Dulcie had figured it out to be either four or five times removed – but their affinity for the obscure author had made the connection seem closer.

Still, here at the college, claiming such a lineage without proof would seem a little odd. One day, Dulcie thought, she'd have proof. Until then, this was something she only shared with a very few.

'Won't you come in?' Mina's voice was also soft. The result, Dulcie thought, of sadness, as well as fatigue.

'Mina, I need to ask you something,' Dulcie said, once they were inside. Mina had gotten them both iced tea – the first of the season – and sat beside her. 'Is your roommate here?'

'No.' Mina shook her head. 'With all that was happening . . .' She sighed, rather than finish her sentence. 'I gather you heard?'

'I'm not sure.' Dulcie took a deep breath. It was time to dive in. 'But I think I know. It was you, wasn't it? The undergrad who filed suit against Roland Fenderby.'

Mina nodded and made a big show of stirring her tea. Dulcie, who also cried easily, waited while the younger woman composed herself.

'I'm not supposed to talk about it,' she said finally, her voice barely above a whisper.

'That's so unfair.' Dulcie heard her own voice rise in anger. 'And you're not,' she continued, more quietly. 'I'm asking you questions, that's all. And, besides, I'm family.'

She was rewarded by a shy smile as Mina looked up. She was, as Dulcie had guessed, blinking away tears.

'I should have come to you,' she said now. 'When he – when it happened.'

'I'm sorry I've been out of touch.' Dulcie meant it. 'I've been cranking on with my dissertation, but this is more important.' She took her cousin's hand. The tea could wait. 'So, please, tell me what happened.'

Mina took a deep breath. She seemed, Dulcie thought, to be gathering herself – and for one awful moment, Dulcie wondered if she was about to confess to something more than filing a suit. Then the younger woman began to speak.

'It was in the fall. I was taking "Politics and Prose", you know, his seminar?' Dulcie nodded. She'd been lucky enough to study the same material with Fenderby's predecessor, Jason Tinderthwall. 'Some of what I was researching touches on your work, and that made it more exciting. And when he picked me for his own section, I thought I was really lucky.'

Dulcie swallowed. She knew how unlikely it was for an undergrad to get one-on-one time with a full professor. Even as a grad student, she hadn't been guaranteed such access.

'When he started asking me to come to his office beyond office hours, saying he wanted to talk about my paper, I thought . . .' Mina shook her head and pulled away, but after a sip of tea, she was ready to begin again.

'Then, at the end of the semester, I was down in the library. I'd been doing some research and I thought I – well, I thought I found something.'

She paused, a faint smile playing on her lips. 'It's funny. I meant to tell you, Dulcie. I thought it would be right up your alley. But when I was leaving, I ran into Fenderby and he asked me if anything was wrong. I was, well, not taken aback, but it did startle me. He saw that and said that I was flushed, that my eyes were shining. He actually said he thought that maybe I was coming down with something, and so of course I started to explain that, no, I was just excited – that I thought I'd uncovered something. And he asked me to tell him about it, to come with him to his office and tell him about it.'

A longer pause this time. Dulcie waited, wondering if she should ask, but then Mina began again. 'At first, I thought he was complimenting my work. He said I was as bright as a shiny new penny.' She shuddered and wrapped her arms around herself. 'I thought, "bright", you know? But then he started touching my hair. Stroking it, and then he tried to kiss me.

'I said no, Dulcie. I was very clear.' She looked up and Dulcie could see that her eyes were now dry. 'He was full of flattery. Said he'd never felt like this and that I was his smartest . . .' She blushed and turned away.

'It wasn't your fault.' Dulcie had rarely felt so torn. She wanted to hug her friend – her cousin. At the same time, she wanted to lash out at the man who had done this to her. Only, she recalled with a start, someone already had. 'And the board . . . did they give a reason why?'

'Someone vouched for him.' Dulcie could hear the anger in her cousin's voice.

'The wife.' Dulcie remembered the angry, beaten-down woman she'd met at the apartment. 'She probably wanted to protect what little security she had.'

But Mina was shaking her head. 'No,' she said. 'I don't think so. I mean, it was all confidential, so I can't be sure. But I got the feeling it was somebody in the university community. I mean, directly. Another faculty member,' she explained. 'Or a student.'

'But who?' Dulcie wasn't questioning Mina's instincts. She'd been part of the university long enough to know what the levels of involvement were. A faculty wife was part of the community, even if she had no salary or specific duties or even a university ID. But no spouse would ever be as much a part of the family, so to speak, as another faculty member. When had Thorpe first brought up the idea of adding Fenderby to her committee? Dulcie tried to remember. 'I mean, I gather he had a reputation.'

Mina nodded. 'That's what I'd heard too, when I went to the Women's Center. They have peer counseling, and a hotline. That's what gave me the courage . . .' She broke off. 'Anyway, someone testified on his behalf. Corroborated his alibi for the times when I said I was in his office, I gather. I mean, why else would my case have been dismissed?'

'I'm sorry.' Dulcie didn't doubt her cousin for a minute. To her mind, the board's refusal to pursue the charges only compounded the crime. 'But surely, the police can't think . . .'

Mina shook her head. 'I don't know, Dulcie. I told them all I knew.'

'You weren't— you wouldn't be down there.' Dulcie didn't even want to say Fenderby's name. 'Not after . . .'

'Yes, I would.' Mina looked up. Her eyes were now clear, her voice strong. 'I'm down there most mornings. I wasn't going to be chased out of the library by one old lech. My carrel's down there. I guess I could have petitioned to have it moved, only I'm still an undergrad and, well, I wouldn't be able to tell anybody why. So I decided to stick it out. That's where the early nineteenth-century political tracts all are. I mean, that's why Fenderby had his office there.

'But I wasn't there that morning.' Mina paused, her face thoughtful. 'Well, actually, that's not true. I did go into the library. So I guess that will be on the record, that I signed in and all. But I ended up leaving right away – I never went down to Level Two at all. Tom could have told them that.'

'Tom?' Dulcie wondered if she'd missed something.

'Tom Walls. He was in your seminar?' Mina looked at her. 'We've become friends.'

'Oh, I'm glad.' Dulcie could see it. She suspected that the quiet man had a bit of a crush on her, but really, Mina was much more age appropriate. And, as far as she knew, single. 'Were you studying together?'

'No, but he works in the library and he's – well, he's been very sweet about keeping me company when I have to go down there. He meets me at the elevator and he hangs around while I work, making sure nobody bothers me.' Mina leaned in. 'He knows about what happened,' she said. 'I mean, I was warned not to tell anybody, but he already knew. He was never a fan of Fenderby's anyway. He always called him a creep, so it just seemed natural.' She shrugged.

'I'm glad.' Dulcie's opinion of the quiet junior rose. 'So he can vouch for you. For that morning, I mean.'

'Well, that's the thing.' Mina sat back, her brow knitting. 'I understand him wanting to be careful and to be honest, but . . .'

Dulcie waited, apprehension growing.

'He says he can't be sure if I was there that morning,' Mina said finally. Her voice was a little breathless, as if she herself couldn't believe her words. 'He says he doesn't always know if I'm there or when I leave. And I went off to meet a friend who kind of stood me up, so the police are saying I don't have an alibi.'

THIRTEEN

D ulcie never thought of herself as a violent person. After hearing this, however, she was seized by a desire to shake someone – Tom Walls, to be specific – or maybe slap him.

'That's crazy,' she burst out with, instead. 'Is he – I mean, he always works on Level Two, right?'

'Yeah.' Mina nodded. 'He always says hi when I come in. I mean, that was it – you know about his stutter. But he would keep an eye on where I was, even when he had a load of books to shelve.'

Dulcie could picture it. Students weren't supposed to try to reshelve books – too many got lost or misfiled that way. Instead, they piled them on the carts positioned at the end of every few rows of stacks. If Mina were working at one of the carrels the library staffer would be able to check in with her every time he finished with a specific row. If that staffer was a friend, he should have been able to safely assure any authorities of Mina's presence – or her absence.

If, in fact, that was what had happened. Dulcie didn't like to admit it, even to herself, but it bothered her that her cousin had kind of changed her story. From not being there at all to going into the library but then leaving quickly . . . it sounded suspicious.

'So, you didn't meet with anyone after you left?'

Mina shrugged. 'Nothing I can talk about.'

That wasn't good. 'And you didn't, maybe, duck down to

your carrel? Just briefly?' Dulcie hated herself for even asking.

'No.' Mina didn't seem to take offense. 'And if I had, I'd have touched base with Tom. I wasn't going to be chased out of the library, but I hated being down there, knowing that creep was nearby. He was so angry after the hearing. He'd threatened me, you know. Said that if I ruined his career, he'd get me back.' She laughed, but it was a sad little sound. 'Maybe he did.'

'No, no way.' Dulcie was too angry to sit there any longer. 'Mina, this is terrible, and I'm really sorry I didn't know about any of it. But I'm going to straighten this out.'

She stood, but Mina did too, reaching out to her. 'Dulcie, you can't,' she said. 'Remember – I'm not supposed to say anything. You can't tell anyone.'

'Don't worry.' Dulcie took her cousin's hands in her own. 'I won't say anything to anyone about Fenderby, or about your suit. But I am going to track down Tom Walls and see why he won't tell the police what he knows to be true. Or I'll . . .'

She stopped herself. No, it wouldn't do to make any more threats.

'Just believe me,' she said as she reached for her bag. 'I'll find out why Tom isn't telling the truth, and I'll make sure he does.'

With renewed vigor, Dulcie marched back up to the Yard, determined to find her student and set things right. She knew that Tom Walls was a retiring sort. But there came a time in a person's life when he had to speak out. When someone else's reputation – even her freedom – were on the line was certainly one of those times.

'Ruby!' Ignoring the huddle of uniformed cops by the front entrance, Dulcie made her way into the library, heading right to the circulation counter to hail her friend. 'Do you know if Tom Walls is working today?'

'Tom? Sure.' Her friend paused, as if consulting a schedule in her mind. 'Though I don't know if they've opened Level Two up completely.' She leaned in, her voice dropping to a loud stage whisper. 'They've been looking at the ID scanners and talking to the guards all morning, and I think they're still looking for the murder weapon. But hang on.'

Dulcie waited while her friend consulted a less ephemeral schedule. In less than a minute, she was back. 'Yup, Fenderby's office is still off limits – I guess the cops are waiting for some test results. But the rest of the floor is open again, and Tom's on till three.'

'Thanks.' Dulcie turned for the elevators with a vague feeling of trepidation. She'd have gone back to Fenderby's office itself to get to the bottom of this. But now that she was back, she couldn't help remembering the grisly shock of the day before. That feeling of isolation and fear. As it was, she realized she was shivering slightly as the elevator descended, and not simply because of the state-of-the-art climate control, which compensated for even the slightest rise in temperature or humidity.

'Tom?' Years of training made it impossible for her to raise her voice. Instead, she called out softly as she began to walk down the rows of stacks. 'Are you there?'

The library was her home. The tall metal shelves with their orderly rankings were where she had forged her academic career. Today, though, they felt a bit spooky. Even the motion-sensor lights, which flicked on as she approached each row and then clicked off behind her, made her feel like she was being watched. Being followed, by something or someone that wouldn't identify itself.

'Mr Grey?' She mouthed the words silently. If Tom were in fact nearby, she didn't need him questioning her sanity. She had always liked the quiet student, but she didn't know him that well. 'Can you help me out here?'

She paused, waiting. But as too often happened these days, the only reply was silence. Or, not silence exactly, but a low-level hum. The air-conditioning, Dulcie told herself. That was all. Still, it was a comforting sound, reminiscent of her late pet's deep purr.

The rumble faded as she walked on. Not that that meant anything either. Although she couldn't help but draw her own conclusions as it grew more faint the closer she got to Fenderby's office. Down three more rows and to the left, over near where the high windows still let in some sunlight. Where, she was sure, she saw a movement – a shadow against the light.

'Tom?' she called. A faint noise – a soft shuffle, like a sneaker on the metal stair – came back, off to her right. Turning, Dulcie craned her neck, searching for the source of the sound. It came from the direction of Fenderby's office, though surely that room had been locked up tight. She did not, she was sure, want to go down there. But there was the shadow again – a flicker of light down one of the long rows of books.

'Tom!' She started down, and found herself in darkness as the overhead switched off. Dulcie paused, a chill running down her back. That flicker must have been a bulb or a switch on the blink. It couldn't have been someone turning off the light manually. That would make no sense. Yes, some light came in to this level – but here, in the middle of the high stacks, the darkness was nearly complete.

Not entirely. As she stood there, Dulcie realized her eyes were adjusting. 'This must be how a cat sees,' she said softly, wondering if a certain ghostly guardian were nearby. 'Am I right?'

In fact, if she got close to the shelves on her left, she could even make out titles. *Riot and Rebellion: A History of the Pamphlet in the Years of Crisis,* she read. *The Dawn of Propaganda*, gold letters on dark red, stood out next to it. Political essays. Of course, Dulcie realized, this was what Fenderby had specialized in. What her cousin had been studying when she had been down here. But where was Tom? As Dulcie turned, another title caught her eye – even in the dark, there was something about the binding, about the type. Could it be?

'*No!*' As she reached up for it, a sudden sharp pain – like a splinter or, no, a claw – raked her hand. She drew back, aware that she had cried out. Aware, as well, that another voice had echoed hers. At least, she thought it had.

Not that she could see anyone around her. Instead, she looked down to see her hand darkened by some tarry substance. It couldn't be blood. That swift pain had been too small, and too recent. Even the prick of a particularly large splinter would not have caused this much bleeding. Besides, even in the dim light, it was more brown than . . .

She looked up at the book she'd been reaching for. Yes, it was out of place. *American Gothic: the First Generation* contained *Susanna Castleton,* among other interesting pieces. And while *Castleton* was certainly political – Dulcie had written several papers on it as an undergrad – it was fiction, a novella that no more belonged here than *The Ravages of Umbria* would. This was why students were not supposed to reshelve their own works. Tut-tutting under her breath, Dulcie pulled the leatherbound volume from the shelf. It wasn't like she was going to make the problem any worse. Besides, she had already half-dislodged the novel. How odd, she thought, reaching for it again, that she could notice a book shelved incorrectly. But that day, when both her cousin and the clerk were working down here, she hadn't seen anything. She had believed herself to be alone . . .

'Dulcie?' The familiar voice made her turn as, with a click, the light went on.

'Tom.' She forced a smile. He was quiet. That must have been why she didn't see him that day. 'I guess you didn't hear me. I was looking for you. And, well, I found this.'

She held out the book. It was sticky, she realized. It was, in fact, covered with the same tacky brown substance that was on her hands. She must have touched it before she pulled back. 'Here.'

'But that's—' Tom's voice had gone softer than usual. Softer, even, than library etiquette dictated.

'Wow.' Dulcie looked down, spreading her fingers. It wasn't brown, she saw now that the light was on. It was rustier. Reddish. 'Oh, no!' Only years of training kept her from dropping the book. 'It's blood!' she exclaimed.

And with a thud loud enough to make the shelves rattle, Tom Walls fainted dead away.

'No, I have no idea.' An hour later, and Dulcie was again up in the library offices. This time she was speaking with an older officer. 'Is Tom OK?'

'Let's not worry about him now,' the officer said, for the fourth or fifth time.

Dulcie bit her lip. She had put the book down and run to

the student when he had fallen. He had blinked up at her, but his gaze had been unfocused as she cradled his head, calling out for help, and he had still seemed a bit groggy as the EMTs rushed in to bundle him on to a stretcher and back up the elevator.

'But I am,' she said. 'I mean, I know it was startling, but he might have hit his head.'

The ambulance crew had pushed her aside, looking – she realized only belatedly – for the source of all that blood. They had relaxed visibly when she had explained that, no, the sticky substance had been on the book – and on her hands – and that she had been the one to get it all over the student's shirt collar and pale cheeks. Still, he had fallen hard, and she knew from personal experience how treacherous head injuries could be.

'Let's talk about why you were there.' The officer's voice was low but firm, and once again Dulcie found herself missing Detective Rogovoy. She had asked for the detective as soon as she surfaced, in the wake of the ambulance crew and their stretcher. Nobody had responded, and she found herself craning toward the door, hoping to see his familiar bulk. 'About that book you say you found.'

'I did find it.' Dulcie didn't understand why the man sitting across from her didn't simply check his own notes. 'I saw that it was misfiled and I pulled it down. I mean, I know I'm not supposed to do that. But really, once a book is in the wrong place, how are the library staff supposed to correct the situation? I was going to tell Tom about it.'

'That's right.' Finally, the cop checked his notes. 'You knew that Tom Walls was working down there. You had asked about his hours and his location.'

'Yes.' Dulcie nodded enthusiastically. This man was no Rogovoy, but he was catching on.

'Were you looking for him to give him this book you found?'

'No.' Dulcie closed her eyes in frustration. In retrospect, she wished she hadn't found it. Hadn't bothered to pull it from its misplaced berth. That she had listened to what was clearly a warning. 'I pulled it out because it was in the wrong place. I was looking for Tom—'

She stopped. She had been about to say that she was looking for Tom because she wanted to find out why he wouldn't acknowledge that he had been downstairs with Mina. That he wouldn't provide her with – awful word – an alibi. But to do that would lead to explaining why Mina wanted company when she was down on that level. Her cousin had shared the details of her lawsuit in confidence. It wasn't Dulcie's secret to divulge.

'I was looking for Tom,' she said. He would have to be content with that.

'And you say you simply "found" that book.' The officer was staring at Dulcie's hands. She'd been allowed to wash them, once an older woman in a white suit had taken photos and scraped bits of the sticky brown substance off her palms.

'Yes, I did.' Dulcie realized she was wringing her hands and made herself stop. The desire to cleanse herself once she realized just what that syrupy substance was had been intense. There was something about this officer's gaze, however, that made her feel as if they were still dirty. 'I'm doing my dissertation on fiction of roughly the same period as *Susanna Castleton*,' she explained. 'So, of course, I recognized the volume, and saw that it was out of place. If I or one of my students were searching for this collection, this would be a hardship.'

She didn't know how to stress the importance of order. The officer was nodding, however, so maybe he'd gotten it.

'So this is a book you know. A book you've used before.'

'As I said, yes.' He was not, Dulcie decided, the sharpest man on the squad. She didn't want to get anybody in trouble, but really, she would have to say something to Rogovoy when he got back. 'Now, may I go?'

'I'm afraid we'll have to ask you to stay a bit longer, Miss.' The officer was signaling to someone behind her, gesturing as if calling someone near. 'I know you're a smart young lady, so maybe you can figure this out. How is it, do you think, that you find a body. And then the very next day, you find a book – a book that you tell us you know well. A book that preliminary forensics suggest was most likely the murder weapon?'

FOURTEEN

'Wait, what?' Dulcie couldn't believe what she was hearing. 'The book?'

The officer was still looking past her, but before he could even begin to answer, the sense of what he'd said hit her. 'Of course.' She started nodding. 'That's why it was misfiled. Whoever did it . . .'

'Ms Schwartz?' She turned around at the sound of the familiar voice, her spirits rising.

'Detective Rogovoy!' she exclaimed. 'You're back!' She could have hugged the big detective, assuming she could have gotten her arms around his boulder-like form. Finally, this mess would get straightened out. 'And just in time, too. Someone's got to talk to Tom Walls. He works down on Level Two. He'd know who had been down there – who might have snuck a book into the wrong shelf.'

'Please, Ms Schwartz.' The detective nodded at the officer who had been interviewing Dulcie. 'If you could just stick to answering Sergeant Milford's questions?'

'But they weren't questions per se. He was making statements.' To Dulcie's relief, Rogovoy looked like he was joining the interview. He had turned to pull up another chair as she spoke.

'You were asking for Tom Walls,' he said, his growly voice deceptively soft. 'A junior in your department?' Clearly, she had made her point.

'Yes, of course.' Dulcie hesitated. Rogovoy was a large man, and the chair he'd lowered himself into didn't look up to the task. 'Detective?'

'Yes?' He leaned over. The chair squeaked.

'Are you—' She hesitated, unwilling to offend. 'All right?'

He leaned back, provoking another protest from the furniture. 'Ms Schwartz, can we at least try to stay on point?'

'Of course.' Dulcie wanted to be helpful. 'Only, you've not been around, and I was a little concerned.'

'Huh.' The big man looked at her, his stone face softening ever so slightly. 'Well, that's nice, but no. Work-related,' was all he said. 'I'm only observing here. There's a tangential connection.'

He nodded to his colleague, and both turned to Dulcie.

'Tangential, as in touching?' She stopped short. 'Has anyone asked Tom Walls if he might be involved in any of this?' Dulcie didn't like incriminating anyone else, especially not a student. But she couldn't avoid the obvious. 'I know he was supposed to shelve books, but mis-shelving a book would be a smart ploy. I mean, if he wanted to throw off suspicion.'

Rogovoy glanced up at the other cop. Dulcie waited. It seemed obvious.

'Ms Schwartz, why were you looking for Tom Walls?'

Dulcie turned to face the sergeant. What was his name, Milford? 'Why are you asking, Sergeant? Is that a crime?'

'Nobody's accusing you of—' Rogovoy put out his broad hands, almost as if he would smooth her fur.

'No, I want to know,' the sergeant interrupted. Rogovoy was going to have to do something about discipline. Surely, this younger man was an underling. 'She stumbles on the professor,' Milford continued. 'She finds a book covered in gore, and she's insisting we talk to a poor kid who fainted at the sight of all that blood. Is she one of your—'

'No.' When he wanted, Rogovoy had a bark like a bulldog. Dulcie looked from him to his junior, wondering what the man had been implying. He couldn't think that he and she . . . 'Ms Schwartz,' the senior detective made a noise like he was clearing his throat, his voice going soft again. 'If you could answer the question.'

'About Tom? That poor kid!' Dulcie made herself focus, but that fleeting suspicion – that suggestion – had sparked her anger. She had all the sympathy in the world for Tom Walls. He was the kind of quiet, retiring young man she could have seen herself with, if she weren't involved with Chris, of course. But to call him 'poor kid' when he wouldn't even speak up. When people were making insinuations about her. About her cousin . . . 'He's a coward,' she burst out with now. 'And I want to know why he's lying about my cousin, about not

knowing whether she was in the library the morning Professor
Fenderby was killed.'

'Your cousin?' Rogovoy's eyebrows had disappeared into
the wrinkles of his forehead. 'I wasn't aware that you had any
family on campus.'

'She's . . .' Dulcie sighed. To her it was clear. 'We're . . .
it's very distant. But we look alike, and there's so much in our
families that mirror each other.' She stopped short of talking
about their common ancestress. That might sound far-fetched
to a non-academician. 'And that's why I feel an obligation to
help her now that she's under suspicion.'

Rogovoy looked up, and Dulcie caught the glance he gave
the younger officer. Saw, as well, the very brief nod the sergeant
made to the older man's silent query.

'Why do you think she's under suspicion?' Rogovoy's voice
was so quiet now Dulcie had to lean in to hear him.

'Because of her suit against Fenderby. The harassment charges
that were dismissed. She was warned not to—' Dulcie caught
herself. She hadn't wanted to say anything. She hadn't meant
to betray Mina's confidence. She looked up at the big detective.
'Detective Rogovoy, I'm sorry I said anything. You can't – she's
not supposed to talk to anybody. But I'm not only her cousin,
I'm a friend and I feel a certain responsibility for her.'

How to explain that she had introduced her young cousin
to the allure of early nineteenth-century prose, to the writings
of the woman she believed connected them both? And that by
doing so, she had set Mina on a path that put her in Fenderby's
way?

'And Tom Walls?' Rogovoy sounded so gentle. Maybe she
didn't have to explain.

'He knows Mina, and he's always with her when she's down
on Level Two. It was an arrangement they had. I mean, I didn't
see him down there. But I'd had a shock. He works there, and
I believe Mina.' Dulcie stumbled over herself to explain. It
was better to have it all out in the open. Besides, she told
herself, talking to the police wasn't necessarily revealing a
confidence. It was more like a civic duty. 'Only now he's
saying he was here, but he can't say she wasn't.' It was all
too much. 'I thought if I could talk to him, to find out why.'

Rogovoy was holding up one of his large hands. 'I don't think you should say any more, Ms Schwartz.' His voice was still soft, only now there was an element of sadness in it that was matched by the droop of his large, tired eyes. 'Not before you speak to counsel, at any rate.'

'It's only logical, Dulce.' Chris was on his way. Dulcie had reached him during a tutoring session that he'd cut short when he saw her urgent texts. 'I'm sure they're simply following procedure.'

'Procedure?' Dulcie had retreated to her office, after Rogovoy had escorted her out. She'd been too upset to head for the café where they usually met, and hadn't even wanted to face the walk home alone. 'Chris, you don't understand.'

'He didn't arrest you, right?' Chris would be there in minutes. Dulcie knew that. She'd asked him to come here for just that reason. 'They're gathering information right now, and what you've told them lays out one clear possibility.'

'Chris!' Dulcie was pacing, the small office beginning to feel more like a prison cell than a refuge. She'd been half hoping, when she came down here, that she'd find Lloyd at work. The company of her long-suffering colleague would have given the afternoon some semblance of normalcy.

When she'd found herself alone in their shared space, she'd turned instead to the one high-set window. At times, when the light had shown down, illuminating the swirl of dust motes that never quite cleared, she had been sure she'd seen Mr Grey, and if she had ever had need of a benign feline presence, it was now. But she'd been too agitated to sit and stare. And it seemed that even as a ghost, her one-time pet tended to make himself scarce when rapid movement or loud voices were involved.

'Dulce, sweetie, I'll be there in five minutes.' He'd given up on attempting to explain his so-called reasoning at least. 'Maybe try Suze again?'

'Maybe that's her now.' Dulcie switched over to the incoming call without bothering to say goodbye. If he was going to take the side of the police in all this, then she was justified in nearly hanging up on him, she told herself. Besides, he'd be here any moment.

'Suze?' she asked the phone, breathless. Her former room-mate was a full-fledged lawyer now, working at a legal clinic over in Jamaica Plain. And although their busy schedules kept them from spending as much time together as they once did, Dulcie had no doubt that her fair-minded friend would come to her aid.

'Dulcie, what's up?' Suze sounded calm, even though she had clearly gotten Dulcie's panicked message. 'Is another one of your strays in a jam?'

'Yes, well, no, not exactly.' Dulcie paused. Suze had helped Dulcie out several times before. Most recently, however, she had been instrumental in getting a former colleague into subsidized housing. 'I mean, yes, sort of. My cousin – you remember Mina Love?' She didn't pause long enough for Suze to answer. 'But it's gotten complicated. Suze, I think I'm under suspicion for a murder.'

Once the words were out, Dulcie felt calmer. She was even able to sit down on the edge of her desk and explain what had happened. 'And then Detective Rogovoy told me that I shouldn't leave the city without telling him,' Dulcie concluded. 'I mean, he's keeping tabs on where I go now!'

'That is scary, Dulcie.' Unlike Chris, Suze knew better than to downplay what she was going through. 'And it sounds a little like they tag-teamed you in there. You know, with this Milford being the heavy, pressuring you so you would confide in Rogovoy.'

'But I didn't tell him anything he didn't know.' Dulcie heard her own lie. 'I mean, not much. It wasn't like I was pointing a finger at anyone.'

'You didn't have to,' said Suze.

Dulcie listened, with growing dismay, as her friend went through the same list that Chris had outlined: Dulcie appeared to be protecting her younger cousin. Therefore, it was possible that she had felt the need to avenge her, as well. And now she appeared to be trying to influence what another party – Tom Walls – had told the police.

'But I didn't know about Mina – about Fenderby.' It was the same objection she had made to Chris. 'So I didn't have – I wouldn't have a motive.'

There, the word was out. Not only that, but someone was knocking. Chris! She slid off the desk to unbolt the door.

'Suze.' She mouthed the name as her tall boyfriend slipped his lanky frame inside.

'Manipulated.' Suze had kept talking. Dulcie had missed something.

'Excuse me?' She closed the door behind him.

'I don't think it likely that the cops – even your buddy Rogovoy – would let you in on the direction of the investigation if you were a real suspect, Dulcie.' Dulcie looked up at her boyfriend, a hint of hope sparking the beginning of a smile.

'You think that I'm not . . .' She didn't dare finish.

'I think it's more likely that they believe that you've been manipulated,' Suze said, emphasizing her last word. 'Both Tom and Mina are documented as entering the library, although neither were around by the time you discovered the body, and it makes sense. They're probably thinking that your testimony can be used against your cousin.'

FIFTEEN

T he lightning flared, illuminating for one brief moment the storm-toss'd trees, as spare and grasping as I had once felt myself to be. I turned from them, as I would turn from my former foolish self, in time to hear another crack and howl. The storm persisted, but in its momentary illumination, I eyed once more the crest upon the gate. My final glimpse, before I fled into the horrid night, burned stark upon my eyes. Three lions, rampant—

'No! I cry aloud, as if that very storm still raged. In truth, I fear another, and in my haste to scrape the page clean, I am the brutal strike. The page is torn, a night's work ruined, and yet I cannot rest. It goes, as have so many, into the fire, its edges redden as they curl, then blacken unto ash. I stand watch, aware of my profligacy. This paper may be both our salvation and undoing. For what I can create with my wit and *pen procures us bread, and yet I must not reveal too much, for I myself am the tinder, awaiting one incautious spark. It is my name that may catch and flare. May cause the conflagration that brings down this house, and she who sleeps the rest of innocence within.*

Dulcie woke with a start, her head throbbing. She had had trouble falling asleep, too worried by Suze's concerns to listen to Chris's common sense rebuttal.

'At least they don't think you did it,' her boyfriend had said, as Dulcie had paced back and forth. Esmé had made herself scarce even before her boyfriend had come home. Unless it was her drama, the little tuxedo cat wasn't interested in a scene. 'They'll get to the bottom of it, Dulcie.' Chris had done his best to calm her. 'Rogovoy's a good cop.'

'Maybe that's the problem.' Dulcie repeated her answer to herself now. 'Maybe Rogovoy is too good a cop.'

It was hopeless, she thought, lying there. She couldn't sleep. Couldn't even apply herself to the puzzle of her nightmare. Why had the old familiar setting – a storm at sea – been replaced by one on land? Why did she see herself now as the author? Well, that one might make sense, she acknowledged. Considering how the recent catastrophe touched so closely on her work.

And on her cousin, too. Was it Mina who *'sleeps the rest of innocence'?* she wondered. She hoped so, wishing her cousin more peaceful slumber than she herself could find. But that was the least of the questions ricocheting around Dulcie's mind.

Dulcie loved her cousin. She'd trust her with her own life. Only, where had Mina gone Monday morning? Where, for that matter, had Tom been? It was true that Dulcie hadn't explored every nook and cranny of Level Two – on her way in, she was too set on finding Fenderby. And then she had found him, she thought, with a shiver. But even before, she had been struck by the stillness of the floor. The darkness, except for that stray flash of light from a high-set window.

She shivered again, thinking through the implications. If something had happened between her cousin and the professor,

Dulcie would understand. Mina had been sorely provoked. Maybe there had been another scene between her cousin and Fenderby – some kind of confrontation that had led to an accident, a horrible, tragic accident. Then it would be quite possible that Mina had panicked. Had run back to her room and, well, invented a story to cover it up. Of course, her cousin would come forward, once she had caught her breath, so to speak. She would explain the circumstance, and how whatever had happened hadn't been premeditated. But now Dulcie had made that impossible. Now if Mina confessed to – well – anything, it would appear that she was merely trying to make a deal. To lessen her own guilt. When, in fact, the whole mess had been caused by that creep Roland Fenderby's gross predatory actions in the first place.

'Damn the man.' Dulcie kicked off the covers. Chris, snoring beside her, wasn't likely to wake. 'He deserved it.'

She climbed out of bed and made her way into the kitchen. The night outside was the opposite of that in her dream, clear and bright with an almost full moon. Still, she felt the loneliness of the dream's central figure – a woman, writing alone at night. Desperate to finish . . . what?

Dulcie leaned her forehead on the cool glass and felt a warm pressure against her shin: Esmé. Sometimes it was good to have even a normal cat around. Calming. Dulcie knew she had been letting her fancies carry her away. Her concerns about her thesis were obviously being translated into dream imagery again, the writer with her old-fashioned pen and inkwell standing in for Dulcie and her computer.

Scooping the soft feline up in her arms, Dulcie mulled over what she really knew. She had had variants on this dream before. She either saw the woman writing at her desk, usually by night, as if this was the only time she could escape the cares of the day. Or, she thought as she stroked her pet into a purr, she found herself in one of the wild adventures the dream figure was creating. Fleeing that fortress-like castle in the middle of a storm, or crossing the sea on a too-small sailing ship, the waves making the journey both dramatic and terrifying. It was all standard Gothic fare. Dulcie didn't need Chris to point this out, although he had learned enough about her research to do so. As her own work neared its peak, it made sense that she'd dream a mash-up of her subject and her own aspirations.

Except that Dulcie had come to believe that these dreams were about more than thesis anxiety. Although she never learned the name of the woman in her dream, never even saw anything that might identify her, Dulcie believed she was a real historical person. In fact, even if Chris eyed her with that worried look when she mentioned it, Dulcie believed that the dream writer was the subject of her dissertation, the anonymous author of *The Ravages*. Previous dreams had helped her deal with some problems – both in real life and her work. And while Chris would have a logical explanation for why that happened, something about her daytime thoughts percolating through her subconscious to some kind of clarity, Dulcie knew better. After all, reason didn't explain Mr Grey either.

Whether because of Dulcie's increasing agitation or the mention of her own predecessor, the little cat began to squirm, and Dulcie released Esmé to jump to the floor.

'*Little one.*' Even as Esmé scurried off, a voice as gentle as the brush of whiskers greeted her. '*You are worried, my child.*'

'I am, Mr Grey.' Dulcie stayed where she was, staring at the darkened window. She knew from experience that if she turned, the warm voice was likely to go quiet. 'I'm worried about my cousin, about Mina.'

'*About family, about connections.*' The voice faded into something very much like a purr. Dulcie had once told the big grey cat that he was her real family, back in the days when her pet had lived with her and Suze in his corporeal form and before he spoke in anything more than the occasional mew. She had been fighting with her mother, she remembered, and felt more alone than usual. '*The ties that bind us can also burden us, my kitten.*'

Dulcie felt herself tear up at the endearment. Unless, of course, her late great cat was talking about Esmé.

A warm rumble – half chuckle, half purr – disabused her of that notion. '*As if love were exclusive.*' The low voice seemed to follow directly on her thought. '*As if the warmth in our hearts flowed in clear paths along with our reason.*'

He could have been talking about their relationship, Dulcie thought. But what he said also pertained to her connection with Mina.

'It's true, I'm not sure what's going on with her.' Dulcie assumed the voice in the dark could sense her thoughts. He had always seemed to, even back when he, too, was a flesh-and-blood pet. She recalled hauling the big cat into her lap and burying her face in his long, soft fur. In true feline fashion, he would put up with the awkward contact for a minute or two, before he too struggled to get down, as Esmé had. 'But I trust her – and I feel close to her. The same way that I feel close to you – and to Chris, of course.'

'You wish to protect her, little one.' The rumble was louder. Dulcie could almost feel it. *'And you are concerned that you have done the opposite, that relationships may influence us both toward the positive and to ill effect.'*

'That's it exactly.' Dulcie stood up, all the while careful to keep her eyes on the window. The moon was visible above the apartment building opposite, full and white.

'What we do to protect our own . . .' The purr began to recede and weaken. *'The conflict of the effort . . .'*

'Dulcie, you're up.' She turned to see Chris walking into the kitchen. He reached for the light switch. 'Why didn't you wake me?'

'I wanted to let you sleep.' Dulcie knew her smile was more wan than welcoming. She couldn't help it. Mr Grey had been fading anyway, but she had hoped for more time with him. 'After all, I made you stay up pretty late.'

'You'd do the same for me.' He pulled the refrigerator door open and stood there, browsing the shelves. It was the kind of thoughtless, wasteful habit that Dulcie had never been allowed to develop, growing up in straitened circumstances. Right now, it was the dearest thing she had ever seen. 'Hey, do we have any of those sesame noodles left?' he asked, his face illuminated by the refrigerator light. 'I had this wild dream. I was running down a hillside – a mountain, actually – in a storm at night. It's left me famished.'

SIXTEEN

Dulcie woke the second time to the smell of coffee. A quick glance at the nightstand clock showed her that it was almost ten. She yawned and stretched, until a combination of that intoxicating aroma and general anxiety propelled her out of bed.

'You didn't wake me.' She found her boyfriend in the kitchen, setting out cereal bowls.

'You needed the sleep.' He turned to pour her a mug, but nodded back at the table where Esmé was keeping a watchful eye on her phone. 'You've been getting some messages though. You might want to check in.'

'Great.' Dulcie felt her mellow mood begin to crumble as she reached for the phone. Esmé batted it away, but Dulcie grabbed the little device before it went flying to the floor. 'I'm sorry,' she apologized to both of them before she could snark more. 'It's just—'

'Here.' Chris put the mug on the table beside her, as Esmé jumped down with a peeved grunt. 'Do what you've got to do.'

'Thanks.' Sipping on the coffee – Chris made it almost as strong as Nancy did – Dulcie listened to her messages.

'Ms Schwartz.' Martin Thorpe sounded worried as usual. 'Would you call me? It's necessary that we speak as soon as possible.'

Dulcie rolled her eyes. '*Thorpe!*' She mouthed the name as if her adviser could hear her, and nearly missed the next message.

'Officially, I'll be a visiting professor through the fall semester. After that, we'll see how it goes.'

'Yes!' Dulcie fist-pumped the air. She didn't need to hear the opening of the message to know it was from Renée Showalter, the Canadian academic who had expedited the transfer of materials to the Mildon Collection specifically because she knew of Dulcie's interest. It was in those papers that Dulcie had found the fragments of the later, forgotten novel by the author of *The Ravages*. Granted, Professor Showalter could be a bit odd – Dulcie had reason to believe the red-haired academic might even be a werewolf – but she was definitely an ally.

'Don't you see what this means?' Dulcie quickly related the news to her boyfriend. 'If Thorpe insists on me having another person on my panel, I bet Showalter will do it. In fact, I'm going to propose her today.'

'I'm glad, Dulce, really.' There was something about the way his forehead furrowed, eyebrows disappearing beneath his too-long bangs.

'But what?' Dulcie knew the signs. She waited.

'Well, maybe don't go around telling everyone just how happy you are.' He paused, as if hoping he wouldn't have to continue. 'I know Suze was optimistic, but once this gets out, it might sound like motive for you to want Fenderby dead.'

Dulcie tried to put Chris's fears out of her mind as she trotted off toward the Square. Nancy had promised her she would squeeze her in with Thorpe, if she came by soon, and Dulcie was eager to set her plan in motion. By the time she went to her eleven a.m. section, she might have Showalter on her board. Showalter – who understood what she was writing and why – would make finishing her dissertation a breeze.

As she hurried through another fine spring morning, she briefly considered Chris's other concern – that Dulcie was committing her mentor without consulting her.

'But she's like family,' Dulcie had remonstrated. 'She's always looked out for me.' Dulcie didn't even mention the other bonds she felt with the academic, another red-haired researcher. The possibility that they both might be descended from the anonymous author, as well as the strange sense of the supernatural both shared. Those were too tenuous for even Chris to believe in. Still, Dulcie tried to remember Mr Grey's words from the night before. 'Something about protecting our own?' The soft breeze blew her own curls back against her cheek, soft like the touch of whiskers. 'That was it, wasn't it Mr Grey?'

'She'll do it,' she said, to a bright-eyed squirrel who paused on the trunk of a maple as she went by. 'She has to, right?' The squirrel didn't respond.

'Nancy?' Dulcie poked her head into the departmental secretary's office. While the coffee pot was full, the seat behind the desk was empty. Dulcie took advantage of the former, filling her travel mug for the long trek upstairs. It was only when she realized how slowly she was pouring that she admitted to herself that she was stalling. The motherly secretary might not be able to offer any real aid in her ongoing struggle with her adviser, but just seeing her made Dulcie feel braver.

The sound of heels on the uncarpeted stairs alerted her to Nancy's approach, and she ducked out of the office to greet her. It was only when her cheery 'good morning' was met by silence that Dulcie noticed that the older woman was wiping her face.

'Nancy, are you OK?' Dulcie stepped forward to embrace the secretary, realizing too late that she was still holding her mug.

'I'm fine, dear.' Nancy's smile was clearly forced, as her eyes blinked back tears. 'Simply a disagreement.'

'With Thorpe?' Dulcie couldn't keep the surprise from her voice. If the senior academic didn't know how lucky he was, he was an idiot. 'I'm sorry. I know we're not supposed to know about you two, but . . .'

'It's fine.' Nancy shook her head, looking more relaxed by the second. 'I feel like you are part of the family now. That's what . . .' She broke off with a sigh, and Dulcie saw her glance back up the stairs. 'Well, you'd better go to your meeting.'

'If you're sure.' Another smile, this one with more heart in it, was her only answer. And so it was with great trepidation that Dulcie ascended those same stairs. Thorpe in a foul mood was not someone she wanted to contend with on the best of days. And anyone who could bring the sweet woman downstairs to tears was not someone to ask a favor of.

'Mr Thorpe?' The door was ajar, but Dulcie knocked anyway. 'May I?'

'Yes, yes.' She heard papers shuffling. 'Come in.'

'Good morning.' Dulcie knew the grin on her face probably looked as fake as it felt and kept on talking. 'I was really glad to get your message this morning, because there's something I wanted to ask you. I was wondering if, what with the – ah – tragic death of Professor Fenderby, I could apply to have another academic added to my review committee. To add Renée Showalter.'

There, she'd gotten it all out. The relevant bits, that is. And if Thorpe raised the objection that Showalter wouldn't actually be a member of the department until the fall, Dulcie was ready to counter with her own timeline. Although she hoped to file the dissertation soon, the final steps toward getting her degree – defending her dissertation – would undoubtedly carry her into the autumn term.

Thorpe, however, was not objecting. He was not, in fact, saying anything.

'I'm prepared to file the paperwork,' Dulcie continued, grateful for the chance to say her piece. 'I'm looking to finish at the end of the fall semester of next year,' she said. 'And Professor Showalter has expressed her willingness to work with me even before she gets here.'

With that, she sat back, waiting for the response. Thorpe was blinking, his mouth slightly open. She had blindsided him, she knew. Thorpe considered Renée Showalter a rival for the position of department chair.

'Ms Schwartz,' he said finally, then paused to clear his throat.

'Yes?' She wanted to be polite, but really, she was going to have to insist.

'Ms Schwartz,' he said again. 'Do you have any idea why I asked you to meet with me today?'

'I assumed it was because of all the unpleasantness.' She didn't want to get into details. 'And I wanted you to know, you don't have to worry about my dissertation any longer. I'm really hunkering down, and I'm completely focused. Especially now that I'm hoping to add Professor Showalter to my panel.'

'But – no.' Dulcie was afraid he was going to choke. 'That's not why . . .' He paused and reached for his own travel mug. After a long draft, he tried again.

'I'm afraid that won't be necessary,' he said, his voice still strangely tight. 'You've been put on disciplinary probation, Ms Schwartz. Yours is an unusual case, I know, and of course none of us are saying that you've committed any infractions of the university code of behavior. However, the university does not feel comfortable with the questions that are being raised about your involvement in the – ah – the unfortunate circumstances surrounding Professor Fenderby's demise.'

He stopped and cleared his throat. Then, as if reading a proclamation, he began again, saying the words that Dulcie dreaded. 'Ms Schwartz, I asked you here this morning to inform you that your privileges as a member of the university have been suspended. All work toward your degree must cease pending the successful resolution of the criminal investigation.'

SEVENTEEN

Nancy was waiting on the first floor, standing by the base of the stairs and wringing her hands.

'Oh, Dulcie!'she said. 'I'm so sorry.'

'You knew?' Dulcie blinked up at her.

'That's what Martin and I . . .' She paused, biting her lip, her eyes welling up again. 'When you came in this morning.' She stopped, shaking her head. 'It's simply not fair.'

'I have to go.' Dulcie made her way toward the door, hoping to reach it before she started to bawl. 'I have a section to teach.'

'Oh, Dulcie!' Nancy's voice stopped her, and she turned around.

'You mean I . . .' Dulcie shook her head. 'But, my section?'

'I've been told to make other arrangements.' Nancy looked hangdog. 'Only for the time being, of course. I'm sure this will all be cleared up in no time.'

*   *   *

Dulcie stumbled out of the little clapboard house nearly blinded by tears. Suspended? On disciplinary probation? But she hadn't done anything! All that had happened was that she was in the wrong place at the wrong time – twice. First, when she found Fenderby's body and then when she had accidentally pulled the bloody book off the shelf. It was almost as if . . .

She stopped short. No, this was crazy. If Trista hadn't put the idea in her head, she'd never even be thinking it. Why would anyone want to frame her for murder? Who disliked her that much?

Even though she had no place to be, Dulcie kept walking. Maybe if she did, she thought, she'd find an answer. At any rate, she wanted to get away from the departmental office. That was where she had first mouthed off against Fenderby. Where – she paused to consider – both Alyson Beaumont and Tom Walls had heard her wish him ill. Alyson and Tom – who, between them, had focused attention on her cousin, as well as on herself. Had there been anyone else in the offices then? Anyone besides Nancy?

Alyson had told the police that she'd seen a red-haired woman near Fenderby's office. Even if she was wrong about Fenderby and Mina, even if she'd misinterpreted, Dulcie didn't think a student of hers would actually lie to the police. Would she? And Mina had acknowledged she'd been in the library that morning. No, it was Tom who had refused to support Mina's alibi. He was the one who Dulcie needed to talk to – not only to clear her cousin's name but also her own.

But first, she had a call to make.

'Professor Showalter?' Dulcie almost felt relieved when she got her mentor's voicemail. There was just too much to explain. 'I got your message and I'm thrilled. But – well, there's been a complication. Would you call me back?'

Her next was to Chris. 'Disciplinary probation!' she was yelling in frustration by the end of that message. He would understand. So, she realized, would Suze – and her former roommate might actually be in a position to help.

'I can't believe I actually reached you.' Dulcie collapsed on the library steps as her old friend answered. She had wandered over here without any specific plan, but her relief on hearing Suze's voice – live and not a recording – seemed to drain all the nervous energy out of her body. 'For real!'

'I hate people who screen their calls,' her friend said. 'Though, believe me, I'm often tempted.'

'You don't think . . .' Dulcie paused, anxiety nibbling away at that relief. 'I was trying to reach Professor Showalter earlier.'

'I'm sure she really is out of her office.' Suze rushed to reassure her. 'But, hey, what's up?'

'Nothing,' said Dulcie. 'Or, everything. The university has put me on probation. Suze, this is serious. They're not even letting me file for completion of my thesis.'

'Wow.' It wasn't the cheery response Dulcie had been hoping for. Then again, it was nice to be taken seriously. 'I was afraid of this.'

'You were?' Dulcie was confused. 'But I thought you were worried about Mina, that the cops were twisting my words to frame her.'

'I thought the cops were manipulating you.' Suze paused, and Dulcie struggled to remember her friend's words. 'That they were simply bringing up Mina's suit to see how you'd react. To see if you'd implicate your cousin.'

'But I didn't.' None of this was making sense. 'At least, I don't think I did.'

'Well, now I wonder if I may have been speaking prematurely.' Suze's voice was serious. 'If they are considering it as a serious motive. Only not for Mina. For you.'

EIGHTEEN

Suze immediately nixed Dulcie's idea of speaking to Tom Walls.

'You can't, Dulcie,' she said, her voice firm. 'You cannot seek that man out. Do you understand?'

'But what if—' She wanted to explain her theory. That someone was trying to deflect blame. That she was a scapegoat.

'No,' Suze said again. 'You cannot.'

'Yes,' Dulcie had muttered finally. Suze seemed to require a response.

'That would be tampering with a witness.' Her friend was determined to spell it out. 'And if charges are filed against you, that would go a long way to implicating you.'

'But what if—'

'No, Dulcie.' Suze cut her off. 'I know you believe that you're the only one who can get to the bottom of this. That you're the only one who cares, but trust me, you're not. I've been hearing about a special operation on campus, though that seems to predate this situation with Fenderby. Nobody's talking, but I'm on it. And you should get back to work – and let me do my job. Don't let this derail you. I promise, as soon as we're off the phone, I'm going to call over there and see what I can find out. After all, if you're not being investigated with an eye toward charges, then they have no right to upset your academic career.'

'You mean, maybe you can . . .' Dulcie didn't dare ask.

'Besides, if they are going to charge you, then we have a right to know that too,' her friend concluded, deflating any hope that Dulcie had left. 'I mean officially, they don't have to reveal their evidence until we go to trial. You know that.'

'I do.' Dulcie had begun sniffling. 'It's just a lot to take in.'

'I'm sorry.' Suze must have caught Dulcie's tone, if not her sniffles. 'I'm pretty sure they're just casting a wide net. I mean, the evidence is circumstantial. Though the chances of such multiple coincidences . . .'

'Great.' Dulcie slumped forward. Only the necessity of letting her friend get back to work roused her to thank her, and then to let her go. Once she'd hung up, she rested her head on her knees, shielding herself from the bright morning around her. What Suze had said made sense, and she was scared. But if she was going to listen to part of what her friend had advised, she should listen to all of it. Suze was a lawyer now, and she was on the case. And Dulcie's time would be best spent focusing on her own work. Not worrying about things she had no control over. She'd talk to Chris tonight, and he'd be full of encouragement. But with his emphasis on logic, he didn't always get what she was about. If only she had someone here to cheer her on.

At times like this, she missed Mr Grey more than she could bear. She didn't have to explain herself to him. Didn't have to justify her moods. Granted, she might not have been able to. He was a cat, after all, and when he lived with her, his means of communication were limited to the occasional soft *mrrrup?* But she remembered what a comforting presence he had been. The way he would brush against her, leaning in so that she felt the soft warmth of his body against her leg.

'Miss? Are you OK?' The gentle voice startled her, and she looked up at a face she vaguely recognized. Freckles, not whiskers, set off green eyes, but still there was something familiar in his look of entreaty. 'Do you want me to get help?'

'No, no, I'm fine.' Dulcie struggled to her feet as it hit her. 'It's Nathan, isn't it From English ten?'

'Yeah.' The freckled sophomore nodded eagerly. 'You gave the talk about political pamphlets.'

'I did.' The memory brought Dulcie back. While non-fiction was far from her specialty, the recent discoveries she had made of her thesis subject's feminist topics had intrigued the section head. He'd asked her to give a supplemental lecture. To her surprise it had been well attended.

'It was the best part of the course for me.' Nathan blushed, red flooding up between those tawny freckles. 'I mean, I was taking it as an elective.'

'I get it.' Dulcie smiled. 'There isn't much else in American lit for a government major.'

He nodded enthusiastically, making Dulcie glad she had dredged his name up from among hundreds of former students.

'Anyway, if you're OK?' He paused, the question in his eyes.

'Thanks,' she said. 'I am.' To herself, she added the conditional: 'now. Thank you, Mr Grey.' It was good to be reminded that she was not, in fact, alone.

Despite that encouraging encounter on the stairs, Dulcie was still unsure whether she should even attempt to enter the library. Telling herself that she might as well find out the worst, she decided to try it. After all, if she could get back to work, maybe she would be able to make good use of her newly freed up morning. Never again, she promised herself, would she complain about having to take on another section, not even of the broadest freshman survey classes. Certainly not English ten, she told herself. Not when her spirits had been so revived by a chance meeting.

Unless . . . Dulcie paused. 'Mr Grey?' Under her breath, she addressed the library's spacious anteroom. 'Was that you?' She remembered quite well another chance meeting, when she had found a bedraggled cat out in a nasty nor'easter. Suze had urged her to keep going. To not check out the faint movement – the soft mewl – she had heard in that alley. But she had, rescuing the wet and underfed cat who would come to mean so much to her. And now she stepped toward the check-in desk.

'Dulcie!' Ruby's voice rang out, as unlike Mr Grey's soft mew as anything could be. Still, Dulcie was never happier to see her friend. 'I'm glad you're here.'

'Me too.' Dulcie looked around. She'd been hoping for the guard to wave her in, so she wouldn't have to risk swiping her ID. But being hailed by Ruby superseded even that, and the older guard simply nodded as her friend walked her in. 'Thanks,' she whispered. They were making their way over to Ruby's desk in circulation when her friend paused and turned to her.

'What's up?' Worry creased her face.

'I— Never mind.' Dulcie shook her head. Ruby was a friend. Someone she could trust, but Ruby also had the loudest voice of any library professional Dulcie knew. She'd explain what was happening once the two of them were out of earshot of anybody who might second-guess her presence here. 'What's up with you?'

'I didn't know if you heard about that book.' She pulled Dulcie behind the desk and rolled over a second chair for her. 'The one you found?'

Dulcie nodded. 'I know. It's the murder weapon.' A vague sick feeling was coming over her. 'The police think the killer put it back in the stacks.' She didn't add the worst part – that the police liked her for both the crime and the cover-up.

'But that's just it.' Ruby leaned in and took Dulcie's hands in her own. 'You didn't hear the latest. That book should never have been in Fenderby's office.'

Dulcie shook her head, not understanding. People took books off the shelves all the time. As long as they didn't want to take them out of the stacks, they didn't need to sign them out. 'Fenderby's office was in the stacks,' was all she said.

'Yes, but the book had been checked out.' Ruby spoke deliberately, waiting for Dulcie to catch on. 'It still was – when you found it.'

'So whoever killed Fenderby brought it back into the library?' The full impact of what Ruby was telling her began to sink in. 'Then hit him with it, and left the book as evidence?'

Ruby nodded vigorously.

'So all we have to do is find out who checked that book out . . .' Dulcie couldn't believe it. The nightmare was almost over.

'Dulcie, they already have.' Ruby's voice sank to an unprecedented whisper. 'It was Thomas Griddlehaus.'

'No!' Dulcie could hear her cry echo in the large and open room. All eyes turned toward her, but then – with the peculiar etiquette of libraries – just as quickly turned away. 'That's impossible,' she hissed at Ruby.

'I know,' her friend replied. 'I mean, why would Griddlehaus check out an anthology of Gothic fiction? Everyone knows he's a medievalist. Never mind,' she waved as if at a pesky fly, 'the other stuff.'

'It makes no sense.' Dulcie's head spun with the lack of logic. 'He wouldn't kill anyone. And he *certainly* wouldn't risk damaging a book.' Her own words stopped her. But Ruby didn't question the ordering of priorities. They both knew the gentle library clerk. 'Where is he?' Dulcie asked.

'All I know is the police questioned him.'

Together, they both turned to where the uniformed officer was still huddled with the library guards. Watching them, Dulcie felt her heart sink. Thomas Griddlehaus was not only a scholar, he was one of her strongest allies. They had bonded over years of research, and he had recently shared some of his history with her. History, she realized now, that had some shady bits.

'But he's never done anything like this.' She voiced the thoughts out loud.

'Well, someone did,' her friend said, her voice glum. 'And you know what they say. It's always the quiet ones.'

'You don't really think that.' Dulcie looked at her friend. 'Do you?'

'I'll tell you, Dulcie,' her friend said sadly. 'I don't know what to think any more.'

'That poor man.' Dulcie hadn't thought she could feel worse. 'Did they take him out in handcuffs?'

'What? No.' Dulcie's question disturbed whatever private reverie the circulation chief had fallen into. Her startled dismay, however, cheered Dulcie.

'Well, that's good.'

'I mean, who else would be staffing the Mildon at this time of day?'

'He's still here?' Dulcie couldn't believe it. 'In the Mildon?'

'Of course.' Ruby looked at her, not understanding. 'Where else would he be?'

'But—' Dulcie caught herself. This was a good thing, the way things should be. Just because the mousy librarian had been connected to the murder weapon and allowed to go about his normal routine, whereas she . . . 'I think I need to talk to him.'

'Dulcie, are you sure you should be getting any more involved with all this . . .' She waved her hands again. 'This brouhaha?'

'He's my friend, Ruby,' Dulcie said. What she didn't say was how conflicted she felt about Ruby's news. Griddlehaus was innocent. He had to be, but if the police were looking at him, then they were indeed clueless. And that meant they'd soon be clutching at any straw. She had to get involved, both for her friend's sake and her own.

NINETEEN

To a stranger, Thomas Griddlehaus might not look any more agitated than usual. After he signed Dulcie in, the small man with the big glasses went back to his files, where he was fussing over what appeared to be old-fashioned, and decidedly dog-eared index cards.

Dulcie, however, noticed his upset – it was hard to ignore the little man's deep sighs – and she was torn. As close as she and the clerk had gotten over the last few years, he was essentially a private man, their relationship still primarily formal. And so she had turned to him, as she walked in, waiting to see if he would bring up what surely must be troubling him. She had even made a tentative query, asking in a general way, how he was doing.

'Fine, fine,' he had responded, before scurrying off to his own desk. It had felt like a reversion back to the early days of their working relationship, when she had not known anything about the studious little man.

But when he didn't elaborate, Dulcie had felt at a bit of a loss. Yes, she wanted to help him. She needed to understand what was going on. But was it worth encroaching on his privacy?

Mulling over her options, she had taken her usual seat at the white table. And when the bespectacled clerk came over, she prepared to speak.

'And which box would you like to start with today?' He blinked at her behind those large glasses, as if he bore no other concerns beyond the everyday ones of his job.

'Mr Griddlehaus . . .' she began. And stopped. The police had questioned the clerk, but then they had let him go back to work. Suze had warned her off pursuing the case on her own. So had Rogovoy, although his warning carried less weight than Dulcie's former roommate's. Meanwhile, Chris – and Mr Grey – had assured her that she would be removed from probation soon. No matter who was on her panel at that point, she would have to defend her thesis. In fact . . .

'May I have box 978 please?' She looked up at Griddlehaus.

'Box nine—?' It was his turn to pause, bewildered. 'But . . .'

'I'm assuming that, with the loss of Professor Fenderby, that his hold on the material is no longer . . .' Dulcie struggled for the right word. 'No longer vital.' The librarian winced. Clearly, he wasn't as unscathed by recent events as he would like to appear.

'I mean, it should no longer hold,' Dulcie hurried to explain. 'And since I am trying to respond to criticism he made, well, it seems like this would be a proper method of honoring him. Don't you think?'

'Of course.' The librarian was clearly distracted, though if it was because of his own troubles or Dulcie's rationalization, she couldn't tell.

'I thought now might be a good time to check my attributions,' she added, when he returned with the archive a few minutes later. Her explanation did little to assuage the stab of guilt she felt, asking Griddlehaus to break the rules. She had spoken without thinking, stretching for something normal to say. But maybe her instinct had been a good one. Surely, a dead man no longer had authority to reserve research materials for private use. Besides, she had already donned the white gloves and the box was already here.

'Of course,' Griddlehaus repeated, lifting out the first page and laying it on the table. And so with her own small sigh and a twinge of trepidation, Dulcie began to read.

'*Such Treasure as we may Salvage from the conflagration's fury, for surely such Liberty is as Priceless as any shining Jewel, we must keep safe,*' she read, mouthing the words aloud. Yes, this was the passage. It formed the basis for her chapter on her author's political writings, tying them in with the theme of *The Ravages of Umbria*, the struggle for women's rights. And also – she noted that one word – the spark, so to speak, of her dream. Though in her current mood, Dulcie began to doubt. Perhaps she had been too enthusiastic in her interpretation. Perhaps the author was simply talking about general liberties. After all, the earlier segment referred to a shift from the Old World to the New.

'Such Jewels we would bequeath, to all our heirs. For it is of Our Daughters that I write.' There, that proved it. Didn't it?

Dulcie shut her eyes, trying to remember. When she had first read this provocative essay, it had all seemed so clear: the author had left England for a new life in Philadelphia. Had survived an ocean voyage like the ones she described so vividly. That she had left her former life for personal reasons was implied in her novels: both *The Ravages* and the unnamed book Dulcie had discovered featured heroines who fled abusive mates. That the author was on the cusp of one of the first great movements for women's rights made the rest fall into place. This essay used the fire imagery for dramatic impact. But its main argument, ostensibly concerning the right of a mother to bequeath her own property as she saw fit, was really an extended metaphor about liberty. Wasn't it?

She had to check. 'Mr Griddlehaus,' she called. He was seated at his desk, back toward her. 'Do you mind if I—'

'No, no. Go ahead.' He didn't even look up, but Dulcie knew the procedure. Within minutes, she had retrieved another folder from the box and carefully removed the document she was seeking, in its clear protective sheath, of course.

'Such Jewels as we Bequeath,' she read. Yes, this was the rough – or *a* rough, at any rate – handwritten version of the printed essay she had before her. Earlier in the same chapter, Dulcie had cited the similarities in phrasing that had made her link this essay and others to the *The Ravages*. To be able to see the same penmanship, a rushed but flowing hand, was exhilarating. And yes, this rough did indeed have the subtitle that she remembered: *On Our Rights*, it read, a heading that was excised from the final, printed version, perhaps by an editor who preferred to leave the writer's inflammatory ideas in the realm of metaphor. Otherwise, the essay was virtually the same, except for a few minor changes.

Dulcie knew she could check this off. Her research was sound, and her footnotes would cite both these documents. Anyone who sought to replicate her work would be able to. She mused on the idea as she gently replaced the document. Lifting the page with both hands, she blinked as the cool fluorescent light reflected off the protective covering. These documents were a treasure, a source for her dissertation and beyond, mapping the path of a literary icon. And maybe revealing a lineage . . .

'Hold on.' She paused, the light playing off the shiny surface. From this angle, the faded ink was barely visible. The lacy holes worn in the thick paper by the iron-gall ink casting shadows. But it wasn't the cursive script she was seeing. It was a difference in the paper – in the surface. Raising the folder up once more, she let the light play over the surface. Yes, one area had been scraped and written over.

Carefully, not even daring to hope, she held the document close. She should wait. Ask the experts at the conservation lab for help, and inquire if a lightbox or some other low-risk technology might be used to show her what had once been there. But looking at the page now, her eyes nearly level with the paper, she could see one difference – *'conflagration'*, it appeared, had not been the author's original choice. Beneath it, Dulcie could make out . . . was it a T? Yes, *'the Tempest's fury'*. How strange, she thought, lowering the document once more. In her dreams, she had divined the original wording. Or, no, she was getting carried away. *The Ravages* as well as the newer work both featured storms on land and sea. It was a natural substitution, for someone who knew the author.

With a smile at her own fancy, Dulcie lifted the piece again. To think she had put herself in the author's place. As if her dream . . . She stopped. She had elevated the document as carefully as always, her gloved fingertips raising it with care. Perhaps it was her distraction, the musing of an overtired mind. She tilted the page. No, there it was again. Another change, a smaller one. It was simple: *'our'*, one word, had been written over another. *'My,'* she read aloud. Yes, in this light the original phrase was clear. *My daughter.*

'Mr Griddlehaus?' Dulcie could barely contain herself. She knew what she was seeing was pure speculation. More important, it would have no bearing on her dissertation. Thorpe and her colleagues – even Chris – had finally convinced her to stop expanding her thesis topic. She was no longer going to hare after the 'new shiny' as Trista had put it. She was writing on what she had. But personally, for her own interest, this could unlock one of her private dreams. 'Mr Griddlehaus?' Her voice was rising with excitement. 'You wouldn't believe what I've just found.'

There was no response. 'Mr Griddlehaus?' Carefully replacing the document, she turned. The librarian was still at his desk, staring at whatever he was holding. He hadn't, Dulcie suspected, moved at all.

'Are you all right, Mr Griddlehaus?' Pushing her own chair back, Dulcie walked up to the little man. From here, she couldn't help seeing over his shoulder. 'Are those from the old card catalog?'

'Why, yes.' He turned, eyes huge behind those glasses. 'And yes, they are, Ms Schwartz. This is the original catalog that arrived with the gift from the Philadelphia bequest. I've been meaning to get around to these for months now.'

The Philadelphia bequest had been the gift Renée Showalter had expedited: a collection of unsorted and often handwritten pages in which Dulcie had found parts of the lost novel. It was also the collection that had yielded the page Dulcie had just been studying.

'They hadn't been stored correctly before we received them,' her friend explained, before she could point out the strange coincidence of timing. Without looking up at her, he turned one card, letting it, too, catch the light. Dulcie could see water damage. 'But nothing beyond my scope.'

'Oh, I didn't mean the cards,' Dulcie rushed to explain. It was a little odd that of all the ongoing projects in the Mildon, the mouse-like clerk should choose this one to focus on right now. Though it was possible that their thoughts ran along the same lines – that her presence had reminded the clerk of this unfinished task. 'I was concerned that perhaps . . .'

He looked up at her, as she struggled to find the right words, suddenly ashamed of her single-minded focus. 'I'm sorry,' she said. 'I've been so caught up in my own worries, and when I first came in, I didn't want to intrude. But I should have insisted. You see, I heard about the book – that collection you had checked out.'

'Oh, my.' He turned toward her, then quickly back to the card. 'Yes, yes, of course,' he said, putting the cards down. 'The *Castleton* anthology.'

'Yes.' Dulcie fought the urge to take Griddlehaus's hands in her own, knowing such a move would make the clerk uncomfortable. 'Ruby filled me in.'

Griddlehaus remained silent, simply staring at the cards. 'I should have known,' he said at last, speaking so quietly that Dulcie wasn't sure he had spoken. Shaking his head, he looked up at Dulcie, cleared his throat, and began, in a slightly louder voice, to speak.

'It all began with this.' He held out the cards. 'With the bequest. I've told the police all I knew. I hated to get anyone else in trouble, but I had to explain. After Professor Fenderby locked that part of the archives, I tried to reason with him. I told him that we had other patrons – one in particular – who were making regular use of these materials. He countered that he had a special student, a particularly gifted young scholar, who deserved private and unfettered access.'

He paused, shaking his head slowly in disbelief. 'I only wanted to follow up. The little bit he told me was so sketchy and so general. It seemed clear he was talking about an undergrad. I wanted to offer him alternative materials from the general collection that would serve the same purpose. That's why I sought him out, as soon as I opened the collection. The morning he—'

He stopped again, this time to remove his glasses, which he wiped with his handkerchief. 'That's why the book was in my name. And that's why it was in his office. But I didn't— I wouldn't—'

'Of course not.' Dulcie had never been so convinced. However, another thought was also making itself felt. 'But if you brought him that anthology, you must be one of the last people to see Fenderby alive.' Those glasses were getting a good polishing. 'Mr Griddlehaus?'

He looked up. Without the thick lenses, his eyes looked small and rather swollen. Dulcie wondered if he'd been crying.

'Mr Griddlehaus,' she tried again, making her voice softer. 'Did you see anybody in Fenderby's office? Did anyone go in after you?'

He shook his head and looked down at the ground, before carefully hitching the glasses back around his ears. 'No, I'm afraid I didn't see anyone,' he said. 'His wife – his widow now, poor soul – had been by earlier. I believe she may have brought him lunch. He was trying to lose weight, you know. I believe they had words about it – about his diet. Her voice was raised, which is how I knew who it was. And I – well, I didn't want to intrude, and so I waited until she left before I knocked on his door.'

'But you saw her leave?' Dulcie felt there was something she wasn't getting. Some pattern she didn't see.

'Yes, I did.' Griddlehaus nodded. 'I thought about approaching her. I thought, perhaps, she might be willing to act as an intermediary with her husband.'

'And did you?'

'No.' He looked at the ground. 'The poor woman appeared upset, and so I hung back and busied myself with one of the reshelving bins, until I was sure she'd passed by. I didn't want to appear as if I'd been eavesdropping, so I gave poor professor a few minutes before I went to his office.'

'And you brought the book into him.' Dulcie felt she was missing something in the morning's chronology. 'And, clearly, he was still alive.'

'Alive, yes. Of course.' Griddlehaus blinked at the memory. 'Only I didn't actually go into his office, you see. He had closed the door again, by then. But he heard me knock and he stepped out, closing the door behind him. The officers asked me that as well as whether anybody else had been around. Only I— well, I didn't want to get anybody in trouble.'

'Mr Griddlehaus.' Dulcie didn't want to make the quiet man feel worse. Surely, he had to realize his own reputation – his own freedom – was on the line. 'This may be important.'

He nodded. 'I didn't tell the officer, partly because it seemed inconsequential at the time. But Tom Walls was working in the stacks.' He looked up at Dulcie, his eyes once again both bright and oversized. 'He was watching as I came out, Ms Schwartz, half hidden behind one of the stacks. I think he was waiting for something. Or for someone.'

TWENTY

'**I** knew it!' Dulcie wasn't yelling, far from it, but the force of her expostulation caused Griddlehaus to roll his chair back. 'I'm sorry,' she said. 'But I knew Tom was up to something. He's who I was looking for yesterday when I found the anthology.'

'When you found it?' The librarian shook his head. 'But I thought – the police led me to believe – it had been instrumental in, well, in . . .'

'Yes, I believe it was.' Dulcie cut off his obvious distress. 'But it had been reshelved. Badly reshelved,' she said for emphasis.

'Well, it can't have been Tom, then.' Griddlehaus said it as if the conclusion were self-evident. 'He wouldn't have put it in the wrong section. He's a trained member of the staff.'

'No, don't you see?' Dulcie appreciated Griddlehaus's quaint worldview. At this moment, however, she needed him to see the larger implications. 'I think it was intentional. That he deliberately misshelved it so that nobody would find it. Perhaps he was acting quickly – you know, he had to get rid of the evidence.'

Griddlehaus's blinking had become more rapid, his face white. Dulcie needed to dial it back a bit. 'I don't believe he was thinking like a proper library clerk,' she explained. 'Rather, he was hoping to hide something that might be crucial to solving the crime.'

'Of course.' Griddlehaus nodded. 'So you think that he . . . that Professor Fenderby . . .'

'Yes,' Dulcie said.

'But why?' Griddlehaus voiced the question she had no answer for.

'I don't know,' she admitted. 'I don't even know that he did – the deed. But I do know that he's involved. Do you remember my cousin, Mina Love?'

The librarian nodded.

'She – well, she had an ongoing conflict with Professor Fenderby, and she was in the library that morning, too.' Dulcie paused. 'Briefly, anyway. You didn't see her. Did you?'

He shook his head. 'Not unless – might she have been in with Fenderby?'

'Not likely.' Dulcie wanted to continue. 'Anyway, Tom was supposed to keep tabs on her.' Dulcie waved away Griddlehaus's attempted interruption. 'It's a long story, but she had asked him to be aware of her when she was down there. It was – a safety thing.' That was weak, but it was the best she could do.

'Anyway, because of that, Mina explained that Tom could vouch for her. Only, for some reason, he's now saying he can't. That he isn't sure if she was here that morning, or not. I mean, it wasn't like she'd stop working, run into Fenderby's office and bash him over the head, and then scoot back to her carrel before he turned the next corner, is it?'

Griddlehaus drew back at that, and Dulcie realized that perhaps she'd gotten a bit carried away. Still, he couldn't argue with the logic of her version.

'No.' He looked as if he were chewing it over. 'No, I don't think it is. And I confess, the reluctance on Tom's part is, at the very least, ungentlemanly. He's always seemed like such a gallant young lad, too.'

Dulcie nodded. Before all of this had started, the junior had distinguished himself primarily by his silent, but obvious crushes. The way he would blush, and the gestures he would make were worthy of an undergrad Sir Walter Raleigh. If he had become fixated on Mina, it might explain an attack on Fenderby. But why, then, would he let her be implicated?

Before Dulcie could reason that one out, Griddlehaus turned toward her again.

'This prior conflict is the reason the police are looking at your cousin?'

'Basically.' Dulcie pondered. 'Or, no, there's more. Someone – another undergrad – said she saw a woman down there. A redhead. That's one of the reasons the police wanted to talk to me.'

'They spoke to you?' Griddlehaus's eyes went wide in astonishment. 'But you can't be – that doesn't make sense.'

'What?' She was missing something. 'Please, tell me.'

'One of the officers sensed my distress. Not your friend – the large gentleman – but a younger officer. He made a point of telling me that although I was being questioned, I needn't have any undue fears. That, in fact, the investigation was proceeding in another direction.'

'Another . . .' Dulcie had a sinking feeling in her belly.

'Yes.' Griddlehaus nodded, his voice going soft. 'I believe he mentioned a task force? But, Ms Schwartz,' he paused, his large eyes staring into hers. 'Didn't you want to tell me something? I thought, perhaps, you had found something in your research?'

The change – the possessive, singular phrase *'my daughter'* – it all came back to her. As did her cousin's situation: a known, comprehensible motive that could implicate them both.

'It doesn't really matter, Mr Griddlehaus,' she said, shaking her head sadly. 'I should really focus on my dissertation. Assuming, that is, that I will get to present it at all.'

TWENTY-ONE

The rest of the morning was a blur, and by the time Griddlehaus mentioned his own impending lunch break, Dulcie realized that she should probably make a point of eating something as well. Although the idea of food didn't appeal, a change of scene or maybe some fresh air might help her figure out what to do next.

It wasn't that what she had found didn't matter. It did, and despite what she had told Griddlehaus, she knew she would want to go back to it. That correction – that faded discrepancy – could be the key she had sought so long to both her subject's identity and their strange connection. But if she had any time now – any time before the police made their case against herself or against her cousin – she should use it for the work at hand. She had promised too many people; she had promised herself. She would focus on finishing her dissertation.

Simply going through the notes she had made during her three hours in the Mildon would keep her busy. She had checked her few facts, and once she added the clarifications and filled out the quotes her chapter would be as solid as any peer review board could reasonably expect. It was time to buckle down.

And so with only the most cursory farewell to Griddlehaus, she had packed her notes up and left, even ducking her head down to avoid Ruby's gaze as she exited the library. She didn't like blowing off her friends, but duty beckoned. Adding to the spur of her conscience was the glowing symbol on her phone as she powered back up. One call missed: Renée Showalter.

'Dulcie, I heard!' The Canadian professor's voice sounded so full of concern that Dulcie felt her eyes welling up. 'I'm so sorry! Please call me back as soon as is convenient.'

A sympathetic ear would do more for her than lunch, and Dulcie settled down on the library's stone steps to return her mentor's call.

'Professor Showalter?' She couldn't help sniffing as she spoke. 'Dulcie Schwartz.'

'You poor thing!' The professor sounded like she was outdoors. Dulcie could hear voices and a truck backing up. 'Are you all right?'

'Uh huh.' Dulcie nodded. Although she was brushing away a stray tear, she already felt better. 'It's just been so horrible. Fenderby . . .'

'You don't have to say it,' the professor interrupted. 'It's inconceivable. How anyone could act like that.'

'I know.' The righteous anger was invigorating, too. 'And to think that I had something to do with it.'

'No!' The voice on the line sounded shocked. 'Why – how could you?'

'I know.' Dulcie had never felt so vindicated.

'As soon as I'm out there, I'll clear this up,' said Showalter. 'Though maybe that won't even be necessary.'

'Thank you.' Dulcie leaned back against the step behind her, overcome with relief. The traffic sounds on the line were getting louder. 'Thank you,' she repeated, not sure if her words had been drowned out by that honking cab. 'When do you think you'll get out here?'

'I'm hoping to come down within the next few days.' Showalter was shouting now. 'I'll probably be back and forth for a while, but I'll talk to Fenderby first thing.'

'Wait– what?' Dulcie didn't know if she was hearing correctly. That beeping truck, the traffic . . . 'I thought you said you knew?'

'That Fenderby was directing all your research material to some undergrad?' The traffic noise had gotten louder. 'Don't worry, Dulcie. I'm on it.'

With one more shout – 'call you when I get in!' – she was gone, leaving Dulcie feeling more alone than before. All around her, the campus was coming back to life. The trees were in bud, the undergrads laughing as they made their way to class or, more likely, one of the college dining halls. Dulcie knew she ought to text the professor. It wouldn't do for her to find out only after she arrived. Only somehow the effort to key in the crucial words was just too much right now. As she sat there, staring at the phone in her hand, it seemed to take on a life of its own, buzzing.

'Dulcie?' It had taken her a moment to answer it, the occasion of a live call in real time taking her by surprise.

'Trista.' Dulcie closed her eyes. She was too tired to deal with one of Trista's conspiracy theories right then. 'I can't—' She stopped. Maybe Trista, with her subversive attitude, would be just the person she needed to help clear her name – as well as her cousin's, from the shadow of guilt and insinuation.

'Where are you?' she asked, instead.

'We've got to talk to Tom.' A half hour later, they were huddled over a plate of warm chocolate chip cookies, and Trista had taken the lead. 'Find out where he was when you were down there, and what he knows about that book you found.'

It was after noon, but Dulcie hadn't felt like anything more substantial. As she sat looking at the plate, she realized that, for once, she didn't even really want sweets.

'I should be able to get him to talk,' Trista was saying.

Dulcie nodded, happy to let her friend take charge. Trista did have a way with men. And after all, she had promised Suze that she wouldn't try to confront the junior.

'I just want to understand why . . .' Dulcie didn't finish the sentence. She could feel Trista's eyes on her. 'I wonder if he's the undergrad who was getting access to the papers in the Mildon?'

'The Mildon?' Trista sounded skeptical. 'Let's focus on the bigger problem, shall we?'

'Sorry.' Dulcie slumped in her seat. 'It all kind of runs together for me.'

'Of course it does.' Her friend pushed the plate her way. 'But come on, you don't want these to get cold. They're your favorites.'

'Thanks,' Dulcie broke off a piece, but then just crumbled it into her napkin. 'I just wish . . . I told you what Showalter said, right?'

Trista nodded. Dulcie had. Twice.

'If everyone knows this, then it makes sense for people to look at me. I mean, taking away my research material? Suze is working on the legality of their move, but as far as it being a motive for . . .'

'Enough.' Trista reached across the table to take her friend's hand. 'It's a violation. I know that, but you can get past it, Dulcie. You're strong enough.'

The friends sat in silence. Dulcie, finally, nibbled a corner of the cookie. The chocolate was still molten soft. Sticky. She thought of the book – of the brown mess – and put the rest of the fragment back down.

'This is hopeless, Tris,' she said, shaking her head in resignation. 'Everything we find out just seems to point back to either me or Mina.'

'Mina?' Trista perked up. 'Your cousin, Mina Love?'

Dulcie nodded. 'She had a beef with Fenderby.' She glanced up. Trista was nodding, her mouth set in a grim line. 'And now it looks like she's a suspect.'

'That bastard,' Trista said. It was a bit of a non sequitur, but Dulcie didn't mind. 'Don't worry,' Trista continued. 'Mina will be fine. That creep isn't going to hurt any more young women.'

Dulcie paused, looking at their friend. As much as she appreciated Trista's confidence, that was a strong statement, even for her. But Trista only responded with her own question.

'I wonder who Showalter was talking about? Do you have any idea?'

Dulcie shook her head. 'I thought I was the only one interested in that material.'

Trista waved the thought away. 'That probably doesn't matter. We've got to focus not on whom Fenderby was helping, but on whom he'd ticked off. Didn't you say his wife was there?'

'She left before Griddlehaus talked to Fenderby. Probably walked in with him.' They both knew how it went: tenured professors often escorted non-university personnel on to university property. 'Griddlehaus saw her go.'

'Maybe a protective boyfriend, then, or some poor girl who didn't want his attention.'

Dulcie couldn't help herself. She looked up in alarm.

'Not you.' Trista looked confused for a moment. Then she shook her head. 'Mina. Poor girl. Boy, that man was a creep.'

'So you can see why she's a suspect.' Dulcie felt both relieved and a bit guilty that her cousin's secret was out. It wasn't like she'd said anything. Trista had simply put two and two together. 'And why I am too. Especially since the cops are looking for a redhead.'

'There are other redheads on campus.' Trista was trying to cheer her up. 'Not to mention in Cambridge. And Alyson didn't positively identify either of you, did she?'

'No.' Something was niggling at Dulcie. 'But Griddlehaus— Bother!' The word burst out of her.

'That little . . .' Trista leaned in. 'He didn't say you were there, did he? Dulcie you can tell me.'

'No, it's what he *didn't* say.' Dulcie glanced up at her friend. 'What I didn't think to ask.'

Her friend shook her head quizzically, and so Dulcie continued. 'I told you, Griddlehaus went to Fenderby's office to give him that book. He was going to try to talk him into freeing up the papers in the Mildon, the ones Fenderby had put aside and locked me out of. Well, it seems obvious that's how the book got into Fenderby's office – only Mr Griddlehaus never actually set foot inside. He said Fenderby met him at the door and put him off. Closed the door behind him. Fenderby had someone in there, I bet. Someone who came by after the wife left. Someone he didn't want anyone to see.'

'Someone who took that book and beaned him with it.' Trista sounded a little too enthusiastic for Dulcie's taste. Then again, Trista hadn't seen the body.

'Well, yes.' Dulcie coughed. A bit of the cookie had lodged in her throat. 'In a word. I wonder – I hope it wasn't Mina.'

Trista looked up, quizzical.

'Mina was in the library that morning, but only briefly. She could have snuck in, while Griddlehaus was waiting for the wife to leave the building,' Dulcie explained, the edge of doubt creeping in. 'And if she left right after . . . before I got there. But why would she? She didn't want to be alone with that man. And whoever it was—'

'Tom Walls would have seen her,' Trista finished her sentence. 'Or him. Tom Walls is key.'

They didn't have a plan, or not much of one. Trista was simply going to seek the timid junior out, hoping to get him to explain the many circumstances that were piling up.

'I'll use the old feminine wiles on him,' Trista raised one pierced eyebrow at Dulcie.

'Don't go too far.' Dulcie warned. 'I mean, he's just a kid.'

Another arched brow from her friend. 'I'll be gentle, Dulcie. Besides, I think he likes blondes.'

Dulcie, meanwhile, was going to try to get some work done.

That was Trista's idea, not Dulcie's. She had been all for going back to question Griddlehaus again. She wasn't comfortable with that – the clerk had seemed on the edge of breaking – but it had seemed necessary. 'After all, Tris, maybe he observed something he wasn't aware of. Maybe he's remembered something.'

That pierced brow went up. 'And you're going to – what?

– hypnotize him?' Trista had shaken her blonde mop. 'No, you should stay out of this, Dulcie. Leave the dirty business to me.'

TWENTY-TWO

With a plan in place, albeit a sketchy one, the two friends parted, Trista to seek Tom Walls, and Dulcie to her office.

'The last few yards are the hardest,' her friend had said. 'Believe me, I know.'

Only as she walked back through the Yard, Dulcie couldn't escape the feeling that she was missing something. A name or a piece, or . . .

'Watch out!' Dulcie jumped aside just in time to avoid being hit by a bicyclist, ear buds firmly in place. 'Hey, you're not supposed to ride with those in!' It was hopeless. The cyclist was already out of earshot, even if he had turned his music down. At least her yell had cleared other pedestrians out of the way.

'So stupid riding like that. But couldn't he see me?' Dulcie grumbled. 'It's not like I'm invisible. In fact, if I were . . .'

That was it. She stopped short, and nearly got pushed over.

'Sorry.' It was her turn to apologize, and she turned to see Alyson Beaumont, wide-eyed with surprise. 'Oh, I was just thinking of calling you.'

'Me?' Alyson's normally lyrical voice squeaked.

'Yes.' Dulcie nodded energetically. 'I realized I didn't ask you yesterday. Why did you say you saw a redhead down on Level Two two mornings ago? You know, the morning that . . .'

The blonde raised her hands as if to physically stop Dulcie from continuing. 'Please, don't,' she said. 'I'm sorry. I should never have said anything.'

'But you did.' Dulcie looked at her. 'Were you down there that morning?'

'Me? No.' She shook her head emphatically, sending those golden curls swinging. 'I must have heard it from Tom. In fact, I'm sure of it.'

Dulcie looked at her, trying to remember everything her student had told her. It was bad enough that Tom wouldn't say definitively that Mina wasn't there. If he was now saying positively that she was, well, that was beyond the pale.

'But why would Tom say that?' Something wasn't fitting, and she looked at Alyson for an answer. 'Why tell you?'

The undergrad rolled her eyes. 'I have no idea. He can get a little obsessed. You know?'

Dulcie nodded. She did, and the idea of a positive absence was rather abstract. Like seeing proof that something had been erased – a thought that led her back to her earlier concern. And her duties. Particularly to the pretty blonde who stood blinking before her.

'I'm sorry to have startled you like that,' Dulcie said, trying to summon a smile. Another thought had begun tickling the edge of her consciousness. 'Alyson, you and I had talked about you writing your senior thesis on *The Ravages*. Have you given any more thought to that?'

'Wow, you are all business, aren't you?' The other woman laughed, shaking her head again. 'No, I'm sorry. I haven't. I know that's your thing but I'm kind of off that whole period.'

'I understand,' said Dulcie. 'We have time.' At least, Dulcie thought as she watched her charge walk away, she hoped she did.

TWENTY-THREE

Dulcie was halfway across the Yard when it hit her. Maybe she couldn't talk to Tom, but clearly Alyson had. In fact, it sounded like Alyson had spoken at length with the shy junior about the morning Fenderby had been killed. And while Dulcie didn't think that anyone ought to be passing along second-hand information to the police –

she'd have to check with Suze, but she was pretty sure that was not considered kosher – it sounded like Alyson had done just that. Which meant that whatever she knew wasn't that private. Surely, she could share it with Dulcie.

Only, where had the pretty junior gone? Dulcie sped up, walking quickly back up the path she had ambled down only minutes before. Alyson, as an upper-classman, no longer lived in a Yard dorm, so she might have been on her way to one of the lecture halls. Or the library. Or maybe . . .

There she was! Dulcie caught a flash of honey-blonde hair striding rapidly, head down, and about to disappear behind a rhododendron. And if the woman beneath it wasn't heading for the administration building opposite, that meant she was heading to the Square. Dulcie broke into a run, eager to catch her student before she disappeared in the tumult of the city.

'Aly—' Dulcie called out, before swallowing the last syllable of the name. Because as she raced around the big green bush, she saw why Alyson was hurrying. She was hailing Tom Walls.

Dulcie stopped short. Here, by the rhododendron, she was shielded from their sight. Nobody could accuse her of being a stalker if she was simply standing around the Yard, waiting for an opportunity to speak with one of her own students. To foster the illusion, she bent over the shrub's dark green leaves. Yes, there were buds. In a few weeks, there would even be flowers. In a few weeks, maybe she'd be filing her last thesis chapter. Or looking for a job.

She snuck a peek. Alyson was leaning toward the tall young man in a manner that clearly made him uncomfortable. Of course, thought Dulcie. Tom Walls wasn't at ease with any woman. Surely a beauty like Alyson would make him tense. As she watched, Alyson gesticulated, raising both arms, and when Tom stumbled back, Alyson stepped toward him, closing the gap. Her head bobbed as if she were talking at a furious pace. This wasn't a discussion about reserve reading material or conflicting interpretations of a sonnet. From what Dulcie could see, the two were having a heated discussion of something personal. Very heated.

She couldn't resist. She stepped closer.

'Excuse me!' Another cyclist whizzed by, forcing Dulcie

into the planting. A sharp branch, one that hadn't survived the winter with its leaves intact, scraped her leg.

'Ow!' She bent by instinct, though what she could do if her jeans were torn or she was bleeding wasn't immediately apparent. Still, she hiked up her pants' leg to examine the damage – a long scratch, much like something Esmé might give her, ran up the back of her calf. Strangely, her jeans seemed undamaged, and as she rubbed the broken skin, Dulcie had an odd presentiment. That scratch . . . could it be a message from Mr Grey?

No, she told herself. She wasn't Lucy. Not everything was a portent. But just then, she heard footsteps and she ducked lower, as if to rub her injured leg. The footsteps stopped just short of the shrub.

'But— but.' Tom. She'd know that halting speech anywhere. 'They would know, Alyson.' He sounded like he was choking on the words, and Dulcie had to fight the urge to stand and comfort him. 'I know they would. They would have your ID.'

This close, Dulcie heard his strangled sob. With that, he turned and took off. Only when he was safely gone did she dare look up through the dark green leaves shielding her. Alyson Beaumont was still standing there, a pained expression on her face. But Dulcie didn't think she could reveal herself now. Not unless she wanted to acknowledge the strange inter-action she had just heard. Which, she realized, she could. After all, she hadn't meant to eavesdrop. She did have a legitimate question for the blonde junior, and she had happened to see her . . .

It wasn't to be. Just as Dulcie was working up her nerve to step out of the planting and confront her student, the junior whirled around. Squaring her shoulders, she walked off, through the gate and into the bustle of the Square.

They would have your ID. Dulcie was still standing, absently rubbing her left foot against the scratched right calf, minutes later. She should have gone after Alyson. Should have asked her about sharing Tom's information with the police, if not about what she had just overheard. But the moment was gone, and Dulcie couldn't help but feel that the rhododendron, if not the cyclist, had been a message from Mr Grey. She was supposed to hear that, and she was not supposed to be detected. But what could it mean?

Clearly, both the undergrads knew more about what had happened in the library than they had let on. Or – no – they both feared being thought to be involved, a subtle but important difference. Tom, it seemed, was protecting Alyson. And Alyson had some reason to be angry with Tom – or had wanted something from him. Dulcie replayed the body language she had witnessed. The pretty blonde had been moving in on her shy classmate. Arguing for – or against? – something.

She shook her head. She'd have better luck starting on the other side. The ID. That had to refer to the library. Alyson had said she hadn't been there that morning – or not on Level Two, at any rate. But if the library, or the police, had her student identification, perhaps she'd been lying.

Out of habit, Dulcie reached into her own bag, feeling for the wallet that held her ID. In truth, she wasn't sure of the last time she'd used it. But, no, there it was. Safe and not lost at the scene of some crime. Nestled in by her laptop and the yellow legal pad on which she still took notes.

Notes, she realized, she should see to. She had missed her opportunity to question Alyson further, and everyone – even Trista – had been after her to get back to work. After all, it was her notes, or lack thereof, that had gotten her into this mess. If she had been more careful with her attributions, then Fenderby might not have been able to make a case against her chapter. And then she never would have uttered those rash, hateful words – or had to seek the professor out, opening herself up to suspicion.

Extricating herself from the shrubbery, Dulcie turned back toward her office with new resolve. As curious as she was about Alyson and Tom, she should leave that to the professionals. Let the police do their work, and focus instead on her own responsibilities. She would type her notes into her laptop. Amend the chapter, and email it to Thorpe. Surely, even if she were still officially on probation, he would take a moment to review the chapter. It seemed quite clear that the investigation had plenty of leads. She would be exonerated in a matter of days. Hours, maybe. She should never have been involved at all.

Only, she was. Like the smarting of the scratch along her leg, the truth of the situation kept at her. Yes, she was innocent, and, yes, she had only become involved through a series of minor coincidences. But no matter how quickly her role was clarified, Dulcie couldn't hide from the truth. A man had been killed, and she had information that the police might not. And even though that man was the horrid Professor Roland Fenderby, she was still Dulcinea Schwartz, a member of the university, soon to be restored to good standing, and a citizen with a moral obligation to help bring his killer to justice.

TWENTY-FOUR

'Detective Rogovoy?' As soon as she'd dialed the detective's private number, Dulcie had been seized by misgivings. She didn't like to think of herself as a tattle-tale – a less harsh word than 'snitch' – but she was looking to provide information about another student. Two other students, actually. And she hadn't thought through how to present it. 'It's me, Dulcie Schwartz.'

The sigh at the other end of the line was familiar. The ogre-like detective worked long hours, Dulcie knew. And if he was also being called on by some university task force, he probably had additional paperwork on top of his regular duties. She hated being a burden. But if her information could make the investigation go more quickly, maybe that would be a good thing.

'Ms Schwartz.' The voice sounded tired, and Dulcie could visualize how he was probably running one meaty hand over his face. 'What a surprise.'

'I'm sorry to disturb you, detective.' She paused and took a breath. Being direct was probably best. 'I just overheard two of my students talking, and I wanted to let you know that I think Tom Walls might be covering for somebody. I think he's covering for Alyson Beaumont. I think she was there, and she saw something that morning.' There, it was out.

'Ms Schwartz, aren't you working on your dissertation now?'

She smiled, despite herself. 'Well, I would be,' she said, emphasizing the verb. 'Only because of the horrible tragedy, the college has put me on probation. I gather I'm being investigated.'

Saying the words out loud to her friend, the detective, took the sting out of them. Made them, in fact, sound ridiculous.

'And that makes you want to call me, Ms Schwartz?' There was a note in his voice that suggested his question was rhetorical. 'That makes you want to tell me about other possible suspects? Please, Ms Schwartz, this is a police matter. A serious investigation, and not something you should be involved in. Do yourself – do everyone – a favor. Take some time off. Go home, and think about something else.'

That was not helpful. In fact, if one could simply choose to think about something else, then one would cease worrying about difficult problems. Like what was going on between Tom Walls and Alyson Beaumont. Or why anyone would want to frame her or her cousin. As Dulcie made her way at last toward her office, she fretted over the futility of those words. No wonder she felt like a pariah. Almost as if she—

'Dulcie!' She looked up. Mina had been sitting on the stairs leading down to her office but now rose and was coming toward her. 'I was hoping you'd come here. I didn't want to call.'

'Of course.' Dulcie hurried forward. 'You're always welcome. What's up?'

Her cousin didn't respond, but the way she was looking around was answer enough.

'Never mind,' said Dulcie, fishing for her keys. 'Let's go where we can talk in private.'

Leading the way, they descended to the basement, where the warren of offices seemed unusually still for such a fine day. Dulcie took the quiet as a good sign, however, and was relieved to have to unlock the door.

'We may be interrupted,' she explained, pulling over the single guest chair for her cousin. 'Lloyd probably thinks I just got out of section. But for now.' She rolled her own chair from behind her desk to sit facing the younger woman. It seemed more collegial and inviting. But the way Mina was fussing made her wonder if it was the right move. By the time Dulcie sat down, the younger woman already had her phone out, as if expecting a text message of vital importance.

'Mina, what is it?' Dulcie reached over and took her hands, stilling them.

'I'm sorry.' With a forced grin, Mina shoved the phone back into her pocket. 'I just keep looking – I don't know what's going to happen next.'

'Next?'

The younger woman squirmed in her seat. 'This is pretty awful, and I feel, well, not culpable. But . . .'

Dulcie waited as her cousin bit her lip and shifted. 'Why don't you just start at the beginning?' she asked at last.

'I thought it was a good idea,' her cousin said. 'I thought it wouldn't hurt anybody. Obviously, I was wrong.'

Dulcie nodded, urging her to continue.

'It's the gag order, or whatever they want to call it.' Mina shrugged. 'I wanted it lifted. It feels like everybody knows that I'm the one who brought suit—'

Dulcie started to speak. Surely, Mina's feelings of vulnerability, of being victimized, were at play here. But her cousin kept on talking.

'No, please,' she said. 'People – let's just say, I know they know. Only I can't say anything about it. And now that Professor Fenderby is – well, it's pretty clear that nothing I say is going to hurt his career any more. So I wanted to be able to clear my name. Stop all the gossip.'

'Mina, who's been talking about you? That's not fair. It's not nice.' Dulcie reached for her cousin. She wanted to hold her, to look into her face. But Mina pulled away and kept on talking.

'Anyway, I went to the dean's office. I figured that's where I should start, right? Only the dean told me that it was out of his hands. That, because the agreement that settled the suit was between me and the professor, if I wanted out – if I wanted the gag order lifted – I'd have to come to terms with his estate.' She looked up to see if Dulcie understood. 'His widow. Did you even know that creep was married?'

'I did, yeah.' Dulcie remembered the angry woman she had briefly encountered. 'Not the most pleasant person.'

'I'm glad you said that.' Mina nodded enthusiastically. 'I mean, I know this must be an awful time for her, but . . .' She was biting her lip again and staring at the floor.

'You spoke with her?' Dulcie spoke carefully. She didn't see this ending well.

Mina nodded. 'I called her. I wasn't sure I should, and I feel bad about it, but I did. It was weird.'

'Weird?' That wasn't what Dulcie had been expecting. 'How?'

'It must be shock. Or a grief reaction, or something.' Mina looked up finally, meeting her cousin's eyes. 'But she didn't seem sad at all, or even angry. In fact, she kind of laughed when I told her who I was and why I was calling.'

'Laughed?' Dulcie tried to picture the angry woman she had met chuckling.

Mina nodded, staring off into the distance as if she could see something there. 'It was awful. I thought she was going hysterical, and that I had done something . . . like maybe she was having a breakdown.'

'I'm sure you didn't—' Dulcie caught herself before she said more. She wasn't sure of anything.

'Anyway, I apologized. I asked her if I should come over or send somebody, but then she got all calm. She said she understood why I'd called.'

'And is she going to release you from the agreement?' Dulcie's voice was lifted by a spark of hope.

'No, that's the strangest part.' Mina shook her head, confused. 'She said she couldn't do that. That she wasn't the one who had vouched for her husband, the reason that my suit had been dismissed – but that she was glad that now I finally understood. That it was my livelihood on the line now, thanks to somebody else's lies.' Mina shook her head in disbelief. 'Anyway, I just had to tell someone. It just creeped me out.'

The two sat there for a moment, lost in thought, until finally the younger woman looked up.

'What is it, Dulcie?' she asked.

Now it was Dulcie's turn to stare off into space, flooded with uncomfortable thoughts. 'I don't know for sure,' she said. 'But I'm thinking that there's another player involved in Roland Fenderby's murder.'

TWENTY-FIVE

'Chris, I think Fenderby's widow knows more than she's saying.'

Dulcie had called Chris as soon as her cousin had left, eager to confide in the one person she knew she could trust. The fact that she was talking to her boyfriend's voicemail made it easier to relate what had happened. She trusted him. Loved him, too, but in person, he was prone to interrupting her with questions about her reasoning. 'Mina had a really odd talk with her,' she began. 'Disturbing.'

What Dulcie didn't tell her boyfriend were her own suspicions. Despite her best attempts to convince her cousin, knowing that she herself was pretty much barred from Rogovoy's office, she had been unable to convince the younger woman to talk to the police once more. The younger woman had stood firm, citing her own conviction that Rogovoy and his colleagues – she referred to them as a task force – knew more than they were letting on. Dulcie wasn't sure she agreed. Wasn't sure, if she were being honest with herself, that she entirely trusted Mina's motives. But she told herself that with everything that had gone down, she understood her cousin's reaction. Mina had undoubtedly decided that the best course of action for her was to lay low and avoid further contact with the authorities. Still, she had to wonder, wasn't it likely that the more the police knew, the sooner Mina – and Dulcie herself – would be cleared?

Chris's voicemail was mum on the issue.

'I can't be certain,' Dulcie concluded, after laying out her thoughts. 'But I'm pretty sure the widow was aware of what Fenderby was up to, and that there's somebody else involved.'

'What was that about?'

Dulcie looked up to see Lloyd, his arms full of student papers.

'Here, let me.' Dulcie grabbed the door while her office-mate shuffled in.

'Thanks,' he released the flood of paper over his desk. 'Was that your cousin?'

'Yeah.' Dulcie was reticent to say more. 'Mid-terms?'

Lloyd nodded, bending to retrieve an exam book that had fallen to the floor. 'Practise tests,' he said. 'I swear, the freshmen are getting more anxious every year. This was completely optional, and yet I've already had students who are asking if they can take it again.'

'Why would you want to take an exam twice?' Dulcie asked the bald spot on the top of Lloyd's head.

'Crazy, right?' He rose and brushed himself off. 'They all want an edge. I've told them they can learn as much from the mistakes on the practise test as from taking it again. I think they want to impress me.'

'Well, that's nice.' Dulcie retreated to her own desk. 'Isn't it?'

'It worries me.' Lloyd began to neaten the pile. 'I mean, what will they do if they don't all get A-pluses?' He picked up a red pencil and pulled one of the booklets over. 'Sue me?'

'What do you mean?' An idea had begun to tickle through Dulcie's mind.

'Like, you know, claim that I had unfair grading practices.' He licked the tip of the pencil and ran it along the page. 'Or maybe just threaten me. I mean, that would do enough damage.'

'Lloyd, you're a genius!' Dulcie jumped up. She'd shocked her office-mate into silence. 'I bet that's why – what happened.'

'Excuse me?' Lloyd looked down at the blue book as if it might cough up an explanation.

'I think someone was blackmailing Fenderby – and that's what got him killed!'

Lloyd didn't act surprised, and so Dulcie elaborated. 'I think someone at the university gave him an alibi about the sexual harassment suit, and then threatened to withdraw it. His wife said as much to Mina. And that's still blackmail, right? Can you have negative blackmail?'

'Dulcie.' Lloyd's voice was soft and low, even as he stood and walked slowly toward her. 'Dulcie, please.'

'They've been treating Polly Fenderby with kid gloves,' Dulcie was warming to her subject. 'I mean, she is the grieving widow and Griddlehaus must have told the cops that he saw her leaving her husband's office. But she knows something, Lloyd. She might even know the identity of whoever gave her husband his alibi.'

'Dulcie, listen.' He stood in front of her and reached to take her hands in his. 'You've had a shock. I know that you believe what you are saying, but, no, I don't think we have to go to the police. I certainly don't think you should talk to Fenderby's widow. I think we have to mourn.'

'To mourn? Fenderby?' She heard it, then. The high pitch and volume of her own voice. 'I'm sorry,' she said. 'I was excited by the idea of solving this.'

'I know you were.' Lloyd was using his best teaching voice, the one she associated with panicked undergrads. 'But I'm hoping you'll have a seat and we can talk about this. And then, maybe, we can go to the meeting together.'

She shook her head, not understanding.

'The departmental meeting,' he repeated. The words made no more sense the second time. 'Didn't you get the message?'

'No,' she said, her voice falling to a soft hush. 'I'm on probation.'

'Ah.' He nodded, as if that explained everything. 'No wonder you're upset. But I'm sure this was just an oversight. Or – have you checked your messages lately?'

'Lloyd!' This was getting to be too much, but when he looked at her, she shut up. 'What's the meeting?' she asked instead.

'About Fenderby, I assume.' He leaned back on his desk. 'Probably one of those things where they talk about distributing his responsibilities and offering grief counseling.' He paused and fixed her with a solemn look. 'Which might not be a bad idea for you, Dulcie.'

'I am not mourning that man.' The idea was preposterous.

'No, but you did have a very rude shock. And then to find out that you were under suspicion . . .'

'That's just it!' She was getting worked up again, but she caught herself. 'Sorry,' she said. 'Do you think I can still go to the meeting? Even though . . .' She couldn't even say it.

'Of course,' Lloyd sounded confident. 'I was going to get a head start on the practise tests, but I think taking a walk will do us both good. Don't you?'

By the time they got to the departmental headquarters, Dulcie felt like she'd had a workout. Lloyd had steered her down to the river and back again, striding at a clip that had Dulcie jogging to catch up. If she had been suffering from some kind of nervous overload, she figured, his cure would have been a good one. As it was, she found herself regretting the day's missed meals. That half a cookie wasn't doing much to sustain her.

'Do you think they'll have refreshments?' A crowd was already gathering as they mounted the stairs.

'Cold funeral meats?' Lloyd at least was able to joke as they squeezed inside. 'Or the equivalent, a cheese plate.'

Sure enough, through a cluster of bodies, Dulcie could see the requisite tray, pale cubes of white and yellow already sparse. If she didn't hurry, the best she'd get would be the celery sticks.

'Excuse me.' She pushed her way through. Half of these people were undergrads, and her years of study had to count for something.

'Dulcie!' Trista greeted her from the other side of the tray. She'd managed to snag a plastic cup of what looked like flat cola. Passing it across the table, she called out. 'Hang on. I'll get another.'

'Thanks.' Dulcie sipped. Not cola: sherry, sweet and rather warm. With her other hand, she grabbed the last orange cube, and a few carrot sticks for good measure.

'I wasn't sure you'd be here.' Trista had worked her way around, her own glass in hand. 'What with the investigation and all.'

'Tell me about it.' Dulcie eyed the room. 'Lloyd had to tell me. So, have you managed to talk to Tom?'

'Not yet.' Trista craned around, as if she would grab the undergrad here. 'In fact, there's another angle I want to follow up on. It could be big.'

'Tris?' Dulcie looked at her, debating whether to tell Trista what she'd overheard. Her friend was even more keyed up than usual. 'I'm a little concerned . . .'

'OK, everybody,' Thorpe, standing on the stairs, called out. 'If everyone can quiet down.'

The presence of the acting chair did little to quell the conversation.

'He's going to have to wait until the food runs out,' said Trista, taking Dulcie's arm.

'People, please.' Nancy had mounted the stair beside him. For her, the crowd quieted. 'Mr Thorpe has some announcements.'

'Thank you.' He looked over at the secretary and cleared his throat. Dulcie couldn't decide if he looked more pleased or embarrassed that it had taken his girlfriend to still the room. Neither could he, apparently, because it took a few more coughs before he began to speak.

'I'm sure you've all heard the unfortunate news.' Low murmurs greeted this. 'The very unfortunate news that Professor Roland Fenderby has met with . . .' More throat clearing. 'We have lost a valuable member of the department. And I'm sure you are all concerned with what this means for the remainder of your school year.'

It wasn't the best transition in the world, but it was to the point.

'I would like to reassure you that the department will make all possible allowances for work that Professor Fenderby had assigned or would have been overseeing. Our own Nancy Pruitt is drawing up a roster of replacement tutors and graders, which we hope to post by tomorrow.

'In the meantime, we understand that people have been understandably upset by all of . . . this.' He paused, the awkwardness of his own speech apparent to all. 'I mean, the university has also arranged for grief counseling to be available to any student currently matriculating in the department.'

'Told you.' Lloyd had come up behind them.

'Some of you may also want to know that there will be a non-sectarian memorial on campus tomorrow at eleven in the Mumphrey room. The funeral will be private, at the family's request, but we felt that such a gathering might be a way for many of us to remember the man.'

'Nancy, I bet,' whispered Trista. Dulcie nodded in agreement.

'Anyone who would like to take part is, of course, welcome. Please talk to Nancy after we are done here. And now to the less pleasant part of my task.' Trista turned, eyebrows raised.

Even Lloyd looked pained. *'Less pleasant?'* he mouthed the words.

'As I'm sure you are aware, the university police are involved in uncovering the facts of the incident.' Thorpe pulled a handkerchief out of his pocket and mopped his brow. 'Many of you have already been contacted. We expect you, as members of the university community, to aid them in this manner, to the fullest extent possible.'

The murmuring grew too loud at that for Thorpe to say any more, and it took Nancy – climbing up several more steps – to restore order.

'Please, people!' she called. 'I do have sign-up sheets for counseling and Mr Thorpe and I will be available tonight and, of course, during our regular hours tomorrow. If any of you need assistance. This is a time for the community to come together.'

'Is that what we're doing?' Raleigh kept her voice low as she squeezed in next to Lloyd. The room had grown uncomfortably close, and Dulcie was regretting the warm sherry.

'Well, the intent is good,' her boyfriend countered. Trista snorted in response and Dulcie turned toward her.

'Fenderby would have loved this,' said Trista. Maybe it was the light, maybe it was the sherry, but Dulcie thought her friend looked pale and sweaty. 'He'd be circulating around the room, offering "sympathy" hugs.'

'Was he really that bad?' Dulcie reached behind her. There was usually a couch here. She really wanted to sit down.

Trista rolled his eyes. 'He never tried the trick where he asks you to slide past him to get a book?'

Dulcie shook her head. A mistake, she realized, as the dizziness hit. 'Ick, no.'

'Or the one where he says you're so bright and shiny—'

'Like a new penny?' Dulcie remembered Mina's words.

Trista nodded. 'Makes sense for you. You're a redhead. But me?'

'He never . . .' Dulcie let it go. 'Did you report it?'

'Nah, I should have.' Trista looked around. 'Might have saved someone. Might have . . . pfft.' Trista paused to pick what looked like a cat hair from her lips, and she paused to examine it. 'How did that . . .? Well, never mind. I'm still trying to figure out what our shy buddy Walls has to do with it.'

'Do you see him here?' Dulcie had found the couch behind her. But before she let herself sink into it, she looked around. 'Wait – Tris?'

'What?' Her friend settled onto the armrest beside her.

'Never mind,' said Dulcie, letting her head fall back. 'That was weird. I just thought I saw you on the other side of the room, talking to Nancy. You don't want to speak at the memorial, do you?'

She opened her eyes with an effort. Trista's pallor had been replaced by an unhealthy flush.

'Nobody there would want to hear what I have to say.' Her voice had grown quieter, too. 'And I've already missed my turn.'

TWENTY-SIX

myself am the tinder, awaiting one incautious flare. It is my name that may catch and flare. May cause the conflagration that brings down this house, and she who sleeps the rest of innocence within. To counter that hungry Flame, that fiery Spark that would consume, I must dampen that within me that would burn all down. Must indeed tamp the very Rage that has fuelled my Flight, the Fear that drove me on, seeking Safety and refuge for us both. Yea, though I seek to slake my thirst and ease my parch'd Throat with the cooling draughts of Truth, so would I find her Goblets o'erbrimmed with Blood, the noble Ichor that flows throw me and thus to her slumber crest'd crown.

Dulcie woke late from a troubled sleep, her dreams haunted by bloodied books that fell from dark shelves without warning and sticky sweet syrups in little cups.

'I can go with you.' Chris took one look at her when she came into the kitchen and jumped to his feet, unseating the cat, who complained with a soft mew. Dulcie had staggered home the night before and barely managed to tell him about the memorial before stumbling into bed.

'No, I'm fine. Really.' She returned his hug, with a silent apology to Esmé, before turning to pour herself some coffee. 'The whole crew will be there. I think a lot of them will be speaking.' She remembered what Trista had said, but felt that somehow she had gotten it wrong.

'If you're sure . . .' He looked doubtful, and Dulcie wondered if she'd talked in her sleep. 'Well, I should be off then.'

As soon as he'd left, Dulcie began to ransack her closet. Unlike some of her students – particularly a certain clique who took her seminar in error – she had little black in her wardrobe. Still, after throwing several blouses and a long-forgotten skirt on the bed, she found something that ought to work: a top and skirt in a somber dark grey. It might not be exactly funereal, but it also didn't show the cat hair as obviously as the black nylon, cobwebbed with Esmé's white belly fluff. How was it that everything she owned automatically attracted the opposite color fur so consistently?

'Mrrrup.' Esmé jumped on to the bed, as if to make her own contribution.

'Oh no, you don't.' Dulcie snatched up the day's clothes as the cat drew back, startled. 'I need to look presentable, Esmé.'

Whatever her pet's thoughts on that, she kept them to herself. Though Dulcie did notice the loud purr emanating from her stout body as she kneaded a midnight blue velvet top discarded as too ostentatious. By the time Dulcie was dressed, the cat was settled comfortably on the tunic, her fur spread around her as daintily as a proper lady in *The Ravages* might have arranged her skirts.

'See you later,' Dulcie called as she swung her bag onto her shoulder. It wouldn't help to view her pet's decorum as a silent rebuke. Better to just see it as a small animal enjoying a new soft bed, rather than project her own qualms on to the cat.

For qualms she had, as she made her way through yet another gorgeous spring day. Even her slight hangover began to dissipate in the fresh warm breeze. As if to deny the solemnity of her destination, the morning was as bright as . . . as a new penny. The phrase jumped into Dulcie's mind and just as quickly she discarded it. Hadn't that been what Fenderby had called her cousin Mina? She shivered suddenly, pulling closer the sweater she had donned at the last moment. No, that wouldn't do. It was a lovely day. A spring day after a long winter, but maybe that was the metaphor she should stick with – the reprieve after something awful and oppressive had passed.

It was a terrible way to think about a man's death. And scary. As Lucy's daughter, Dulcie couldn't help but think of the repercussions of such ill wishes. But surely she hadn't caused the professor's demise, no matter what anyone might think. And she wasn't rejoicing in it. What she felt was simply relief.

TWENTY-SEVEN

Dulcie was relieved, as well, when she pushed open the door to the Mumphrey Room. With its wood paneling, darkened by years of sweaty hands and exasperated sighs, the chamber had the gravitas for a memorial event.

'Funereal enough for you?' She turned, to see Lloyd, a slight smile playing over his pale face. His girlfriend, Raleigh, didn't look as amused. Then again, the pretty senior would be graduating this year. As an honors candidate, even as an under-grad, she'd be expected to defend her thesis here in this room, and now she looked around, as if imagining these walls closing in on her.

It wasn't just the walls. The Mumphrey couldn't have been designed worse for exams. Its high ceiling, for example, swallowed up the voices of examiners and made orals even more difficult, while the tall stained glass windows that lined two walls cast distracting colors on one's bluebook.

Right now, the morning sun was shining through the left-hand wall, where the yellow robe of some kind of cleric was washing the usually ruddy Raleigh in a sickly glow that even yesterday's sherry couldn't explain. But although her head was inclined upward, Dulcie could see that she wasn't taking in that bright figure or any of its colleagues, 'The Portraits of the Honorable Dead', that lined the high windows. With a drawn expression only heightened by that sallow glow, her upturned face had turned to the other side, the windows that had yet to be cleaned and restored. 'The window of those who died ABD' – all but dissertation – some wag had christened those dark figures, their faces obscured. For those who would take their exams here, the joke had long since gained the weight of portent.

'Really,' said Dulcie, coming up behind her. 'Talk about final exams.'

Lloyd smiled, a tight-lipped smile, and turned to comfort his girlfriend. Her office-mate looked tired. Dulcie knew it wasn't just the occasion: he was one of the students who'd been drafted to handle her classes.

'It's not your fault, Dulcie,' he'd said, when he'd broken the news a few minutes earlier. 'And I know you'd do the same for me.'

'It would be nice if we each had the choice, though,' she had grumbled, guilt making her feel worse about her punishment.

'What, at the university?' Lloyd had chuckled. 'Have you forgotten that we're academics?'

Looking at the couple, Dulcie was acutely aware of the toll Fenderby's death was taking on all of them. Although he had put on a brave face, Lloyd was plainly anxious. Though whether out of concern for her or his own workload, Dulcie didn't know. He also might be worried about his girlfriend. Dulcie wasn't used to seeing the self-assured senior look quite so rattled. Then again, she too would be facing a panel of examiners here soon enough. She looked over at where the examiners usually sat. A podium stood there now, replacing the long table where her interrogators would wait, facing her. That is, if she were allowed to complete her degree.

Looking past the couple, Dulcie saw blonde hair shaded lightly by the green of the glass. Not Trista, she saw as the figure stepped into the room. In the light of day – even multicolored light – and without the haze of hunger, fatigue, and cheap, sweet sherry, she wondered how she could have confused the two. Alyson's hair was a darker, richer shade, her figure more lush. Standing behind the stooped figure of Polly Fenderby, whose unrelenting black suit and dramatic veil somehow escaped the colorful illumination from above, the junior looked like one of those stained glass figures. They both did, Dulcie realized. Youth and age, or beauty and mourning: an impression heightened by Polly Fenderby's apparent frailty, as she leaned heavily on the arm of a fat man in a dark suit.

'Wow, they sent Grossgirt,' a voice behind her commented in hushed tones. Dulcie recognized the name, if not the corpulent figure who now led the widow to a seat behind the podium.

The administration had sent out the heavy hitters for this supposedly informal event.

'They must be grateful that it ended this way.' A second voice, to her left. But even as Dulcie turned, the speaker defended himself against an unheard expostulation. 'Yes, it's a tragedy, but cheaper in the long run.'

'I knew it.' A voice to Dulcie's right caused her to swing around. Trista apparently had overheard the same voices. 'The petition,' she said, nodding grimly. 'I heard the university had assembled a task force. I mean, they had to. The place was going to be declared a hostile work environment all because of him.'

'You don't think that's why . . .' Dulcie didn't finish her sentence. To openly accuse the university of murder was a bit much.

'Suits have been discouraged?' Trista misread her. 'Yeah, I do. Foolish, though. Should've let the cops do their job. If they'd just gotten rid of Fenderby, they'd have been in the clear. "Positive corrective action", and all.' She mimed air quotes. 'Though that wouldn't have helped Morticia Addams much.'

'Tris.' Dulcie, chastened, motioned for her friend to hold her voice down. 'She's lost her husband.'

Trista shrugged, following Dulcie as she joined the assembled crowd sliding into the pews. She'd wanted to talk to Alyson – and to the widow herself, if possible – but not in Trista's company. Her friend's edginess was clearly exacerbated by the surroundings.

Besides, now that everybody was settling in, the proceedings had begun. Grossgirt, if that was indeed the functionary, had escorted the widow to a chair beneath the carved mantelpiece and now ascended to the podium.

'Thank you all for coming this morning.' His voice, low and ponderous, sounded stage perfect, leading Dulcie to wonder if he'd done this kind of thing often. 'We here at the university have come together to acknowledge a great loss.'

Beside her, Trista made gagging sounds, and Dulcie shot her a glance – resisting the urge to elbow her. But the fat man appeared to be there solely to start the proceedings – or show university support to the widow – and moments later, resumed his seat.

'Hello, everyone.' Dean Grulke had taken the podium – grasping the wood frame in both hands, the mike amplifying her usually whisper-quiet voice. 'I'd like to speak to you today about Roland Fenderby, my colleague and a scholar of great renown.'

'Great,' Trista growled. 'Our least likely public speaker.'

'I don't think she'll be on long.' Dulcie nodded to the widow, who had risen and now stood behind the sweating speaker. 'It looks like Mrs Fenderby is waiting to be introduced.'

'Look who's right beside her.' Trista leaned over, and Dulcie followed her line of sight. Sure enough, Alyson Beaumont had stepped out of the shadows beneath the darker windows and now stood behind the widow's chair. Grasping its back, she leaned forward, staring at the grim-faced widow as the dean droned on fervently but inaudibly, apparently about the dead man. 'Ready to speak ill of the dead?'

'I don't know, but I've got to talk to her,' Dulcie said.

'We'll grab her after,' Trista whispered, leaning over. 'In the meantime, look who's here.'

She didn't have to point. Following her gaze, Dulcie could see: Tom Watts, sitting front and center, apparently transfixed by the dean.

'At least someone is listening to her,' Trista whispered. The student in front of them glanced back, eyebrows raised. But before Dulcie could caution her friend, the droning stopped. The dean, it seemed, was done, though whether she had bowed her head in prayer or exhaustion wasn't immediately apparent. A smattering of applause from the befuddled crowd roused her, however, and she looked up, blinking, before leaning in once more to the mike.

'Widow of our colleague,' was all Dulcie could make out. 'Penelope Fenderby.'

'Linda.' With a nod, she dismissed the dean and took her place, lifting her veil as she approached the mike. As she did, an audible gasp went through the crowd. Polly Fenderby was clearly a mess, her eyes red and swollen, her face white even under the rainbow lighting. Dulcie cast a glance at her colleague. Trista might have had her beef with Fenderby, but there was no way she could deny the raw grief before them.

'Roland Fenderby was my husband,' she began, and stopped, raising one black-gloved hand to her mouth. Grossgirt appeared at her side with a glass of water. She took a sip and began again. 'Scholar, teacher, whatever else he may have been, that is what he was.'

The room had fallen silent. Even Trista seemed cowed, as the widow scanned the crowd, and then began to speak again.

'I am not here to eulogize Roland,' she said, scanning the room. 'I leave that to the university that valued him and understood his incalculable contributions to scholarship and pedagogy.' Another sweep of the room left Dulcie wondering if she was expecting a challenge. 'The university that understood the importance of his great work. No,' she said, her voice taking on a steely edge. 'I am not here today to eulogize the man I married. I am here to address his enemies. To speak to those who brought him down.'

Behind her, Grossgirt took a step forward. Even Dean Grulke started to rise, waiting for a cue. But the widow didn't turn and nobody, it seemed, felt comfortable interrupting her as she kept on talking.

'Like a dog to its own vomit, the evil shall reveal themselves.' She scanned the room. Nervous titters broke out behind Dulcie. 'As the poets say, "some rise by sin, while others do by virtue fall".'

'The lady doth protest too much,' muttered Trista.

Dulcie resisted the urge to elbow her friend. 'She's been through a lot,' she said instead. 'And she's not a scholar.'

Trista eyed her sidelong. 'She was one of Fenderby's students, you know.'

'Yeah, but that was how many years ago?' Dulcie squirmed. It was bad enough she found herself cast in the role of the widow's champion; she certainly didn't want to have a conversation in the middle of an increasingly strange memorial.

'Too late.' Trista was staring straight ahead. Dulcie followed her gaze. Sure enough, the widow must have heard them. Mouth set in a tight line, she was staring straight at them. 'At least she's shut up,' Trista murmured.

This time, Dulcie did elbow her. But Trista was right, though whether the widow had reached the conclusion of her talk or been interrupted was anyone's guess. Grossgirt came forward as she turned from the podium, wrapping one arm around her protectively as he led her back to her seat. Alyson, Dulcie now noticed, was no longer standing behind the chair, and in fact seemed to be making her way toward the far door. In the hubbub following the widow's speech, Dulcie stood.

'People, please.' The dean had taken the podium again, but her voice barely registered above the crowd.

Working her way out of the pew, Dulcie made a beeline for her student.

'Alyson!' The junior turned at the sound of her name, and for a moment Dulcie froze. Whatever her involvement, the past few days had been hard on her. Up close, Dulcie could see the broken blood vessels in her eyes, the dark purple patches below them.

'Did Tom do this to you?' It was the first question that popped out of her mouth, not what she'd intended. 'Was this because of him?'

'What?' Alyson shook her head, though whether in denial or disbelief, Dulcie couldn't tell.

'You can tell me, Alyson.' Dulcie was face to face with her student now. She spoke quickly, aware that the other student had to be nearby as the pews emptied. 'I heard what Tom said. I know you were there.'

'You've been found out.' The voice, like a hiss, came from behind her. Dulcie turned, startled, to find herself staring at the widow. 'It's all your fault,' Poppy Fenderby spat the words. 'It's your fault my husband is dead.'

'Mrs Fenderby!' Whatever she had thought, this was certainly not the way to handle it. She took a breath, the better to reason with the aggrieved widow, and saw Tom, his back toward them both as he headed toward the door.

'Tom?' she called, curious. Surely, he had heard what was happening. But he didn't turn, and just then another voice cried out, whipping her around again.

'Watch out!' A young man pointed at Alyson. The pretty

junior had gone a ghastly shade of green, for which the stained glass above could only be partially responsible.

'Alyson!' Dulcie rushed to her student, as her eyes rolled back in her head and she collapsed to the floor.

TWENTY-EIGHT

'Step back, Miss.' A dark blue shoulder slid in front of Dulcie. 'Let us do our job.'

'It's OK, Dulcie.' Raleigh was at her side, pulling her out of the way. In the minutes since Alyson had collapsed, Dulcie had found herself in the middle of a maelstrom. Someone had screamed, and Dulcie had jumped forward to cradle the fallen student's head. Now she watched as the EMT checked for vital signs. As a second uniformed worker pushed by with a stretcher, Dulcie and Raleigh were forced back further. All around, the previously sedate gathering was buzzing.

'What happened?' Someone had grabbed Lloyd. He shook his head and turned back toward his friends, his arms up to shield them from the crush. 'Did she faint?'

'Hang on.' Dulcie strained forward. Alyson's eyes had opened and her head was turned toward Dulcie. One hand seemed to reach out to her, too, before the EMTs placed it back by her side and buckled her in. 'She's trying to say something. Wait.'

Dulcie grabbed the emergency worker's arm, but he only shook her off.

'Coming through,' he called, as he and his colleague rolled the stretcher out, forcing the crowd to step back into the pews as they passed.

'She was trying to tell me something.' Dulcie turned to her friends, as they waited to step out from between the confining benches. 'I've got to find out what it was.'

'Maybe she was confessing.' Trista spoke softly, but suddenly the buzz in the room changed.

'Guilt?' Dulcie heard a male voice murmur.

'I hear she's been suicidal.' A woman this time, speaking in a whisper. 'That it's a cry for attention.'

'I think you should leave this alone,' said Lloyd. Raleigh nodded in agreement. 'It's probably nothing, but things have a way of happening around you.'

'That's not fair,' Dulcie protested. 'I didn't make Alyson sick.'

'No, but we don't want people asking why you were pushing to talk to her right before she collapsed.' Raleigh had Dulcie's arm and was maneuvering her toward the door. 'Especially not if she made herself sick. What if she is involved in some way?'

'Poor girl.' Trista's voice conveyed something other than sympathy. 'I wouldn't be surprised if this was all a stunt to focus attention away from her and leave you in the hot seat.' Trista paused, considering the ramifications. 'Well, you and your cousin.'

'What?' Raleigh asked, looking at Lloyd. He turned to Dulcie, a mute plea in his eyes.

'I'm being investigated,' Dulcie said. 'Just because, well, the bad timing, me finding the professor and then the murder weapon and all. That's why Lloyd is covering my classes.'

Raleigh blinked. 'I'm sorry,' she said. 'And here I was, worrying about my own silliness.'

'It's nothing.' Dulcie insisted. 'Bad timing. Only, well, my cousin Mina – you remember her? – she had a run-in with Professor Fenderby, so in a certain light, it's possible that the authorities . . .' She couldn't bring herself to say it.

'The cops think either Mina killed Fenderby and Dulcie's covering. Or Dulcie killed Fenderby to avenge her cousin.' Trista had no such problem. 'Which is why Dulcie and I have been trying to get timid Tom to explain why he told Alyson that he saw "a redhead" around the time Fenderby was killed, even though he knows full well Mina wasn't there at the time. And why he planted the bloody evidence where Dulcie would find it.'

'Now, we don't know—'

'We didn't before,' Trista interrupted. 'But the circumstantial evidence is building up. And I know you are sentimental about your students, Dulcie. But if it's you or either of them, I know whom I'm going to protect. You're my friend. They're not.'

'Thanks, Tris.' She knew her smile was weak. It was hard to summon up any more. 'It's all so horrible. Why do you think she did it?'

'I don't know and I don't care.' Trista looked around the room. 'I wish I'd gotten a chance to grab that Walls, but he ducked out of here fast enough.'

Dulcie nodded. Tom's exit, just when all hell was breaking loose, did seem suspicious. 'At least I ran toward her,' she said. 'Maybe I stopped her from hitting her head.'

'Yes, you did,' said Raleigh. 'And if anyone thinks Dulcie did anything wrong, Lloyd and I can vouch for her. I wonder what Alyson was going to say anyway? Did anyone get a chance to talk to her?'

Lloyd shook his head. 'No, she was standing behind the speakers, over by Fenderby's widow.'

'Was she looking sick then?' Dulcie remembered her student's wan face, her shadowed eyes.

'She looked guilty,' Trista snarled. 'Like reality was catching up to her.'

TWENTY-NINE

After the brouhaha of Alyson Beaumont's collapse, it had taken at least fifteen minutes before order was restored. Even though other speakers were clearly waiting for their turns, the atmosphere was more reminiscent of a barroom in the aftermath of a brawl than anything more respectful. Voices were raised and everyone looked uncomfortable. When Thorpe got up to speak, he stumbled over his notes and re-read the same page twice. Dulcie saw Nancy on the sidelines, wringing her hands. And front and center sat Polly Fenderby scowling. Tom Walls did not return.

People were finally beginning to settle down and slide back

into their seats when Dulcie had an idea. 'If you don't mind,' she kept her voice low. 'I think I'm going to duck out.'

'You want some company?' Trista looked ready to take off, but Dulcie shook her head.

'I'll let you know if I find out anything.' Trista was too much of a loose cannon right now, Dulcie thought. Besides, it would look odd if two members of the department left. One advantage of having found the deceased and of being under suspicion – perhaps the only plus – was that she would be given a pass from the usual expected behavior.

'Maybe it was a virus,' Dulcie said under her breath as she made her way down the row of seats. 'Plus it is hot in here.' This last was to an older woman – one of the techs from the library, Dulcie thought – who'd given her a nasty look as she stumbled over the oversized bag at her feet.

In truth, the air outside was a welcome relief. Cool and fresh, with the hint of warmth to come. It was so pleasant, in fact, that Dulcie was tempted to abandon her quest and play hooky. A more leisurely stroll by the river than the one Lloyd had led her on, or a latte and croissant in the sun.

But no, she had left the convocation with research in mind. And, with Lloyd otherwise engaged at the memorial and covering her sections, she had the office to herself. Fifteen minutes later, she was hard at work. Not tracking down criminals, she acknowledged. But maybe just as important.

'Dogs to their vomit,' she typed into the university search engine, finding the phrase lifted from Proverbs. What else had Polly Fenderby said? Something about 'rising by sin'. It was, as she'd suspected, Shakespeare, not the vague 'poets' that the widow had credited. But this was just a warm-up, and so with a little trepidation, Dulcie typed in her next query: Polly Fenderby herself. Who was the sad, angry woman who had made such a spectacle of herself in front of her late husband's colleagues?

A quick search surprised her. The widow – Dulcie counted off the years – was barely forty, a good twenty years her husband's junior. And while the most recent mentions were all gardening related – she had leveraged her green thumb into boards of various suburban garden societies – she did not appear to have ever been much of a scholar, no matter what the gossip had said.

Then she found it: a wedding announcement from Midwestern daily. 'Penelope Wrigley to Wed,' read the headline. 'Bride-to-Be Marries Professor.' The body of the short article confirmed what Trista had already shared. Polly Fenderby might not have set the world on fire with her scholarship, but she had been studying with Fenderby when their romance started, here at the university. 'The new Mrs Fenderby intends to give up her studies to focus on homemaking,' the article ran. The implication, Dulcie knew well, was that the pretty young woman in the picture had come East to hunt for a husband, her goal all along a Mrs rather than a PhD.

What was strange was the follow-up. When the Fenderbys hadn't had children, Polly appeared to have focused on her gardening. 'Blue ribbon lilies', read one caption. The photo showed a slightly older photo of the young bride, but one who was still smiling and hopeful. 'Daffodil days', read another, extolling in particular her poet's narcissus. Dulcie remembered the young plants she had seen in the Fenderbys' house, the damp spring earth still clinging to the bulbs.

But over the years, as her focus on horticulture had grown, the couple appeared to have downsized. Those first photos were of bigger yards in the outer suburbs, and Dulcie wondered if the woman she had met had resented losing the large yard for the convenience of Cambridge. City townhouses could be pricey. Then again, Dulcie thought, so could settling a case of sexual harassment.

That, Dulcie knew, was speculation. And certainly not something she could ask the widow about. Still, it was interesting to confirm that Fenderby did indeed have a history of involvement with his students, dating back to his marriage. Maybe, Dulcie thought, the widow's scowl – not to mention that wild accusation – had some precedent.

Dulcie took out her phone. *Mrs Fenderby was a student*, she texted Suze. *Maybe others?* She paused. Her cousin's suit was still confidential. *Harassment?*

There was no reply, and Dulcie found herself thinking of Polly Fenderby's garden. The woman had a gift, even if age and her husband's philandering had dulled the bright prettiness of that first photo. It wasn't like Fenderby had been any prize. Fat, balding and sickly when he died, he'd probably never been her match – except in status. Maybe that was inevitable, she thought, when a pairing was so unequal. Maybe it was a good thing that she and Chris were both struggling grad students. Maybe she shouldn't graduate before he did.

No, that was fear talking. And when further queries turned up nothing more, Dulcie knew she should distract herself with some useful activity: work. Opening the notes file on her computer, she got to it, typing up her notes from the Mildon. She might not know why her author had changed the wording in that passage, but at least now she had it recorded. At some point – maybe even after she had filed her dissertation – she would be able to go back to it and figure out what it meant.

What it meant. Dulcie sat back. The office windows let in the afternoon sunlight, a slanting beam that raked the overflowing bookshelves lining the wall. One word, or, no, three, and here she had spent hours on it. Not far from here, people were trying to make sense of a man's death, while she was documenting a change in wording in a draft of a book that probably hadn't been read for two hundred years. A change that probably wouldn't even make it into her dissertation, assuming she got to finish it. Assuming she was able to graduate.

She had to. Dulcie sat back, allowing the screen before her to go blank. No, what she did wasn't a life or death concern. But words mattered – not only to her but to other readers and scholars. To anyone who loved books and cared about how they were created. About why people made choices. Maybe it was about life, anyway. It certainly was how Dulcie wanted to spend her life. Unless . . .

Dulcie pushed the chair back and blinked up at that shaft of light. The movement made the dust motes swirl, and for a moment, Dulcie thought she could see the faintest outline of a cat – a grey cat – in the slow dance. The swirl like a cursive 'S'. Like the document she had taken notes on, so elegant and old-fashioned. Like something else as well. Staring at the dust, she tried to remember. So much of what she read these days was typed. Even memos tended to be printed, if they were even on paper at all. Her thoughts went back to Fenderby, his head cradled on all that paper. And that one little note – *your little blossom* – three words. Surely, the police had noticed it. Had picked it up for testing or analysis, or whatever the police did these days.

No, Dulcie shook her head, the movement dispersing the dust in the light. She had been told to stay clear. To let the professionals do their jobs. She had questions that the police might not know to ask. She had heard things – she knew things – about Fenderby and her cousin. About the way the department functioned. But everyone had warned her against getting involved. It wasn't like she didn't have enough on her plate. Especially now, with her life's work at stake.

A faint vibration made her start, and she reached for her phone. If Detective Rogovoy was asking for her help . . . But, no: Suze had sent a brief text: *Courage! Working on things.* That was all. And while Dulcie knew that her mother would take that as an encouraging sign – an omen that the universe was aware of her frustration – for Dulcie it was enough to drive her to despair.

Things? Dulcie typed in – and then erased her text unsent. She knew she wasn't being fair, that she should be grateful for the update, as vague as it was. Anything to do with the law took time, Suze had taught her. The two had been roommates all through Suze's law school years and into the early part of her career, when she'd clerked at the legal aid clinic. That had helped Dulcie to understand first-hand how much research went into everything, how much evidence was compiled before any proceedings – from an appeal to an arrest. That was why, Suze had told Dulcie, she shouldn't be unduly worried about being involved in an investigation.

'Everybody who has come into contact with Fenderby is probably part of the investigation,' she had said. Not that this helped Dulcie relax much. After all, Suze was no longer at the university. She might have forgotten how byzantine it was, how easy it would be to lose standing, to lose her students and fellowships, her placement – even her opportunity to file her dissertation – if she wasn't quickly cleared.

And then it hit her. Suze might have forgotten what things were like here, but Dulcie remembered what her roommate had taught her. Opening an email file, Dulcie started typing a direct appeal to the dean. As quickly as she could type, she was citing due process and habeas corpus. Even if she didn't get all the details exactly, Dulcie felt like she was making a good case for herself. You don't room with a law school student for that many years without having some sense of how things worked. What about innocent until proven guilty? With a final poetic flourish, she finished the missive, CC'd Thorpe, and sent it off.

Closing her computer with a soft thud, Dulcie reached for her bag. Even if her research into Polly Fenderby hadn't yielded much, it had served to explain a little about the widow. Besides, that search had made her get down to her own work. It had been wonderful to focus on her findings for a few uninterrupted hours, to be able to properly record what might yet prove to be a breakthrough. Now, she needed to take action. She owed it to her cousin and to herself to try. Besides, she told herself, it was only common courtesy to visit someone who was ill.

'Alyson Beaumont?' She waited at the reception desk of university health services. 'She would have come in about an hour ago?'

Dulcie wasn't sure what her student's condition would be or if she'd be allowed visitors. What she had realized was that Trista, in her defense, was putting the worst possible interpretation on her collapse. Dulcie owed it to Alyson to find out what the truth was, and, if necessary, intercede.

'Hang on.' The receptionist picked up a phone and turned away for privacy. For a moment, Dulcie feared the worst. Wasn't that what they did when someone died? Called for a doctor or a supervisor to come down and break the news? But just as Dulcie steeled herself to ask, the woman turned back around.

'She's been admitted,' she said. 'Third floor.'

It had to be the heating system. Dulcie licked her lips, as she waited for the elevator. The infirmary hadn't adjusted to the warmer weather, she decided. Why else would her mouth be so dry?

The door pinged and Dulcie jumped. Only when the doors started to slide shut again did she step forward, stopping them with her hand. She couldn't be nervous, she told herself as she pressed the button for the third floor. Alyson was her student, no matter what else she may or may not have done.

Still, Dulcie couldn't deny her reluctance as she stepped out on the desired floor. What was she going to say to her student? How, after all this time, was she going to ask her what she needed to know?

'May I help you?' A young man in a white coat addressed Dulcie in a soft voice, his dark brown brows bunching in concern. Of course, she probably looked like she was in pain.

In response, she forced a smile. 'Alyson Beaumont?'

'Room 302,' he said. 'I've just visited with her. She's tired, but I think she's still awake.'

'Thanks.' Dulcie took a deep breath as the young doctor walked away. He had neither asked for ID nor forbidden her entrance. Letting the breath out slowly, she headed toward the room.

'Alyson?' Dulcie knocked gently on the opened door before entering. 'It's me, Dulcie.'

'Ms Schwartz?' A movement in the far bed, by the window, drew Dulcie in. Alyson Beaumont, her face as white as the pillowcase, had turned her head. Dulcie walked up to the bed. If Alyson's eyes had been shadowed before, they looked practically sunken now. Her lips were a strange bluish grey. 'Thanks for coming.'

'My pleasure.' Dulcie relaxed, pulling the flimsy guest chair up to the bedside. 'How are you?'

'Tired.' Alyson looked it. 'But better, thank you. I thought I was just getting sick.' She had closed her eyes, and Dulcie wondered if she was going to sleep. 'I feel . . . faded, somehow. Like I've been erased, you know?'

'I guess.' It had to be a coincidence, Dulcie told herself. 'Like you've been scraped out?'

'Exactly.' A feeble nod. 'Removed from the picture.'

Dulcie started. There was something about that image that

sparked a memory. Alyson saw her reaction. 'You don't think that I . . .' She paused. 'I didn't do this. Honest.'

Dulcie nodded. That hadn't been her concern. 'But you are involved,' she said, screwing her courage up. 'I wanted to ask you about Tom. You said that he was the one who saw a redhead. And I . . .' She paused. It wasn't going to be easy to admit that she'd eavesdropped on the undergrads, but there was so much she wanted to know. 'I wonder if there's anything you want to tell me?'

It didn't seem possible for the face on the pillow to get any paler, but Dulcie thought it did go a bit green.

'Tom.' Alyson sighed. 'He says he can't vouch for anyone. That he can't be sure. But . . .' She stopped and for a moment, Dulcie thought she'd passed out. Then, with an effort, Alyson started speaking again. 'I can. I was there.'

'Did you tell the police?' Dulcie kept her voice gentle. She couldn't help but think of that note, with its feminine writing. A suspicion was forming in the back of her mind.

'It isn't what you think – I was gone before.' She opened her eyes and gave Dulcie a beseeching look. 'They know. Tom does, too. Only he's a little . . .' She stopped, her eyelids fluttered closed. 'He can get a little needy. Oh!'

'What?' Dulcie leaned in. Alyson was struggling to sit up. She was in distress. In pain. 'Alyson! Should I call someone?'

'No, it's – I have a cat. She's only a kitten.' She fell back at that, leaving Dulcie to make sense of the apparent non sequitur. 'And, well, they're keeping me here.'

Dulcie bit back her first response – surprise that Alyson seemed to have only remembered her pet at this point. After all, the woman was ill. And she understood her concern. 'Do you have a roommate,' she asked. 'Someone I can call?'

Alyson was shaking her head. 'I moved off campus over the winter break, to the River Tower. It was – I wanted the privacy. But now . . .'

'I can go over.' Dulcie spoke without thinking, but then the repercussions of what she'd said kicked in. 'I mean, if you want me to. I've got a cat too, so I know how demanding they can be.' She smiled, as if to make a joke out of it. To her relief, the woman on the bed smiled back.

'That would be wonderful. My keys are in my jacket.' She paused, her eyes closing for a moment. 'I guess I have another reason to thank you,' she said, once Dulcie had retrieved the jacket, pulling her student's ID and a large brass key ring from the front pocket. 'That one,' Alyson pointed, and Dulcie worked it loose, noting how the oversized 'A' on the ring almost matched the one in the signature on the ID. 'They told me it was your fast action that saved me.'

'Saved you?' Dulcie re-hung the jacket.

'Yeah.' Her voice had faded to barely above a whisper, Alyson reached for a plastic cup with a straw in it. 'Sorry,' she said, after taking a sip. It was clear that she was fading.

'Alyson, I don't know what you remember, but all I did was call for help.'

'That's just it,' she said. 'The EMTs got me here in time. I'm lucky it was slow acting.'

Dulcie shook her head.

'They pumped my stomach,' said the girl in the bed. 'It sounds so crazy, I know. They're saying I was poisoned.'

THIRTY

'Are we ready for dinner?'

Dulcie jumped, but the orderly behind her motioned for her to sit back down as she removed a tray from a cart and placed it before Alyson.

'I'm afraid there's nothing very interesting for you today,' she said, consulting a chart. 'But let's try to get a little something in your belly.'

The woman on the bed glanced up, but didn't move, even when the orderly pushed the tray up.

'How're we doing here?' A nurse walked in. 'Are we going to eat something?'

Dulcie stepped back as the nurse slid by her to secure a blood pressure cuff. 'She was just telling me . . .' She stopped. Had Alyson really said she'd been poisoned? Might she have meant food poisoning – or something more innocuous?

'Visiting hours are about over,' said the nurse, without waiting for her to finish. 'And I'd say our gal here has had more than enough excitement for the day.' She paused to read the meter by the cuff. 'You can come back in the morning.'

'But—' Dulcie's protests only garnered her an evil look. 'OK,' she said finally. 'Goodnight, Alyson. I'll take care of your kitty, don't worry.'

Alyson was smiling, Dulcie was pretty sure, as she took her leave.

'Hey, sweetie.' As soon as she was out on the sidewalk, Dulcie turned her phone back on. Chris's voicemail popped right up. 'Do you have any thoughts about dinner? I was thinking I'd stop by Mary Chung's again on the way home.'

Dulcie smiled. One of the best reasons not to live alone was messages like this one. Then again, not everyone had the option of a loving mate. Even before listening to the rest of her messages, she called Chris back.

'More takeout sounds great,' she said to his voicemail. Well, at least he would hear her voice. 'You wouldn't believe the day I've had. I'll tell all when I get home. I've got a stop to make first.'

Dulcie found herself re-evaluating her thoughts on undergrad living when she got to Alyson's apartment. Living with a roommate might be more social, but not even the renovated residential houses were as nice as this place. A modern high-rise, down by the river, with a lobby bigger than some university common rooms, the River Tower was the kind of building that Dulcie associated with bankers or socialites. Anyone but an academic.

'It's not very Cambridge,' she griped to herself as she waited for the elevator. 'I'm surprised they allow pets here.' Only the soft hum of machinery responded.

Once Dulcie had let herself into Alyson's apartment, though, any complaints she had were silenced. She had stepped into a sunken living room, empty but for a spare, modern-looking sofa and a coffee table. Neither of these were Dulcie's style – Esmé would have shredded that white upholstery in a day – but that wasn't what had taken her breath away, and she walked past the cool chrome and linen with barely a second glance, transfixed instead by the sliding glass door at the room's end and the small deck it opened on to. Alyson hadn't put furniture on it. In truth, the little landing was barely big enough for a chair. But even through the closed door the porch offered a sweeping view of the river and Allston beyond.

'Oh, my!' Dulcie walked toward the doors, transfixed. Only as she was reaching for the latch did she feel the soft pat of a paw and look down to see a marmalade tabby kitten sitting to attention at her feet.

'Hello, darling.' Dulcie scooped the kitten up and examined her. Young – Dulcie estimated her to be only a few months old – and plump and well socialized, the kitten responded to the attention with a robust purr that set her whole body vibrating. In turn, she examined Dulcie with round blue eyes that seemed to hold a question.

'Are you looking for your person?' Dulcie had been in the habit of talking aloud to cats even before Mr Grey's transformation. It only seemed polite, and besides, who could tell what the thoughtful little beasts understood? 'She'll be back in a day or two.'

Maybe it was the wide-eyed nature of that direct stare, but Dulcie felt she was being questioned. 'She's been ill,' she said, hoping to settle any qualms. 'Or, isn't that what you're asking?'

It had to be those eyes, so round and innocent. 'Alyson? Your person?'

The kitten turned in her hands and began to wash, and Dulcie felt she had hit on the right answer. This was clearly a new pet, so perhaps it made sense that she – he? – hadn't been sure who Dulcie had been talking about. That would also explain Alyson's lapse. A long-time pet person would have thought of her cat immediately upon awakening in a hospital, at least Dulcie was pretty sure she would have.

The kitten's careful bathing, meanwhile, had exposed a pretty blue collar under the white and orange fur, and Dulcie settled the kitten against her chest to reach for its tag. 'And who might you be, little one?' But the move unsettled the animal, and with a twist she jumped down to the floor.

'Have it your way.' Dulcie couldn't take offense. Esmé wouldn't have stood for a stranger holding her at all. Besides, she hadn't come here to cuddle. And so she followed the kitten's bouncing rump into the kitchen, which like the rest of the apartment seemed a little too spare and modern. It was, however, roomy, and Dulcie felt a twinge of jealousy as she reached for a brushed nickel pull and opened a cabinet, looking for cans or kibble. The first two were almost empty – leading Dulcie to think the apartment was as new as the kitten. But on the third, she struck gold, finding not only cans but also a cute dish with a graphic of a fish on its side.

'This has got to be for you, right?' Dulcie looked down at the feline, who had taken up a post by the granite island. Although the kitten didn't answer, the intensity of her stare – blue eyes wide – convinced Dulcie she was on the right track. She opened the can and deposited the dish on the hardwood floor. Like the rest of the kitchen, it appeared spotless – barely used. Except . . .

'What's this?' Under the island's edge, a balled-up bit of foil caught the light. Dulcie reached for it, drawing back as the kitten looked up from her food. 'No, we can play when you've eaten,' she told the cat. It was good to see that not everything in this place was high end.

In the meantime, Dulcie made herself useful. She found the litterbox and scooped it, and then wiped a sponge across the island and moved on to the counter. Both were virtually spotless. Dulcie got the impression that Alyson didn't cook much. The only human food visible was a loaf of what looked like a poppy-seed lemon cake, wrapped loosely in more foil, over by the refrigerator. A scant few crumbs had escaped from that, and so Dulcie brushed them into the sink. She then neatened the end of the loaf, evening it out with a knife she'd found in one of the half-empty drawers, before crimping the foil back into place. Surely, her student wouldn't begrudge her a little sweet, if she noticed that the loaf now had a cleaner cut at all.

Another slice – very thin – and the foil fit better. After all, there was no point in wrapping the cake up again if it were simply going to go stale. But that was enough. Dulcie washed off the knife and placed it in the rack to dry, then checked the drawers for more foil but found none; no wonder the sheet around the loaf was a tad short.

A soft rattle reminded her of another reason. The kitten had finished her meal and was batting the foil ball across the floor. It bounced with a tantalizing irregularity that had the little cat jumping and scurrying, until it landed by Dulcie's right shoe.

'Hang on.' She bent to throw it, and only then noticed the bit of red ribbon peeking out. 'This is not good.'

While the kitten cast a quizzical and – Dulcie thought – a rather disappointed look up at her, Dulcie began to unravel the makeshift toy. Foil balls had been a staple at her house, when Esmé was small. Even Mr Grey had been known to bat one around, all traces of his staid maturity disappearing as the crumpled toy careened around her dorm room. But ribbons were just too tempting and too dangerous. Dulcie had heard of kittens needing emergency surgery when they had ingested such temptations. Alyson was clearly a first-time cat owner – the ball was scrunched more tightly than either Esmé or Mr Grey would prefer – and Dulcie would have to have a word with her about feline safety.

'Mrrrup?' The kitten reached up as if to grab at the dangling ribbon.

'I'm sorry, kitty.' Dulcie had gotten more of the ribbon out finally and pulled, only to find it stuck fast. Carrying it back over to the counter, she opened the foil further – this was getting to be a lot of work for a toy she could have constructed in thirty seconds at home. Once she had the foil flat, however, Dulcie could see the problem. The ribbon had been taped to the foil, along with a bit of paper. *'Penny,'* the paper said.

'Is that you, kitty?' Dulcie pulled the ribbon, tape and all, free and loosely bunched the foil up again. 'Did she name you Penny because you're copper colored?'

The kitten only tilted her head and blinked those big blue eyes.

'Well, there you go, Penny.' Dulcie tossed the ball and was gratified to see the energetic young beast bound after it. When the kitten collided with an ottoman, tumbling over on her back onto the hardwood floor, Dulcie had a moment's concern, but the fall didn't seem to faze the small beast who bounced back on the attack, knocking the foil ball back toward Dulcie as if making an all-star pass.

'Go for it!' Dulcie kicked the ball, careful not to catch the little cat with her toe. The kitten obliged and as she ran off, Dulcie heard a rap at the door.

'Hello?' Dulcie opened it to see a middle-aged woman with short grey curls. 'May I help you?'

'Oh.' The woman blinked, looking for all the world like the kitten, her eyes round and blue behind her big glasses.

'I'm sorry.' Dulcie shook her head. 'I'm a friend of Alyson's. You must be a neighbor?'

'Yes, I'm Sara Dodge.' The woman extended a hand. 'I heard some noises.'

'Sorry,' Dulcie apologized again. 'I'm sitting her kitten and I guess we got a bit rambunctious. I'll try to keep things calmer.'

'No, no, it's not that.' The other woman, Dulcie now noticed, was waving a piece of paper. 'I was only hoping that someone was home. You see, we've got a condo meeting coming up, and I'm trying to get support for some capital improvements.'

'I see.' Dulcie nodded, although she didn't really. She took the flier, however. 'I'll leave this for Alyson. Was there any other message?'

'No.' The grey curls bobbed as the woman shook her head. 'No, thanks. Just if Alyson wants to talk before the meeting, she should call me. We're really hoping either she or her boyfriend can be there.'

'Well, isn't she a sly one?' Dulcie said to the kitten, after the visitor was gone. 'I didn't know she had a boyfriend at all. I wonder if this is his condo?' Dulcie took the flier into the kitchen and, after a little consideration, decided to leave it on the counter. Odds were, she knew, the apartment was a rental – she and Chris had looked at a few condos when they were searching for a place. Although the city had pretty much recovered from the real estate crash, there were always a

number of absentee landlords who rented out their places.
Graduate students, she'd learned, were usually considered good
tenants – if they could afford the sometimes steep fees.

'A place like this must cost a pretty penny, don't you think?
Though you're the real pretty Penny, aren't you?' But the
kitten was no longer listening. Exhausted by the bout of play,
she had stretched out on the rug, her blue eyes closed in sleep.

THIRTY-ONE

There was no point in lying to Esmé. From the moment
Dulcie walked into the apartment, the round little cat
was aware she'd had contact with another feline.

'I'm sorry,' Dulcie knelt on the living room rug, holding
her hand out to her pet. 'I had to. Her person is sick.'

'Huh!' With a sniff of her mostly pink nose, Esmé turned
away, showing Dulcie her smooth black back. Even though
she was facing away, Dulcie could hear her thoughts, almost
as if the young cat were on her shoulder. *'And you smell funny,
too.'*

Sometimes, Dulcie felt with a pang of disloyalty, she wished
things would go back to the way they were – that she couldn't
hear what her cat was thinking. Before Mr Grey had died – and
then returned to her through his occasional visitations – Dulcie's
relationships with cats were simpler.

For now, however, she was reprieved by the sound of
the door opening. It was Chris, carrying a large paper bag.

'I wasn't sure if you'd want the dumplings again or the
noodles, so I got both,' he said as he carried the fragrant bag
into the kitchen. 'Plus, they were having that duck special, so
I got that too. I figured that after last night, you'd be ready
for a proper dinner.'

'Awesome,' Dulcie replied, with another twinge. Her
snacking at Alyson's had left her without her usual appetite.
'I'll set the table.'

Twenty minutes later, the dumplings were gone, as were

most of the noodles and a good portion of both the duck and the tofu. Most of that had been consumed by Chris, as was usually the case. Tonight, however, he did pause to look at his girlfriend with concern.

'Are you feeling all right?' he asked, chopsticks still in hand. 'You've barely touched anything but your rice.'

'Yeah, I'm fine.' Dulcie put her own down and reached for her glass of water. 'I guess I'm just trying to figure things out.'

'Tell.' Chris grabbed a sliver of dark mushroom and waggled it. 'I'm all ears.'

It was just as well he was still eating. As Dulcie went through her day, he paused several times. But he was as good as his word and only chewed thoughtfully as she explained about visiting Alyson and then going to her apartment afterward.

'I thought you were going to stay out of this,' he said, his voice gentle, once she was done.

'I was. I am,' Dulcie corrected herself. 'I mean, I had to go to the memorial out of respect. Fenderby was on my thesis committee.' Chris looked like he was about to interrupt, but Dulcie kept talking. 'And then I realized that I'd never gotten a chance to ask Alyson about what she'd told the police – and what she'd said is having an impact on me.'

Chris put his chopsticks down. 'Dulcie?'

'Only now I'm not sure if she's involved.' Dulcie was on a tear. 'I mean, Chris. She's got a cat.'

The rest of the evening didn't go well. Dulcie knew that Chris was upset, but she couldn't simply drop it. Not now. Besides, she had gotten work done.

'If I'm ever reinstated,' she'd explained, while they were doing the dishes, 'I've got all my citations in place. That chapter is bulletproof.'

He'd winced, and she'd moved on. 'Maybe having this extra time is a good thing, you know? Lucy would say everything happens for a reason.'

'I don't know, Dulce.' Chris took the rice bowl from her and began drying it. 'If you're quoting your mother, you must be desperate.'

Dulcie couldn't remember the last time she was grateful for the Red Sox. But Chris had switched the game on, and she relaxed on the sofa beside him, happy not to talk.

'Hey, Esmé,' she called softly. The players all seemed to be talking to the pitcher about something. 'Come join us?'

'Meh,' the cat said aloud. She had taken up a post by the television and was staring at Dulcie as she sat there. *'You still smell funny,'* was all the little tuxedo said as she turned tail and stalked out of the room.

The cramps started sometime after two. At first, Dulcie tried to ignore them, shifting in the bed in her attempt to find a more comfortable position. Esmé had jumped off before she had woken, if she had joined them in bed at all. But Chris was snoring gently, and especially after their touchy evening, Dulcie didn't want to be the cause of a sleepless night for him.

When a particularly sharp pang made her gasp, she realized this wouldn't work. Bent over, she made her way to the bathroom and opened the medicine cabinet. Surely, in with all the Band-aids and half-finished bottles of cold medicines, they had some antacid.

'What's up?' Chris, rubbing sleep from his eyes, was standing in the doorway. 'You OK?'

'No,' said Dulcie. Another cramp hit and she sat on the floor. 'My stomach hurts like anything.'

'Hang on.' Thanks to his height, Chris was able to check the higher shelves, and in a minute he'd pulled out a bottle of something foul-looking and pink. 'It's from 2011, but it should still be good. Let me get a spoon.'

'Thanks.' Dulcie knew he wanted to help, but sitting there, looking at the sickly pink bottle, she wasn't sure this was the answer. In fact, at the idea of swallowing it . . .

Another cramp, and she found herself retching.

'Oh, Dulcie!' Chris was behind her, holding her curls out of her face as she vomited into the toilet. One heave, then another, until finally she collapsed, empty and exhausted. Leaning back against the tub, she let her face rest against the cool porcelain and shut her eyes.

'Hang on.' She blinked. Chris was holding a glass of water to her lips, and she summoned the tremendous energy necessary to take a sip. 'I guess you don't need that Pepto now.'

'Guess not,' Dulcie struggled to answer. She could not recall ever feeling quite so tired. 'I think it was the color, that horrible pink . . .' She waved feebly, indicating the toilet and the dinner she had just lost.

'Poor dear.' Chris sat beside her. He'd gotten a damp washcloth at some point and was gently wiping her face. 'But I'd put my money on it being the duck. Maybe it was on special because it had been sitting around for a while. Though I've never known Mary Chung's to give anyone food poisoning.'

'I don't think it did. Besides, you ate most of that.' It was an effort to speak. Even more to talk, but Chris's words had sparked the germ of an idea in Dulcie's mind. 'Before dinner,' she said, her voice little more than a whisper. 'At Alyson's. I had cake.'

'Ah, the truth comes out,' her boyfriend teased gently. 'No wonder you weren't that enthusiastic about the noodles. And I guess we know what happened.' He paused. She shook her head, as much as she could. He wasn't getting it. He didn't understand.

'Spicy Szechuan on top of cake maybe wasn't the best idea.' She could hear the tender chiding in his voice.

'No,' she said. It was too much effort to say more. She could barely shake her head. 'No,' she repeated.

'Especially, when maybe you've been drinking too much coffee?' His voice had a smile in it. 'That stuff is pretty acidic, you know. And the brew they serve at the English department could take the paint off a car—'

She pulled away and lurched toward the toilet. It was hopeless. She was empty. Spent, and after a moment the spasms subsided. An overwhelming wave of fatigue swept over her, but at least the horrible sickness had passed – at least for now – leaving her exhausted, but a little more in charge of herself.

'It's not the coffee, Chris,' she managed to say, her voice weak. 'I've been poisoned.'

THIRTY-TWO

*G*oblets o'erbrimmed with Blood, the noble Ichor from that Most Ignoble crown . . . Even in her sleep, Dulcie recognized that the quote had been altered. The imagery turned from something mystical into something bloodier and more coarse. *That those so Bonded could so Bloody be, that Words once Scripted could be Overwrought . . .*

Still woozy, Dulcie tossed and turned, the image of a bloodied hand writing and crossing out those words recurring through her dreams. Only in the dream, the ink became blood, the page itself bleeding as the words were scratched out, the 'bloody ichor' spreading through the paper to obscure the text.

She woke, at last, to find Esmé staring at her, the cat's green eyes inches from her face. 'What is it, Esmé?' Dulcie murmured as she blinked away the dream. 'Was I talking in my sleep?'

In response, the cat turned and jumped off the bed, leaving Dulcie to assume that the little tuxedo had stayed behind only to watch over her and, perhaps, to safely wake her from her nightmare. But although her pet may have saved her from night terrors, Dulcie couldn't entirely shake the grisly image from her mind. If anything, the memory only added to her conviction that something much worse than spoiled duck was at work.

'I don't know, Dulcie.' Chris looked somber when she joined him in the kitchen, stating her intentions for the day. When she blanched at his offer of coffee, he renewed his protest. 'I think you should be in bed.'

She was determined, however, only acceding to his request that he accompany her. 'I don't want you passing out on the way in. And if you start feeling sick again,' he had said, as he helped her into the cab – another of his conditions, 'I'm taking you to health services.'

'I'm OK,' she insisted. In truth, she felt more like the wet washcloth that Chris had used to wipe her face the night before than anything like herself. 'And this is important.'

She'd given up trying to convince him that Esmé had tried to warn her. Although he, too, could hear when their pet chose to communicate, he'd put the little tuxedo's apparent rebuke down to a much more selfish reason: Dulcie had held another cat.

'Alyson didn't try to harm herself. She was poisoned,' Dulcie repeated now. 'As was I.' It was hard to enjoy the luxury of a cab when it jolted so. Still, the fresh air coming through the open window helped counter the movement. It also reminded her of the view from Alyson's apartment. 'I wonder if she'll get out today?'

'Dulcie, please.' Chris put his hand over hers. 'She's not your concern any more. Especially not . . .'

He caught himself, but it was too late. Dulcie closed her eyes. There had been no answer to her email when she'd checked this morning. Nothing from Thorpe, nor from the dean. She was still on disciplinary probation.

'Detective Rogovoy, please.' Despite Chris's offer to seek out the detective himself, Dulcie made herself walk up to the reception area. It wasn't that she didn't trust Chris, but that she feared his skepticism might translate somehow. What was it Alyson had said? It was so easy to judge people by their appearance – and Chris's pale face tended to broadcast his emotions.

Rogovoy's, however, was usually as stolid as granite. He was looking past her as he emerged from his lair, though, so maybe it was surprise at seeing her boyfriend that provoked the slight rise of his eyebrows.

'Ms Schwartz.' His voice was a grumble. 'Mr Sorenson. My office, please.'

'Thank you.' Dulcie had requested this meeting, so the feeling – hard to shake – that she was being summoned to a dean's office for a talking-to didn't make much sense. To counter it, and reclaim the upper hand, she began to speak as soon as he had shut the door behind them.

'You undoubtedly know that Alyson Beaumont was admitted to health services yesterday,' she said. 'What you don't know is that I was sickened last night, as well, most likely by something that I ate at Alyson's off-campus apartment. And while I don't have any conclusive evidence of who might be trying to poison Alyson, I do have reason to believe there is collusion between her and another undergrad, Tom Walls. He—'

'Wait a moment.' Rogovoy's big hand came up like a stop sign. 'You were at Ms Beaumont's apartment?'

'She has a cat,' said Dulcie. 'A kitten, really.'

He nodded, as if he really did understand.

'I didn't know she was going over there,' Chris broke in. 'I would have stopped her.'

'You would have— Wait.' Dulcie turned to face her boyfriend. 'Have you two been talking about me? Are you trying to control me?'

'Not control, exactly.' Chris reached out as if he would take her hand, but Dulcie drew back.

'I can't believe you.' She had rarely felt so betrayed. 'I trusted you.'

'Dulcie, I—'

'Ms Schwartz.' The detective's booming voice interrupted them both. 'It was my idea to reach out to Mr Sorenson, and you should be grateful.' He paused. Dulcie could only stare. 'You are not helping. In fact, you are putting yourself at risk. I've said it before and I'll say it again, please do not conduct your own "investigations".' He accentuated his final word with his fingers, making little air quotes. 'You are not trained for this kind of work, and your involvement both hinders the efforts of those who are and endangers you and other bystanders.'

'Well, then.' Dulcie could feel the blush climbing up her cheeks. 'I guess I have no choice. But at least I'm honest.'

Chris's brow had knitted up as if he might cry. Right then, Dulcie didn't care.

'I assume you have no objection if I provide the minimal amount of pet care,' she continued, her voice dripping with sarcasm. 'Seeing as how Ms Beaumont herself asked me to?'

'I believe Ms Beaumont is being released today,' said Rogovoy, his own voice calm and, now, rather quiet. 'Therefore, the problem is moot, and so I reiterate, Ms Schwartz, please, focus on your own work.'

'If I could . . .' It was a complaint, nothing more, but Rogovoy perked up at it.

'I believe I may be able to help you there,' he said. 'Call it an acknowledgment of your good intentions. In fact, I'll call the dean as soon as we finish up here. Do we have a deal?'

Dulcie looked from the stone-faced detective to her own boyfriend. In neither did she see any alternative. 'Deal,' she said at last, and rose to go.

'Dulcie, you've got to understand . . .' Chris was talking to her as she strode out, easily keeping pace despite her best efforts to leave him in her metaphorical dust. 'You've never— There's a special—' He stepped in front of her, forcing her to stop. 'Detective Rogovoy is worried about you.'

Dulcie glowered at him, but didn't respond. Arguing was difficult while maintaining this pace, and when her phone rang, she was grateful for an excuse to turn aside – toward an elegant wrought-iron fence – and answer, as if Chris was not even there.

'Hello?' She struggled to keep her voice even. No way did she want Chris to hear how breathless she had become.

'Dulcie!' The voice on the other end was excited. 'I'm sorry I haven't gotten back to you!'

'Professor Showalter!' Dulcie leaned on the fence, relief leaving her exhausted. 'You wouldn't believe what's been going on.'

'I have some idea,' her mentor said. 'I've spoken with the dean – and with your thesis adviser as well.'

'Oh?' Dulcie stood up. Somehow she had never imagined that Showalter and Thorpe would talk.

'Of course,' the Canadian professor continued. 'As soon as I heard about Fenderby, I got in touch with your department. I thought, this can't wait until I'm actually on campus.'

'Thank you so much,' said Dulcie. She looked up at Chris and even smiled. 'With you on my dissertation committee, everything will go so much more smoothly. You're the only one who understands—'

'Wait, Dulcie,' the voice on the phone interrupted her. 'I think you may have the wrong idea.'

'You're not going to take his place on my committee?' Dulcie couldn't believe her ears.

'I'm not sure,' said Showalter. 'That's not what I was asking about. What I've been looking into – and what I was querying the department about – was the segregation of papers.'

'You don't have to worry about that.' Dulcie tried to temper her disappointment. Professor Showalter was championing her, she was just a little behind the times. 'I've already gotten access to the segregated box – number 978 to be exact. In fact, I found something very interesting in one of the documents.'

Dulcie paused, waiting for her mentor's curiosity to mount. The response that followed was not what she expected.

'I'm sure it was, Dulcie,' said the professor. 'But that's not what I wanted to talk to you about. And, in fact, although I do not yet have any standing to do so, I would advise you not to delve into that box any more. Not until the investigation has been closed. You see, I had an unusual call after I spoke with the dean and then Mr Thorpe. It seems my queries had triggered some kind of alarm with your university security services, and I found myself the object of some rather disturbing questions. My own went unanswered, as is too often the case. But it doesn't take a detective to unravel what was going on. And, Dulcie? I am hoping you can avoid any further entanglement with them. I believe those pages are somehow linked to the murder of Professor Fenderby.'

THIRTY-THREE

'I can't believe Chris betrayed me.' An hour later, tucked into the couch with a mug of weak tea, Dulcie was still feeling a bit weak herself, as well as peeved. Esmé, who had been bathing when she started to speak, appeared unfazed. Chris had done what he could to make amends for his betrayal, escorting her home and pampering her, and that seemed to be enough for the chubby tuxedo at the foot of the sofa. Then again, thought Dulcie, cats are born with a natural skepticism. 'He actually colluded with Detective Rogovoy behind my back.'

'*Men?*' The thought – half enunciated as a soft mew – came to Dulcie as a question, and she immediately felt a stab of remorse.

'I don't want to turn you against an entire gender,' she said. 'I mean, *some* men are reliable.' She searched her mind for examples. Her father, for example, had always meant well. He had simply gone off the grid when Dulcie was still quite young. And Lloyd had always seemed quite a respectful and responsible partner to his girlfriend Raleigh. And hadn't Alyson's boyfriend given her that lovely marmalade kitten, Penny?

'*Mrrrup?*' The bat of a paw, with just an edge of claw, interrupted Dulcie's thoughts. It must have been the praise for another feline that Esmé had picked up. The little tuxedo had a hard enough time dealing with Dulcie's love for her predecessor. Maybe it was just as well that Mr Grey seemed to be receding from her life. If Dulcie was going to truly commit to Esmé, maybe she had to accept that her great, grey cat was no longer with her. That Esmé and Esmé alone was her pet, even as the cat sat with her back toward Dulcie, ignoring her as only a feline could.

'I am sorry, Principessa Esmeralda,' apologized Dulcie, using the cat's full title to show deference. 'I haven't paid you proper respect, have I? No wonder you've been acting out.' She stopped. Something about the pose – the sight of the cat's back, especially as she jumped to the ground and sauntered away, turning a deaf ear to Dulcie's voice. The memorial – before Alyson had fainted – Dulcie pictured the scene. Pictured Tom Walls walking away.

'I can't believe I didn't think of this,' she said, grabbing her jacket. 'It must have been because I was sick too. Thanks,' she called to the retreating feline. 'Thank you, Esmé!'

Throwing her bag over her shoulder, Dulcie ran for the door. She had to catch Alyson before she was released from the health services – before she went back to her own apartment. What was it the junior had said about her classmate – about Tom Walls? That he was 'obsessed'? He must have known she had a boyfriend. Maybe he never intended to hurt her – maybe his target was Alyson's secret love – but at this point it didn't matter. Someone had sickened Alyson – had poisoned her – and Dulcie was pretty sure she knew who.

Turning on her phone as she raced down the stairs, Dulcie saw that a text had come in. Thorpe had called another meeting, she read. There was no agenda given, but it was promising that he'd even reached out. Torn between hope – had Showalter gotten through to him? Had Rogovoy? – and fear, she texted back, confirming that she'd be attending, and nearly collided with one of her neighbors. 'Sorry!' she called out, as he jumped aside.

Maybe it was the text – a sign of things turning around. Or maybe it was her own near collision, reminding her of her own heedlessness. But Dulcie was suddenly gripped by doubt.

Even as she hurried on, all the other possibilities began to race through her thoughts. Was it possible that Alyson had faked her illness? Or, worse, made herself sick? Dulcie mulled over her interaction with the junior's neighbor as she trotted down the street. The woman had mentioned the boyfriend – but she also seemed to think that Alyson owned the unit. Maybe, her trot slowed to a walk . . . Maybe Alyson didn't have a boyfriend, Dulcie thought. The neighbor could have been confused or mistaken. Dulcie had taken the neighbor's word for it because of the presence of the kitten. But Alyson hadn't specifically said who had given her the kitten. For all Dulcie knew, the little marmalade tabby could have been a gift from Tom. Or from another classmate or—

No. She stopped short. It didn't make sense. It was the kind of crazy hypothesis that Rogovoy warned her about. Better to stick with what she knew. For starters, she began to enumerate the facts as she started to walk again, Alyson had been attacked. Rogovoy might not have said as much, but his reaction made it plain. He'd warned Dulcie off because she wasn't helping. Ergo, it made sense that there was an investigation into whatever had made her sick. Ergo, she was at the center of something. Add in that Rogovoy was clearly keeping tabs on the junior – he knew she was being released – and it all began to add up.

*   *   *

The only certainty Dulcie had was that Chris had been right. She shouldn't be up. She felt that before the end of the block, a wave of nausea nearly doubling her over on to the sidewalk. She should be in bed, with her tea and the cat – the real, live cat who now lived with them, despite all Dulcie's callous ingratitude.

She certainly shouldn't be pushing her poor, sick body as she was then, running up toward Massachusetts Avenue. But as she hit the main drag, in time to grab a bus heading in the right direction, another thought hit Dulcie with a certainty that made every other concern fade away. Everything else might be speculation, but Alyson Beaumont was in danger.

'Please, sit down.' The young woman who approached Dulcie didn't look like a receptionist. For starters, she was wearing scrubs. But Dulcie had been out of breath by the time she had pushed open the main door to the health services, and so she'd let herself be led to an empty examining room.

'Is this for a new procedure?' She looked around. 'For privacy or something?'

'Please, let's focus on you,' the woman answered. 'How may I help you?'

'I'm looking for a patient,' Dulcie answered. 'Alyson Beaumont.'

'Oh.' The woman sat back. 'You looked so pale . . . I'm sorry, this is triage. I thought . . .' She shrugged.

'Thanks, anyway.' Dulcie rose, feeling herself wobble as she stood, and turned to the uniformed woman. 'But maybe you can tell me. If a person has been poisoned, how long before she works it out of her system?'

The other woman blinked. 'Ah, do you mean food poisoning?'

'Never mind.' Dulcie waved her off. It was all too complicated. Besides, she'd spied a familiar shade of rich blonde hair passing through the lobby.

'Please, Miss.' The nurse, or whatever she was, took Dulcie's arm. 'If you think you may have been poisoned, you should let us run some tests. Keep you here for observation.'

'This isn't about me.' Dulcie summoned a smile that she

hoped would compensate for the cold sweat on her forehead. 'I'm fine. Really.'

It was Alyson. Dulcie could see her now, over by the door. 'Alyson,' she called. And then shut up. Alyson was talking with Tom Walls, and the tall young man appeared to be near tears. Dulcie paused, unsure of whether to interrupt. The two were leaning together, Tom towering dark and gawky, regarding the golden Alyson with that intense look Dulcie had come to know so well. She'd wait, she decided.

The moment passed, and Alyson turned to go. Tom, it seemed, didn't want her to.

'But I was trying to help,' he said. Dulcie could hear his voice straining upward, even as Alyson motioned for him to keep it down.

'Don't you have a job to get to?' Her voice was low but clear. Tom nodded. 'I wouldn't want to keep you,' she said, and turned to go.

But Tom wasn't done. 'Alyson, please,' he called out, even as Alyson pushed open the door. 'You don't know!'

'Save it,' Alyson snapped back, her voice suddenly harsh. 'For Mina Love!' And she was gone.

Dulcie felt her jaw drop. Here she had assumed that Alyson had been victimized. That an obsessed classmate had poisoned her and coolly walked away. For a brief moment, she had thought she understood why. But as she stood there, frozen, she had to consider that she'd had it all wrong. And that somehow, between Alyson and Tom, her cousin Mina was in danger.

THIRTY-FOUR

'Pick up!' Dulcie commanded her phone, even as she heard her cousin's ring. 'Please, Mina.'

'Hi, you've reached Mina Love . . .' Dulcie sighed and hung up. There was no way to communicate this all in a thirty-second message. Instead, she tried to text: *Mina,* she typed, *we have to talk. Important. Soon!*

It wasn't enough, but it was all she dared. Alyson and Tom had stepped out on to the plaza as she fiddled with her phone, and now she followed, hanging back in the shadow of a pillar as she watched the mismatched pair turn once more toward each other. They were too far away, now, for her to hear anything, the warmer weather having brought a lunchtime crowd out of the surrounding towers.

'Let's try that new pizza place.' A couple barged in front of her, their voices raised. By the time they passed, Alyson was gone and Tom was standing alone, his face drawn and distraught.

The decision had been made for her. Besides, she realized as he started walking, she knew where he was headed. He'd mentioned work. She could find him at the library. Down on Level Two.

Even with the milling crowd as cover, Dulcie held back. Partly, that was expediency. She had no idea still what to say to the junior. How to ask him about his role in Alyson's illness – or in her cousin's troubles. She had promised people she wouldn't talk to him. Had trusted Trista to find out anything relevant.

Partly, she realized as a fat figure on a cell phone barreled into her, she wasn't up to following him. Tom was as tall as Chris, and despite his apparent gracelessness, moved quickly through the crowd. Dulcie had never been more aware of her height – or lack thereof – somewhere below the eye level of the average pedestrian. Add in the fatigue and waves of nausea, and it wasn't long before she lost sight of his bobbing head.

Well, she consoled herself, she knew where to find him. What she needed to focus on was what to say. How to get the truth out of him without endangering Mina – or herself. Simply by his refusal to give her cousin an alibi, he had framed Mina, and no matter how she worked the problem over in her mind, Dulcie didn't see how she could get him to retract his statement.

There had to be a way. And so, with a deep breath to settle her stomach, Dulcie took off in the direction of the library, searching for his lanky form as the plaza opened up to the sidewalk and the street. Her focus helped, keeping the nausea at bay, but Dulcie was reminded how tightly wound she was when her phone buzzed and she jumped.

'Mina!' Seeing her cousin's name pop up flooded her with relief. Still, she covered the receiver, not wanting anyone to overhear. 'Where are you? Are you OK?'

'I am, thank you!' Her cousin sounded surprisingly normal. 'For a change, I've got the best news.'

'We have to talk,' said Dulcie, anxious to break through. 'I've overheard something.' A twinge of belated compunction made her pause. 'Two of my students were – well, they were talking about you.'

'Alyson Beaumont?' Mina asked, as if it were the most natural thing in the world 'I'm so glad.'

'Wait – what do you know?' Dulcie was confused. 'Is this your news?'

'It is,' her cousin sounded positively joyful. 'I knew I should pressure the dean. That I could get the judgment thrown out. I mean, the man was a creep, but he's dead, right?'

'Yes?' Dulcie's head was spinning.

'I guess that made all the difference,' Mina said. 'There's another woman, one who never filed. She – well, I gather Fenderby pushed her further than he did me, and she was afraid of how it would come out. But she's going to make a statement. It's all confidential, but I know Alyson was taking a class with him. I'd seen her name on his schedule.'

'And do you really think it's Alyson?' Dulcie paused to consider. The facts just might fit. 'But why now?'

'Maybe she was ashamed.' Dulcie could hear the shrug in Mina's voice. 'Maybe she knew what would happen. I mean, look what they did to me. And in a way it doesn't matter as much now, since he can't be censured or fired any longer. But it will go a long way toward clearing my name, and really that's all I want now. But, hey, you texted me? You said there was something important?'

'Yeah.' Dulcie thought back. Could she have misinterpreted what she heard? 'But first, Mina, how did you find this out? I mean, about the other woman going to testify?'

'I'm sorry, Dulcie.' In the background, Dulcie could hear other voices. Someone called Mina's name. 'This is all confidential.

And I'm about to go into Sever Hall – not that I'm in the mood
for late lyric poetry right now. Was there something you had to
tell me?'

'I don't know any more.' If Mina's conjecture was correct,
it would change everything. 'I'm sorry. I should let you go.'

'No problem.' Her cousin sounded happy, her voice more
buoyant than it had been all week. 'Call or text if you
remember!'

Dulcie knew she should be happy. Still, something about
the exchange she had witnessed didn't sit right, and she
decided to follow Tom to the library. Odds were, nothing had
happened.

'Ms Schwartz.' Once again, the guard on duty waved her in,
past the line of undergrads waiting to swipe their cards. With
everything going on, she'd forgotten her earlier anxiety until
she'd joined the queue, and she accepted the courtesy with
relief.

'Thanks,' she called over her shoulder as she passed the
courtly guard. At times, it was nice to be part of a community,
she mused as she descended to Level Two. In fact, the idea
of anyone in this community turning on anyone else . . . she
stopped herself. She was being naïve. Fenderby had been a
member of this community, too. And not only had he been
unpleasant to her, he had assaulted her cousin, as well as some
other member of the university. Even if, as she liked to think,
his death had come about through some random accident,
she couldn't change that one undeniable fact. Not unless she
doubted Mina – but before she could even go down that rabbit
hole, the elevator doors swung open, and she found herself
face to face with Polly Fenderby.

'Hello.' She straightened, momentarily taken aback by the
widow's unexpected appearance.

The woman before her was holding a large, open cardboard
box. A pair of bookends – lions couchant – were piled on top,
next to what looked like a bud vase and a stained coffee mug
with the logo *Wordsmiths Do It Write*. The box only seemed
about half full, but the widow held it awkwardly, balancing
its weight on one hip.

'Here, let me.' Dulcie reached for it. The widow jerked it back.

'I'm sorry,' Dulcie apologized. 'I thought maybe you needed help.'

'You've already done enough,' the woman growled.

'Excuse me?' Dulcie knew that grief affected everyone differently. However, she hadn't heard of anyone becoming delusional. 'I'm sorry, Mrs Fenderby.'

'You should be.' The woman pushed past her, the corner of the box pressing Dulcie out of the way as she stepped into the elevator. 'It's all your fault. If you hadn't gotten involved, Roland would still be alive.'

Dulcie had no comeback to that, and watched the elevator doors close in silence.

'Dulcie?' At the sound of her name, Dulcie jumped. Seeing Tom, she stepped back. Too late, the elevator was gone. 'I'm s-sorry,' he said. 'Did I startle you?'

She exhaled, shaking her head. 'It's not you. It's Mrs Fenderby. I seem to have irritated her. Not that she doesn't have enough reason to be upset,' she added quickly.

'I know.' He nodded, and Dulcie wondered if it was simply his speech impediment that sealed his lips now.

'She's packing up his office?' Dulcie asked. It seemed a good neutral way to work up to the subject at hand.

'The c-college is going to,' he said. 'She wanted some things,' he managed to get out.

Dulcie nodded and followed him as he turned and walked back into the stacks.

'Personal items,' he said, as he retrieved a cart and began to file books. Grief, she thought again. It was strange. While she didn't quite see the value in a stained mug, but then again, if she'd lost Chris maybe such things would take on meaning. It wasn't like the old mug or the bookends had been involved in the crime that had taken his life.

She waited until he turned her way, to make the question seem more casual. 'So the police gave their permission?'

Tom shrugged. 'I guess so,' he said. 'She's been in and out.'

Dulcie nodded, distracted. 'Hey, Tom, I never got to

apologize. I didn't mean to scare you the other day – with the book and all.'

He shook his head. 'I'm sorry, too,' he said. 'I guess I . . .' His voice trailed off, but whether his stutter or something else held him back, Dulcie couldn't tell. 'It was a shock to see,' he said, after a long pause.

'Tom.' It was now or never. 'I know you care about Alyson. She's a lovely person. But – is there anything you'd want to tell me about her?'

He blinked, his face twisting in misery. 'No,' he managed to choke out. Dulcie thought he was holding back tears. 'No,' he repeated.

'Nothing?' Dulcie felt for him, but right was right.

'Only that she's a good person. No matter what—' He stopped to run his sleeve over his eyes. 'Wait.'

He paused and seemed to look beyond her.

'May I help you?' he said. Dulcie turned to see a familiar silhouette in the shadows beyond the stack's overhead lighting. She gasped – something about that shape, tall, looming. But then the figure stepped into the light, and she recognized Renée Showalter walking toward her.

'I'm sorry,' said the professor, stepping forward. She had a trench coat draped over her shoulders and the slight dishevelment of someone who has been traveling. 'I didn't mean to interrupt.' She turned to Dulcie. 'Dulcie, may I speak with you?'

'Uh, sure,' Dulcie turned back toward Tom, hoping to secure a promise to speak later. But he was already back at work, pushing his cart of books down the aisle between the stacks. And as tempted as she was to go after him, Dulcie couldn't help being excited at the unexpected appearance of her mentor. 'I didn't know you were coming so soon,' she said, turning back to the red-haired professor.

'I just got in,' she said, shedding the coat and folding it over one arm. 'I came straight here. I thought I'd go down to the Mildon to see if I could straighten things out with Thomas, but then I ran into Penelope and thought I should stop by here first.'

Elation turned to confusion. Dulcie would have loved to

escort Showalter down to the Mildon. In fact, she couldn't think of a better way to get on with her day. Something was clearly troubling her mentor, however, and Dulcie looked up at her quizzically, not sure what she had missed. 'Penelope?'

Showalter waved her free hand dismissively. 'Or Polly or Poppy or whatever she calls herself these days,' she said. 'Roland's wife – widow, I guess I should say: Penelope Fenderby née Wrigley.'

'You know her?' Somehow, Dulcie couldn't see her self-assured mentor socializing with the woman she had just encountered.

But Showalter was already nodding. 'Yes,' she said. 'Or I did. Roland and I did our post-docs together. Penelope was one of his students. He always did go for the pretty ones.'

Dulcie shook her head. While she couldn't see the washed-up, angry woman she'd just passed as pretty, she'd already figured out that Fenderby had married a former student. 'I guess some people don't change. What a wolf.'

'Please.' Showalter drew back, offended, and Dulcie bit her lip. Not that long ago, she'd had her suspicions about the red-haired professor. Her appearance on campus right about the time that a large canine had been spotted had made her wonder if, perhaps, there was something supernatural about her. That and Showalter's uncanny knack for sniffing out the truth.

Dulcie had dismissed those thoughts long ago as simply fancy. Still, there was something about Showalter. Maybe it was her unusual golden eyes. She paused, realizing that the professor was regarding her with those eyes, only now her face looked drawn. And not, Dulcie thought, because of her own derogatory use of 'wolf'.

'I'm sorry,' said Dulcie. 'Did I say something?'

'No, not you,' said her professor. 'It was the strangest thing. Polly told me you were down here nosing around her late husband's office. Said she wasn't surprised at all. Dulcie, she basically accused you of having an affair with her husband.'

THIRTY-FIVE

'Dulcie, I'm sorry.' The professor winced, her brow bunching up as if she shared her student's discomfort. 'You look unwell. I shouldn't have— You weren't having an affair with the late professor, were you? I would never forgive myself.'

No!' Dulcie shook off the idea. The implications were horrible. 'I wouldn't—'

The very concept was appalling – but even as she played it over in her mind, Dulcie had an inkling of what might have spawned it. 'You must have misheard.' Dulcie was vehement. 'I know she's angry at me, but not – what you said. I think she blames me somehow for what happened. Blames my involvement – which was purely academic. And not something I ever wanted.' She looked up at Showalter, suddenly aware of their surroundings. In the library. Near Fenderby's office. 'I couldn't stand the man,' she said, softly but quite clearly. 'And I suspect the feeling was mutual. I know he arranged to be on my committee, but I have no idea why. He only critiqued one chapter of my dissertation,' Dulcic explained. 'And he really hated it.'

Now it was Showalter's turn to look perplexed.

'How odd,' she said. 'You see, he called me – oh, it must have been two months ago – to ask me about the Philadelphia bequest. I hadn't heard from him for years, and I'll confess I was a bit shocked. Not only that he remembered me or my area of expertise, but that he sounded so excited about it. He said he had an extremely promising student whom he wanted to mentor and whose studies in the bequest he wanted to direct. I thought he was talking about you, of course.' She looked a bit hangdog about that last admission.

'So, did you suggest he serve on my committee?' Dulcie had to ask.

But her mentor only frowned. 'No,' she said. 'He's not – he

wouldn't have been my choice. You're sure he wasn't interested in your work?' Showalter regarded her. 'That there wasn't some kind of falling out?'

Dulcie shook her head, aware of the other woman's intense gaze.

'Never mind that. You really don't look well.' The professor appraised her. 'Do you feel all right?'

'It was something I ate.' It was easier not to have to explain. The sneaky edge of a suspicious thought creeping into her consciousness wasn't helping either. 'So he didn't say who his "promising student" was, did he?'

'No, I'm sorry. I should have asked.' Showalter had the grace to look chagrined. 'Though clearly there was some confusion about the materials and access, and now the police are involved. Which is why I was heading to the Mildon. I assume I can sit down with Thomas Griddlehaus and clear things up.' She paused, those golden eyes taking in Dulcie. 'Would you care to join me?'

Dulcie hesitated only a moment. Tom was nowhere to be seen, and so she turned to her mentor. She'd been so distracted recently, and this was what she had long hoped for. What everyone told her she should be doing. 'Yes,' she said. 'Let's go.'

Thomas Griddlehaus's eyes grew almost as wide as his glasses when he saw the two approach.

'Professor!' The little clerk actually came out from behind the counter to greet them, reaching to take Showalter's coat. 'Welcome.'

'Thank you, Thomas,' Showalter responded, leaving Dulcie nearly speechless.

'I didn't know you two . . .' She managed to form the words, looking from one to the other as Griddlehaus led them into his domain.

'We go back forever,' said Griddlehaus, hanging her coat in a closet Dulcie had never noticed before.

'Thomas was a major force in the accession of the Philadelphia bequest,' Showalter added. 'Of course, we both wanted you to have access, but most important was that the material go to a library where it could be properly cared for and catalogued.'

'Of course,' said Dulcie, still taking it all in. What had Mr Grey said about relationships? This one certainly seemed to be a positive force. Out of habit, she wandered past the two, to take a seat at the reading table. Neither, she noticed after a moment, followed her.

She turned to see the tall professor bending over, in quiet conversation with the bespectacled clerk. 'My, my,' Griddlehaus was saying, as Showalter turned toward Dulcie.

'I'm afraid I can't stay for long,' she said, taking in the table and the white gloves. 'I'm supposed to meet with Thorpe soon. But I did want to clear up this Fenderby matter.'

She turned back toward Griddlehaus, who typed away at a computer keyboard he'd slid out from under the console cabinet.

'Well, that is odd,' he said. 'So, perhaps it was all an error. We might never know.'

'May I ask?' Dulcie got up and went to join them.

'The late professor's injunction,' Griddlehaus said. 'I knew he had pulled those materials for an undergrad, but it appears that the student in question never read them. Never, as far as I can see, requested them.'

He turned to Dulcie, his eyes wide behind those glasses. 'Maybe it was all a mistake, Ms Schwartz. Maybe he did intend for them to go to you.'

'I doubt it,' Dulcie said softly. The man might be dead, but she felt no compunction about speaking the truth.

'Never?' Showalter had begun leafing through the ledger but she looked up at that.

'Not that I can see.' A few more taps on the keyboard. 'No, there's no record of an Alyson Beaumont ever checking in here.'

'Alyson?' Dulcie did a double take, and Showalter slid the ledger over. Together they looked through the pages. Most of the signatures were nearly illegible, but Dulcie skimmed, looking for the big 'A,' like that brass key ring. Flipping through pages, she saw her own looping scrawl and a few others. Very few others. But it wasn't that. There was something else.

Something she felt she was supposed to remember. 'She's my student,' she said, distracted. 'I don't know . . .'

'Were you aware of her interest in the bequest?' Showalter turned her strange golden eyes on Dulcie.

'Well, I knew of her interest.' Dulcie paused to consider. 'In fact, I'd been steering her toward *The Ravages*, or at least toward one of the lesser-known Gothics, as a topic for her thesis. She's a junior, and I was hoping to get her started early. But, to be honest, she's always seemed a little distracted to me, if not, well, maybe not that interested.'

'Maybe Fenderby was hoping to pique her interest,' Showalter posited, turning back to the ledger. 'After all, when we spoke, he did say that he'd found something quite intriguing.'

'What was it?' Dulcie thought of her own discovery – of the corrected page, the altered phrasing. To her that had been tremendously exciting. Would it have been so to Fenderby, a man who claimed not to care for the fiction of the era? As she waited for a response, she felt a frisson of anticipation – for all of her issues with Fenderby, he had been a tenured professor. If he had thought that page important . . .

'I don't know,' said Showalter. 'He was quite secretive about it.'

'Oh.' Dulcie couldn't help feeling let down. 'I guess I'm the only one interested in those pages.'

'Well, the only reader of any consistency,' said Griddlehaus. 'There was a request late last semester. Though, that was before the items were put on hold.'

'Who was it?' Showalter voiced the question in Dulcie's mind.

'One moment, please.' Griddlehaus typed a few more keys and then turned to them. 'Box 978 was requested on December third from a different junior. Mina Love.'

'My cousin?' Dulcie shook her head. 'That doesn't make sense.'

'That she wouldn't share your interest?' Showalter sounded amused.

'No, that she wouldn't have told me.' Dulcie paused, a memory tickling the back of her mind. 'Unless . . .'

'Well, this is odd.' Griddlehaus had gone back to his computer, and his comment interrupted her train of thought. 'Very odd.'

They waited.

'Fenderby put in the request for the papers to be held two days later.' He turned to the ledger and flipped open the pages. 'Yes, two days.'

'But I've been using it.' Dulcie looked at the librarian. 'I used it all through the winter, in fact.'

'I don't know what to tell you.' Griddlehaus had a pained look. 'The request seems to have been held up. Perhaps some confusion in circulation?'

'Circ—' Dulcie paused, catching herself before she said anything else. Anything that might incriminate her friend. What had Ruby said? *'None of us here like him very much.'* 'He must have been angry,' was all she said.

'Oh, he was,' said Griddlehaus. 'At the time, I thought perhaps he was overreacting, but now that I see this . . .' He sighed.

'Were you aware of this?' Showalter turned to Dulcie.

'December?' Dulcie thought back. 'No.'

'Perhaps he pulled the material to check your work?' she suggested.

Dulcie shook her head. 'He wasn't on my committee yet and, well, I hadn't finished writing this chapter yet either.' She remembered, with a twinge of embarrassment. 'I kind of got distracted by some other things that were going on. Though, I'm much better now,' she reassured her mentor.

'I have no doubt,' she smiled back. 'Well, perhaps he was the right person to critique it, then, since he seems to have had a prior relationship with the material.'

'But that's just it.' Griddlehaus looked up at them. 'Fenderby never saw that box. He hasn't been here since before Thanksgiving.'

'Then how . . .' Dulcie asked. Showalter broke in.

'That's ridiculous,' she said. 'He told me he'd found something important. Something key.'

'I don't know what to tell you,' Griddlehaus reached for the ledger. 'Ms Schwartz?'

But Dulcie had paused, the memory poised to break through interrupted by another. 'The key,' she said.

They both turned to her. But Dulcie was already standing and pulling her coat on. 'The key – I'm sorry.' Dulcie reached for her bag. 'I've got to run. You see, I have Alyson Beaumont's house key. I dropped by to feed her cat last night, when she was in the infirmary, only now she's been released and I've forgotten to return it.'

THIRTY-SIX

D ulcie didn't have the money to throw away on cabs. But the thought of her student locked out of her own apartment made such concerns trivial. Besides, she had to admit, although with the passing of time – or the congenial company of Showalter and Griddlehaus – she was beginning to feel more like herself, she was still under the weather. And as the taxi weaved through Cambridge traffic, she was grateful for the opportunity to sit and think. Something had been bothering her, and now, she decided, was the time to put it to rest.

'Alyson!' When Dulcie didn't see her student in the lobby, she'd let herself in. But instead of finding the junior slumped in a doorway, she found her taking out the trash – her apartment door wide open behind her. 'You got in!'

'The building manager was in,' Alyson said, hefting the bag in her arms. 'And I got my spare. Did you rush over here? I'm sorry, I could have told you.'

'That's fine.' Dulcie felt weak with relief. 'I'm just glad you weren't locked out. Hey, little girl.' The marmalade kitten had poked her head out of the open door.

'Oh, would you grab her?' Alyson called back over her shoulder. 'You can go in. I'll be right back.'

Dulcie did, cradling the kitten up to her face. 'Who's so sweet?' she asked, inhaling the baby powder scent of the kitten as she stepped into the apartment. Alyson had been busy, she noticed, as she pulled the door nearly shut behind her. The mat under the kitten's food dish was clean and the empty counter looked like it had just been wiped down, too. Still holding the kitten, Dulcie sat on the sofa and took in the river view. It was only after the kitten squirmed to be let down that Dulcie noticed something unusual. Unlike every other student apartment she had ever seen, there were no books in evidence. Only a few journals – two fashion magazines and something on the dialectics of feminist theory – were in evidence, spread across the glass coffee table.

Rising, with a glance at the door, Dulcie began to explore. Many of her students read their assignments on e-readers, she knew. And other disciplines – like Chris's – tended to rely on two or three bound volumes, the rest of their material existing solely online. She had just peeked into the bedroom when she heard the front door open, and she stepped out, a little abashed at having been found out.

'The bathroom's to the right,' said Alyson, seemingly unfazed, as she pulled a shallow dish from a cabinet. Dulcie saw the graphic of a fish on its side. The kitten, apparently recognizing the dish as well and twined around her ankles, making for a scene so familiar that Dulcie felt right at home.

'No, I—' She paused, unsure how to continue. 'How are you feeling?' she asked at last.

'A lot better,' Alyson replied as she opened a can. 'I think the doctors must have been wrong. I mean, I was sick and everything, but today I feel like myself again.'

'Do you think it was something you'd eaten?' Dulcie was hesitant to use Alyson's own word: poison. It seemed too close to the gossip that Alyson had sickened herself to arouse sympathy. 'I confess, when I was here yesterday, I had a bit of that cake you had left out, and I wondered . . .'

'No,' Alyson said definitively, as she set the food dish down and stroked the kitten's back. 'There was nothing in that that could go bad. Stale, maybe.'

'But if someone put something in it?'

Another shake of the head as she watched the kitten eat. 'That was from my boyfriend.'

'Is he the one who gave you Penny?' Dulcie squatted beside

them. The little marmalade ate with gusto, eyes squeezing shut
as she lapped furiously at the soft food.

'Penny?' Dulcie looked over to see Alyson staring at her.

'The kitten.' Dulcie stood, but pointed to the orange and
white cat.

'Oh, it's funny you should say that.' Alyson got up too and
turned to the sink to rinse her hands. 'But, yeah. I used to be a
redhead when I was younger, and so when he saw this kitten . . .'
She shrugged and seemed quite caught up in her washing.

'Is he the reason you live here?' Dulcie asked, her voice
gentle. Another shrug. 'The reason why you don't have any
books?'

'What?' Alyson turned, reaching for a cloth to dry her hands.
'Oh, no. That's – I don't like the clutter.' She shrugged and
smiled. It was an awkward smile, full of apology. But suddenly,
Dulcie understood what was going on.

'May we sit down?' She motioned to the sofa, and with
a sigh of resignation the junior followed her. Dulcie positioned herself carefully, aware of the pristine white fabric,
and looked over at the coffee table – also so spare and clean.
Alyson did too, but said nothing.

'Alyson,' said Dulcie, when enough time had passed for
the kitten to jump up between them – unselfconscious, despite
the pricey fabric – and start to wash. 'I just came from the
Mildon. I didn't know that Professor Fenderby had put
materials on hold for you.'

Alyson caught her breath, a pained look passing over her
face, and Dulcie realized she needed to tread gently.

'I gather you never made use of them?' she asked. It would
be better to just state the obvious, rather than force the poor
student to confess to her lapse.

'No.' Alyson hung her head. In shame, Dulcie thought. A
shame she understood. Dulcie had never been a slacker, not
like that. But there were areas where she did the least possible
work to get by. The requisite math course she had taken as an
undergrad. And Physics for Poets, her one required lab class,
for which she had had to beg for both extra tutoring and additional time simply to get a passing grade. Still, to have access
to a resource like the Mildon and not make the most of it . . .

She stopped herself before she said anything harsh and looked around again. Clearly, this was not a woman who shared her love of literature.

'Alyson,' she said, finally, as the junior looked up at her with large, sorrowful eyes. 'Why are you even considering doing your thesis on the Gothics?'

The junior shrugged. 'I don't know,' she said, and exhaled. It was the sound of exhaustion or, Dulcie thought, relief. 'It's really not right for me.' She turned from Dulcie to stare straight ahead. From here they could see the little deck, and the bright blue day beyond. 'It sounded like fun. I guess, I thought that, like, there'd be more magic in them. More mystery. Like some puzzles to solve – maybe something hidden in the pages of a lost manuscript. Something like that.'

Dulcie bit her lip. She had helped uncover a rare printer's mark not that long ago. And that correction she had found . . . but, no, her student was talking about something more prosaic.

'Something out of a novel?' she suggested, keeping her voice gentle.

Alyson shrugged. 'Yeah, I guess,' she said.

'I thought as much.' Dulcie collapsed back into the sofa. Even as her tutee seemed reinvigorated – freed by her confession – Dulcie felt deflated, as if the spirit had gone out of her. 'I shouldn't have talked the genre up so much. I can get . . .' She paused, searching for the right word. 'Enthusiastic,' she said, eventually. 'Everyone tells me so, but just because I'm gung-ho on late eighteenth-century fiction doesn't mean it's right for everyone.'

There, she'd said it. It had been difficult, but it was out.

'But that's not the problem, Dulcie.' Her student was looking at her with wide eyes. 'Your enthusiasm has been wonderful, really. You've brought the books to life for me in a way I never thought possible. I mean, you've almost convinced me that I could do this.'

Dulcie looked at her without understanding. If the junior wanted any more of a mea culpa, she didn't know what she'd do. She'd tried her best to convey her interest, and now she had virtually released her student from any obligation.

'If you don't love it, Alyson,' she said, 'don't waste your

time on it. Doing a thesis, even an undergraduate thesis, takes up so much of your resources.'

'My resources, yeah.' Alyson looked at Dulcie and then down at the kitten. 'I guess I should make it official then,' she said. 'I don't even think I want to do honors.'

'Wait, I don't mean to dissuade you.' Dulcie interrupted.

'No, it's for the best.' Alyson began stroking the kitten. 'I need to do some major re-thinking. Maybe take a year off. But it's not you, Dulcie.' She looked up, her eyes clear. 'You've been the best adviser I could ask for. As close to a real mentor as I can imagine. Only, I think I need to make a change.'

Dulcie didn't know whether to feel relieved or despondent as she left Alyson Beaumont's apartment, taking the elevator down to the large, empty lobby.

On a totally selfish level, she'd gotten off easy. Not having a junior to steer toward her thesis meant she'd have substantially more time for her own work, assuming she was reinstated.

On the other hand, she had failed. Or, worse, maybe she had unconsciously sabotaged the girl. Just because Alyson didn't share her own interests didn't mean she should drop out of the honors program. And what did she mean when she said, 'as close to a real mentor as I can imagine', anyway? Hadn't Alyson referred to Dulcie as her mentor? Dulcie thought back – no, maybe that had been another student, Dale, Alyson's former roommate, who had told her that. Just another undergraduate misinterpreting what Alyson had said. Or worse – buttering up the instructor for a good grade. But there was something else – something tickling the edge of Dulcie's consciousness as she pushed open the door to the street. Something she should have asked.

Dulcie paused to consider, standing by an evergreen hedge that looked so hopeful with its glossy green. Was it that she should have pushed Alyson more? She looked down at the green sprouts along the hedge. Crocuses, maybe, or daffodils, sheltered by the evergreen. Should she have been doing that? Maybe shared some of her own discoveries to excite and engage the undergrad? The winter had been hard on everyone, and maybe with a little more effort, she could have prompted the younger woman to flower.

Dulcie bent to look at the green sprout, its tip already expanding into a bud. Already bent, she noticed, either from the wind or an errant foot. With one finger, she lifted the drooping tip. Was this what she had been trying to think of? Duties she had missed – opportunities that she hadn't taken, or offered to a student in her charge?

No, that wasn't quite it. But once again Dulcie's thoughts were interrupted, as her phone began to buzz.

'Hi, Lucy,' she said, working hard to keep her voice neutral. It was never easy to explain the complicated politics of student life to her mother. Today was not the day to try.

'Dulcinea, I'm ashamed of you.' Her mother's tone was bracing. 'Giving in like that.'

'Excuse me?' For a brief moment – very brief – Dulcie wondered if her mother was, in fact, as psychically gifted as she had always claimed to be. Surely, her two-word greeting hadn't revealed that much of her mood. 'Lucy?'

'Letting yourself be railroaded out of the university,' her mother said. 'I received the notice today, and I must tell you, I expect any daughter of mine to put up much more of a fight.'

'Railroaded?' Dulcie paused. 'No, I'm not, Lucy. Honest. In fact, I have someone working on it.' Rogovoy had said he would. Hadn't he?

'I certainly hope so,' Lucy's voice sounded a shade less stern. 'When I saw that letter from the university, I knew I had to call you right away.'

'Thorpe?' Dulcie was taken aback.

'Did you swallow something?' Lucy asked. 'Are you all right?'

'Yes, I'm fine.' Dulcie reassured her. 'It's just – Martin Thorpe wrote you?'

'No, it's not any Thorpe. Hold on.' Lucy put the phone down with a thud, leaving Dulcie to run through the possibilities. It couldn't have been—

'Dean Grulke,' her mother announced. 'Isn't he someone important?'

'She,' Dulcie corrected her. 'Linda Grulke is the dean of

the college. So, yes, she is important – very – but . . . I can't explain right now. Just – please don't worry about this. I'm taking care of it. And now I've got to run.'

'If you're sure,' her mother jumped in before Dulcie could disconnect. 'I'll burn some sage for you, anyway.'

'Thanks, Lucy.' Dulcie hung up and turned around – the question she had forgotten to ask now pressing. Alyson Beaumont may have considered writing her thesis on the Gothic novel because of Dulcie. But – especially considering her lack of interest – why had Roland Fenderby set aside research materials for her?

THIRTY-SEVEN

Alyson's apartment wasn't typical student housing. Dulcie knew that already, but the fact was made clear as she turned and walked back to the sleek high-rise. Two men in business suits and a woman in heels converged on the entrance as she approached, blithely ignoring the new flowers on either side of the white concrete plaza. Two were on their phones, and all three looked a little the worse for wear, clearly returning after hard days in the office. The men, at least, didn't look any older than Dulcie. The woman was wearing so much makeup it was hard to tell. But in her jeans and sneakers, Dulcie felt like a child compared to them – or maybe a different species entirely – a stray from the university who had drifted over to a foreign city.

'You coming?' One of the men turned back toward her. He was holding the door open as his colleague, cell to his ear, passed through. But he was looking at Dulcie, an inviting half smile on a face that had probably been clean shaven nine hours before.

'Oh, thanks!' She grabbed at the door. On campus, she'd have been asked to show ID, but maybe out in the real world, security was less of an issue. Luckily, her benefactor was too busy texting as the elevator came to inquire as to her business in the building. But as the elevator made its halting way up – all three of the new arrivals appeared to live on different floors – she found herself mulling over possibilities in her head.

'Thanks,' she repeated to the stubbly man, who nodded back as he got off. And Dulcie realized she'd missed another opportunity. As much as she didn't like to gossip, it might have been useful to inquire if any of these people knew their neighbor, Alyson. Maybe one of the young businessmen was the boyfriend both Alyson and her older neighbor had mentioned. That would be better than the ghost of an idea forming in the back of her mind as she got off the elevator and started down the hall. That such a bright and lovely young woman as Alyson would be . . .

'Tom!' It was Alyson, her voice high and tight – though with a whine at its end that spoke more of frustration than anger. Dulcie pulled up short when she heard it, that final quaver stopping her like a siren would. 'You've made a mess of everything!'

Dulcie hesitated. She'd meant to return to Alyson's apartment and confront her student. She'd assumed she'd be alone still. Now not only was it apparent that she had a guest, but it seemed that she was in the middle of an argument – or at least a very loud discussion. Although, Dulcie thought, Alyson could be on the phone. After all, she'd probably raised her voice while talking to Lucy, and it was possible that in such a modern building the walls were thin.

'No, I— I . . .' No such luck. Even without the stammer, the voice was clearly identifiable as Tom Walls – and clearly projecting from behind the door that, Dulcie could now see, hadn't quite latched when he arrived. Tom and Alyson were having a fight.

'You what?' Alyson wasn't waiting for the poor man to finish. 'You thought that maybe you could step in? Take his place?'

'N-no!' Even from outside the door, the hurt in Tom's voice was clear. 'I would never.' A catch of breath like a sob.

'You hated him. Admit it.' Alyson was moving. Dulcie could hear sounds like furniture being pushed aside, drawers opening. A squeak, a thud. Was the junior packing?

'This isn't about me.' Tom was clearly crying now, his voice choking on the tears. 'It's you! And I— I don't blame you. Alyson!' This last cry one of desperation.

'Get out!' Her voice was ragged, and Dulcie wondered if she, too, was going to cry. 'Just – get out.'

Dulcie barely had time to duck into a recessed doorway before Alyson's door opened. She held her breath as Tom stumbled past, his face in his hands. Blinded by tears, he didn't even look up until he reached the elevator. She peeked out to see him punch the call button and ducked back into the doorway as he turned back toward the woman who had just kicked him out.

'Alyson,' he called, his voice pleading. 'I did it for you, Alyson. To save you.'

The elevator door opened then, and he stepped in and was gone.

'Whoa.' Dulcie leaned back against the door where she had sheltered, unsure of how to proceed. She had been about to confront her student, hoping to dispel a horrible suspicion that had crept into her head. A suspicion that Tom's parting words only seemed to confirm. Now, however, she had reason to believe that this suspicion was not only true, it may have had fatal consequences.

'Alyson?' She knocked gently on the junior's door. 'It's me, Dulcie,' she said. 'I've come back.'

'What?' The woman who opened the door was a far cry from the cool, collected junior she knew. Alyson Beaumont was red-faced, her eyes swollen. 'Oh, this is not a good time,' she said, and began to close the door.

'Please.' Dulcie put her hand on it. She was small, shorter than her student, but Alyson gave way, and Dulcie followed her student in. 'Alyson,' she asked, taking a seat once more beside her student on that fancy sofa. 'What was your relationship with Roland Fenderby?'

The face that looked up at her said it all. Swollen eyes wide and blinking, mouth already trembling with more of the tears that stained her pale cheeks. Still, Dulcie had to confirm what she suspected. She fished a pack of tissues from her bag and pushed it toward her student before continuing. 'I know Professor Fenderby set aside research material for you. He wanted to give you an edge on your thesis. Help you out more than he would many other students. Was he . . .' She left the sentence open, waiting.

Alyson sniffed and nodded. 'I didn't know he'd done that – with the papers,' she said. 'I didn't ask him to. In fact, I told him I didn't care. That the Goths weren't my thing.' She stopped to reach for a tissue. 'We had such a fight.'

'And he did that because . . .?' Never, Dulcie realized, had she so wanted to be wrong. Only everything she was hearing pointed at one conclusion.

Alyson blew her nose and looked toward the window, and Dulcie feared she was concocting a story. 'Alyson,' she said, keeping her voice soft. 'Whatever happened wasn't your fault. You were the student. He was—'

'You don't understand.' The junior cut her off, turning back toward her with a new urgency in her voice. 'Nobody does. It wasn't what you think. Wasn't – ugly. Roland Fenderby and I were in love.'

It was all Dulcie could do not to interrupt. In fact, she found herself biting her lip to keep silent as the golden-haired junior described what had happened.

'It started when I was taking his class freshman year,' she began. She'd been foundering, she admitted. College had been harder than she'd anticipated, and the combination of beauty and brains that had made her a star in high school didn't seem to have the same effect here. Only Roland Fenderby, a tenured professor, had recognized her brilliance. He had taken a special interest in her right from the start.

As she spoke, her kitten came into the room, jumping up on the sofa beside her and began to wash. 'He said he wanted to mentor me,' said Alyson, as they both watched the kitten, and Dulcie heard the echoes of Alyson's excitement and pride.

Roland had believed in her, Alyson was saying. He'd given her extra tutoring, even loaned her books from his personal library.

Grooming her, Dulcie thought. As a predator does to a

potential victim, a young and impressionable student, for example. Alyson, of course, saw it differently.

'I know he was older than me, but I've dated a lot of older men,' she said. 'And we shared something.'

Before long, the pack of tissues was empty, and Dulcie got up to hunt down more and then to refill Alyson's glass of water. 'I knew how he'd committed to his wife when they were both too young. She was his student, too, you know. Only she never fulfilled her promise.'

Dulcie was glad to be in the kitchenette then, where Alyson couldn't see her face. Still, she nearly dropped the glass as Alyson kept talking.

'That happened a lot to Roland,' she was saying. 'Women were drawn to him, and sometimes they got jealous and lashed out.'

'Wait.' Dulcie put the glass down before she could spill it. 'You don't mean – the harassment suit?'

Alyson nodded, apparently unaware of the look of horror on Dulcie's face. 'Exactly. Roland told me all about it. It had happened before. Some girl came on to him, but he wasn't interested. He told me all about it, right afterward.'

'So you gave him an alibi.' Dulcie felt sick.

More nodding. 'From what Roland said, I think he and I were together then. I mean, I didn't give all the details but . . .' The hint of a smile played over her lips. Dulcie had to put her head down to fight the dizziness.

'Of course, that was before the whole thing with the Mildon.' Alyson kept talking. 'In fact, I wonder if she was involved with that. Wanting to make trouble between us.'

'But she didn't know—' Dulcie caught herself. Tom must have figured it out. *I did it for you.* He must have alerted the authorities about the inappropriate relationship, and Alyson must have blamed Mina. It didn't matter. Alyson was never going to testify on Mina's behalf. She hadn't reached that point yet. Hadn't let go of the illusion of love. An illusion that Fenderby himself had seemed poised to shatter.

'What do you mean "make trouble"?' Dulcie asked, an even more horrible thought forming in her mind. 'Why would the confusion at the Mildon have caused any trouble for you?'

'Well, you know.' Alyson shrugged, her tone becoming strained. 'Roland thought that maybe I didn't appreciate what he'd done for me. That I wasn't properly, I don't know, appreciative?'

She looked at Dulcie as if her tutor might have the answer.

'As if,' Dulcie began, her voice stuck at a whisper. Alyson had been used, badly. Worse, from the young woman's viewpoint, she may have sensed that her lover was getting ready to discard her. Dulcie cleared her throat and tried again. 'As if you weren't fulfilling your potential?'

'No! It wasn't like that,' Alyson burst out. She might be deluded but she wasn't a fool. 'He loved me. I know it. I just made a mistake. He wouldn't have left . . .'

She broke down sobbing again, leaving Dulcie with no response beyond patting her back. The movement – or perhaps it was the heart-rending wail Alyson gave as she caught her breath – roused the kitten, who jumped to the floor.

'Oh, Roland!' Alyson cried, leaving Dulcie little option but to continue petting her as if she were the little marmalade.

It was an odd experience, Dulcie thought, as the kitten brushed up against her shin. With her free hand Dulcie reached to hoist her up, needing some comfort herself. Because in light of what Alyson had told her – the lies, the opportunity, and the heartbreaking motive – Dulcie couldn't escape the conclusion that Alyson may have killed her lover. For many reasons, and not just for the sake of the little cat who now nestled by her side, she could only hope she was wrong.

THIRTY-EIGHT

As Alyson's sobs slowly subsided, Dulcie considered what to do next. She didn't think it likely that Alyson would go to the police. For starters, if the young woman had looked wrung out before, she'd be exhausted now. Besides, Dulcie doubted she would see the need. Alyson was in such deep denial she didn't think she'd done anything wrong.

Dulcie had to admit, she felt sorry for the younger woman. If – and it was still a big if – Alyson had in fact killed Roland Fenderby it was in large part because he had manipulated her. Used her and then was ready to discard her. It would be enough to break many women. When Dulcie thought of the small part she may have unwittingly played – after all, she was probably the reason Ruby had delayed Fenderby's request about the papers – she felt a twinge of, well, not guilt, exactly. But culpability. Which for now expressed itself in murmurs of 'there, there,' and when Alyson at last hiccupped and swallowed, the offer of a handful of Kleenex and a fresh glass of water.

'Do you have anyone you want me to call?' It was weak, but it was the best she could offer as Alyson wiped her face. 'Like, maybe a support group?'

'You mean, because of his – because of my loss?' Alyson blinked.

Dulcie bit her lip. She'd been thinking in terms of sexual harassment, but clearly Alyson wasn't there yet. 'Not exactly,' she said. 'But I know, on campus—'

'No, no way.' For a moment, Dulcie thought Alyson understood. Until, that is, she began to speak again. 'I can't do any of my grieving publicly. Despite everything, Roland's wife insisted on hanging on to their sham of a marriage. And now that he's— that he's gone, she'll never let go.'

'Did she know?' Despite herself, Dulcie was shocked.

'Of course.' Alyson replied. 'He had told her he was going to leave her as soon as we became involved. Only she was making life difficult for him.'

'Ah.' It was the best Dulcie could do. She might have been raised in the woods, but even Dulcie knew better than to believe a story like that one.

The real question was whether Alyson believed it – or if she knew she was in the process of being dumped. Men like Fenderby were serial offenders, and it was only a matter of time before he found another young woman as – what had Ruby's word been? – as malleable as Alyson. But now that the junior had calmed down – she was letting the kitten bat at her finger – Dulcie didn't see how she could push that one. Better, she decided, that she should bring this latest bit of information to Detective Rogovoy. He had told her to stay out of it, but surely this bombshell put everything in a different light.

With what she hoped were sympathetic sounds, Dulcie rose to leave. Alyson's outburst appeared to have done her good, and she barely looked up as Dulcie got her coat and headed out.

'I hope she rots in prison.' Alyson's voice reached her as she opened the door.

'His wife?' Dulcie's voice cracked on the question. Surely, this was too much.

'No,' Alyson responded, still playing with the kitten. 'That girl who set out to ruin him.' She didn't even look up as Dulcie gasped. 'I think it's pretty clear that she must have killed poor Roland.'

THIRTY-NINE

Dulcie was dialing Mina's number even before the elevator had descended.

'Pick up, pick up,' she urged the phone. When voicemail responded, she hung up and tried again.

She had to tell her cousin about Alyson. Not only that it was the junior who had destroyed Mina's case, but that the other girl would most definitely not be testifying on her behalf. In a way, it didn't matter. Alyson's experience – whether she recognized it or not – supported Mina's suit, and although Dulcie would do her best to keep the junior's confidence, she was certainly going to report it. Fenderby had been a predator: a user of young women. And even after his death, his actions – and Alyson's lies – were still causing Mina harm. Dulcie didn't know if they'd get Alyson to tell her story to the dean, but just knowing the truth about why her suit had been dismissed had to give Mina a boost.

'Mina, it's Dulcie.' She finally gave in and addressed the voicemail. 'Call me?' There was too much to explain.

Plus, Dulcie realized, she had questions of her own. And as she strode out of the building, she decided to try her cousin's phone again. For starters, Dulcie was curious as to why her cousin had been in the archives. Why in particular she had been looking at the materials the late professor had procured for his girlfriend. Dulcie didn't think that Mina had any connection to Fenderby, and she would swear that her cousin was no murderer. But Mina had been oddly elusive about her whereabouts the morning of his death – saying only that she had left the library after making a brief appearance. In anyone else, Dulcie acknowledged, such evasiveness would be suspicious. For now, she put such thoughts out of her mind and focused on Alyson's misdirected anger. Mina wasn't safe.

'Mina, it's me again.' She paused to think of a message she could leave. Some quick warning that would give her cousin a heads-up without causing undue panic. 'I've got some news,' she said at last. 'Kind of mixed, good and bad. For starters, I think I may know what happened with – you know – the thing.' For all Dulcie knew, Mina might play her messages where others could hear them, and officially she was still bound by the gag order.

'I also have some questions for you.' Dulcie spoke quickly, before the automated system could cut her off. 'About the library,' she was talking a mile a minute now. 'And, well, Mina, I don't think you should say anything to anybody. I'll explain. Call me!'

She turned the phone off, then realized her mistake. Although her time in the library had gotten her in the habit of powering down all her devices, in this case, she wanted to be reached. In fact, she wanted the ring tone to be as loud as possible, to make sure she didn't miss Mina's call while she was walking home.

'Damn.' In the growing dusk, it was hard for Dulcie to see what she was doing. All the buttons seemed to bring her back to the message function. Had Chris programmed some kind of shortcut for her that she'd forgotten? After a minute or two of fumbling, she thought she had it. Both her ringtone – Esmé's most aggrieved mew – and the vibrate function were on their top setting. Dulcie tucked the device back into her bag and looked up to see a figure striding toward her.

'D-Dulcie!' Tom Walls stepped into the light, but not before Dulcie had jumped back. 'Are you—?'

'I'm fine.' Dulcie snapped, fear causing her to momentarily forget her manners. 'You startled me.'

'I'm sorry,' he managed to say. He turned toward the high-rise, the light from its lobby illuminating his face, and sighed, leaving his sentence unfinished. He looked tired, Dulcie thought. And torn, as if he were suffering from some great heartache.

Why hadn't she seen it? All the signs had been there. Tom Walls was in love with Alyson Beaumont. He'd even – if she'd heard correctly – tried to help her win free of Fenderby. To come clean about the older man's parasitic attentions.

It might have been at her urging – or maybe a misplaced gallantry – that had prompted him to misdirect police attention, refusing to acknowledge that Mina had not been near Fenderby's office. For that matter, Tom had also been responsible for shelving the murder weapon – essentially muddying a crime scene and concealing evidence. Dulcie thought back to the afternoon she had found it, and how at the sight of the blood and gore on its binding, he had fainted dead away. Unless, it suddenly hit her, he hadn't fainted at the sight of the book, but at her discovery of it.

'I did it for you.' The memory of that anguished cry rang again in her memory. But this time, Dulcie heard it as it had been – not through the filter of her own concern for Mina, of her own wishful thinking.

'I did it for you,' Tom had cried out. Filled with regret now, sure, but also with passion. And another scenario began to take shape in her mind. Tom had been in the library that morning, too. He always was. Only he was such a quiet young man, such a reliable worker, that nobody had questioned his presence or absence except as a witness.

Surely, Dulcie thought, the police must be considering the possibility. Detective Rogovoy must have at least wondered. But had any official ever seen the young man as he now stood in front of her? Broken, hurt – and angry?

An alternative narrative began to unfold before Dulcie. A

narrative hidden from all others. Rejected, his frustrations compounded by his difficulty in expressing his love, Tom might have struck out at his rival – at a man he knew was taking advantage of a young and vulnerable woman. The woman he loved. Alyson had been a fool, misguided and manipulated. But she had appeared honestly bereft at Fenderby's death. Tom Walls would have no such regrets. All he had was a motive for murder.

'I heard what you said.' He was speaking, forming each word carefully as he turned back toward her. 'About the library.'

'What I . . .?' He must have heard her talking to Mina, but she'd been intentionally vague. Hadn't she? She didn't want to get her cousin in any more trouble.

'It's not what you think,' he said, stepping closer. 'What you're saying.'

'I didn't say anything,' Dulcie responded, unsure what she was defending herself against. 'Just that it's interesting.'

'No.' He shook his head, the deep sadness now leaching into his voice. 'I heard you. I saw you.'

From deep within her bag, Dulcie felt a vibration: her phone. She reached for the flap, only Tom was too quick for her. He had his hands on her bag. He was holding it.

'Tom.' Dulcie kept her voice level. Calm. She was not going to panic. 'Let go of my bag, Tom.'

'I can't let you tell them.' He choked the words out, his hand holding the bag shut. Inside, the phone buzzed like an angry bee. A muffled mew, as if Esmé herself was imprisoned there, followed.

'The police know I'm here, Tom.' It was a bluff, and as soon as the words were out, Dulcie regretted them.

'You can't.' He shook his head, his despair written on his face. Inside her bag, the phone fell silent, and Tom let go, taking a step back. 'It's not her fault.'

'Oh, Tom.' Now that he was retreating, Dulcie was over-whelmed by the sadness of the situation. 'You must have felt you were saving her.'

'I would do it again.' He stood up a little straighter, but his head hung low. He paused again, looking up at her. Willing her to understand. 'She was so hurt.'

'Fenderby wasn't going to leave his wife, was he?' There was no point in pretending any more.

'No.' He stared at the ground. Carefully, trying to move so quietly that he wouldn't notice, wouldn't look up, Dulcie took a step back. 'She visited that morning,' Tom sounded lost in his memory. 'Visited in the library.' He broke off, shook his head. Dulcie took another step. 'The bastard.'

'Yes, he was.' Dulcie kept her voice level. She had such sympathy for her student, but really, she had to get out of here. 'He was extremely selfish.'

She took another step and stopped as Tom's shoulders began to heave. He was crying, she saw. Silently, his head bent, his body wracked with sobs.

'Tom?' She should leave; she knew that. And yet he was her student, and he was in pain.

'It wasn't—' He had his hands over his face now, his voice further muffled by his tears. 'It wasn't her fault!'

And like that Dulcie's phone began to vibrate again. Tom looked up and locked glances with Dulcie. Esmé's mew followed, and Dulcie grabbed for it, just as Tom reached forward. Reached for her.

'No!' Dulcie stepped back and then turned and ran. She heard Tom behind her. Heard him stumble and then begin to sob once more.

'Don't tell them about Alyson!' he called after her, his voice choked by tears. 'It wasn't her fault!'

FORTY

The phone was no longer buzzing by the time Dulcie stopped running, winded. She'd reached Mass Ave, where the combination of pedestrian traffic and bright storefronts made her feel like it was safe to moderate her pace. By then she had begun to wonder if she had imagined it all. She'd been sick and the scene with Alyson had been terrible. And even if . . . she paused, panting, to consider.

Even if what she thought was true, wasn't Tom her student, too?

'Are you OK?' Dulcie looked up to see an elderly woman peering at her through thick glasses, eyes bright with concern.

'Yes, thanks,' she responded, trying to muster a smile. 'I was just running.'

'You look like you've had a fright,' the woman said. 'I don't mean to pry, young lady, but I would be quite willing to accompany you to the police.' The woman had to be eighty, Dulcie thought, and looked to weigh maybe a hundred pounds. But she stood as straight as a lamppost.

'No, really.' The smile became genuine. It was nice to have someone care. 'I did get spooked,' she explained. 'But I think it was all in my head.'

'You should trust your instincts,' said the grey-haired old lady, with a stern look. Dulcie paused – those words. She had heard that before. But before she could query her would-be protector further, the woman turned and disappeared, her slight shape lost in the Cambridge crowd.

'I'm imagining things,' said Dulcie to herself. 'Aren't I?' She looked around. No, there was no sign of Mr Grey. Not even a similarly colored squirrel or leashed dog in sight. What she did see was a coffee house, and suddenly Dulcie realized how famished she was. The day – the previous night's sickness – had drained her. She had a million things to do. Choices to weigh. *Trust your instincts.* But which one? The urge toward fear and blame – or compassion for her students, driven beyond their limits? She had to think this through. Her students' lives could be at stake.

'All baked goods are half off after five,' said the barista as she rang up Dulcie's tab – a latte and large blueberry muffin. 'In case you want another.'

'No thanks,' Dulcie replied automatically and then stopped herself. Why not bring a treat home for Chris? 'Yeah, sure,' she said. 'How about that cranberry nut one?'

Two minutes later, she was sitting on a high stool by the window, drinking a frothy latte and nibbling on a muffin so moistened by blueberries that even after a day on display it hadn't gone stale. In such a cozy environment, and with a little food inside her, Dulcie was feeling calmer. Not that she was prepared to totally dismiss her fears. After all, she didn't need a stranger repeating Mr Grey's words to make her see sense. 'Trust your instincts.' She thought that one over. Her original instinct had told her that the whole thing was a horrible accident. At this point, she was willing to dismiss that thought as more of a wish. More recently, she acknowledged as she broke off more of the muffin, she had believed Alyson was likely responsible. The girl had been horribly used by Fenderby and it did sound like she was being rejected, which might have triggered the kind of angry outburst that would have resulted in the death of the sleazy professor. Only then she had run into Tom, and he had seemed to have good reason to attack the professor, too.

'I did it for you,' he had said. Wasn't that tantamount to a confession? Even his absence fit the theory. He must have killed Fenderby and fled. Unless – with the warmth and the sugar, together almost as comforting as a kitty, Dulcie's tired synapses sparked again. Could he have meant . . .

'Excuse me.' A bearded man to Dulcie's left was looking toward her bag, which was mewing. 'Isn't that your phone?'

'Oh, thanks.' Dulcie said, as the man turned from her to stare pointedly at a sign. *Don't Be Cellfish*, it read, a picture of an iPhone with a circle and a red bar across it. 'Sorry,' she added belatedly.

'Mina?' She was whispering as she answered. 'Did you get my message?'

'Yes.' Her cousin sounded worried. 'I've been trying to reach you. Where are you? What's going on?'

'I'm—' The beard was staring daggers at her, so she turned away. 'I'm at the coffee house in Central – the no-cell one? Hang on.' Holding the phone with one hand, she started to push the muffin back into its paper bag. It would be a pity to give up her seat, but she needed to talk to her cousin.

'Wait, Dulcie!' The voice reached her as she pulled her bag up. 'I'm not two blocks away. I'll come meet you.'

'Great.' Dulcie turned to stare the bearded man in his beady little eye. 'I'll be right here.'

*   *   *

By the time Mina arrived, Dulcie had managed to snag a table, much to her hirsute antagonist's apparent disgust. She had also finished her muffin. Laying out the other for her cousin, she waved her over.

'What's up?' Her cousin sipped her own mug, wincing at the heat. 'You sounded upset.'

Dulcie nodded. 'I found out who testified against you,' she said. 'It was – it was one of my students. She gave Fenderby an alibi.' As she spoke, she leaned forward, lowering her voice. The café was crowded, after all.

'Who?' Mina looked at her, eyes wide. It was the obvious question.

'I don't know if I can tell you.' Dulcie sighed, wondering if she should reveal Alyson's identity. On one hand, she wanted to help Mina clear her name. On the other, if Mina confronted Alyson, it could simply make everything worse. 'It's complicated.'

'Complicated.' Mina sat back and shook her head. 'I bet. But why would another student do that? Do that to me, in particular?'

'She might not have understood.' Dulcie thought back. 'Not really. Fenderby was good at manipulating people.'

'I guess.' Mina didn't look convinced. But after a moment, she came up with another question. 'What does this have to do with the library?'

Dulcie shook her head, not understanding.

'You said something in your message about what I'd found?' Mina said.

'Now, that's weird,' Dulcie responded, relieved to be on safer ground. 'I don't know if you even remember, but back in December, I gather you were doing some research in the Mildon?'

'Oh, yeah.' Mina nodded. 'Yeah, of course I do.'

'Well, it turns out the documents you were looking at were the ones Fenderby wanted put on reserve for – for another student.' Even as she said it, Dulcie wondered. 'I don't know how this is all tied up, but I think – did Fenderby try to get you to tell him about your research? Was he interested in what you found?'

'No.' A look of confusion came over Mina's face. 'He didn't
– he wasn't. Once I turned him down, he lost any interest in
what I was doing. Then, with my suit and everything, I kind
of forgot about it with everything else.'

'But surely, when you saw him at the hearing, you must
have said something. Given him some kind of clue . . .'

'No, not at all,' Mina was insistent. 'The only person I told
was your friend Trista – Trista Dunlop.'

FORTY-ONE

'W ait – what?' Dulcie was sure she'd misheard, or
that her cousin had misunderstood her question.
'I'm talking about your research – the papers you
were looking at in the Mildon.'

'I know.' Her cousin nodded. 'I'd found something. At
least, I thought it might be something, and I wanted to tell
you. I was really excited, but I ended up talking to Trista
first, and, then, well, everything went crazy and I kind of
forgot about it.'

'And Trista wouldn't have been talking with Fenderby.'
Dulcie sipped her latte, thinking of her friend's aversion to
the late professor.

'No.' Mina was adamant. 'No way. She hated that
sleazebag.'

'Huh.' Dulcie considered. 'Maybe it's just a coincidence,
then. Did you know Fenderby was looking at the same materials you were?'

'No.' Mina shivered in disgust, hands cradling her mug.
'I'm glad we were never there at the same time.'

'Strange.' The pair were silent for a moment, but just as
Dulcie was about to ask her cousin what she had found, she
remembered something Griddlehaus had said. Something about
Fenderby not having visited the collection recently. She'd have
to ask, only for once, there were matters more pressing. 'I
think we have to go talk to the police,' she said.

'Because of the alibi?' Mina's face clenched up. 'Because I've already filed the petition with the dean, and I think I ought to wait, Dulcie. Let that go through the official channels.'

'There's more.' Dulcie paused, unsure of how much to share with her cousin. She wanted to trust her, but she couldn't avoid the feeling that Mina was hiding something. She stared down at her mug, but it was nearly empty. 'I think that the other victim you were counting on isn't going to come forward. I think she was being pushed.'

'No.' Mina shook her head. 'You're wrong.'

'I'm afraid so,' Dulcie hated bearing bad news. 'And it's worse than that. She may be . . . well, Fenderby's behavior may have gotten him killed.'

To Dulcie's surprise, her cousin blanched. 'No, you can't think that,' she said, cutting Dulcie off. 'She wouldn't—'

'I don't think she did.' Dulcie kept her voice soft. 'But I think she was involved, and that someone very close to her was provoked into defending her. I'm sure the law will take the circumstances under consideration. But if she won't come forward, I have to.'

'But she's your friend.' Mina pleaded, leaning over the little table. 'She trusts you.'

'And I feel sorry for her. I do, but I think she's key to a murder investigation.' Dulcie fought to keep her voice low. She'd caught the looks from the other tables. 'And I've got to do what's right.'

'At least give her a chance to explain.' Mina was either oblivious or didn't care.

Dulcie shook her head. 'I was just with her. She's not going to come forward.'

'But I thought you were with the student who lied about me – about Fenderby.' The two women stared at each other, uncomprehending. Finally Mina spoke. 'Wait,' she said. 'I'm confused.'

Dulcie wasn't. 'I'm afraid it makes perfect sense.'

'No,' said Mina. 'You're talking about a friend. You're talking about Trista.'

'Trista wasn't—' Dulcie caught herself. Trista had been the one to tell her about Fenderby. She'd been so active in the battle against him, volunteering to help Dulcie escape his clutches. 'No – wait – Trista was victimized by Fenderby too?'

Mina nodded. This time she was the one to drop her voice. 'You didn't know?'

Dulcie shook her head.

'She didn't tell a lot of people,' Mina said, the sadness clear in her voice. 'But I thought she – that maybe she'd finally agreed to come forward. I wasn't supposed to tell, only you can't think that she was involved in any way with his death.'

'No,' Dulcie reassured her. 'It's complicated.' She thought about Tom. From what Trista said, he'd had a crush on her too. If he knew, well, it only added to his motive. 'This wasn't about Trista,' she said, wondering if she was lying. Better to stick to what she knew for sure. 'This was about someone who thought she was in love.'

FORTY-TWO

I n the end, Mina declined to accompany Dulcie. 'I can't say anything,' she reasoned. 'And to just sit there will feel like lying.'

'I understand,' said Dulcie. 'But I guess I should get moving.' The sugar rush from the muffin had worn off by then, and she felt herself flagging. Whatever had gotten to her last night had left her weak, and she wobbled as she rose.

'Are you OK?' Mina reached to steady her. 'Maybe I should walk over with you.'

'No, I'll be fine,' said Dulcie with a conviction she didn't feel. 'I'm just glad we talked. I'm sure that when this is all straightened out, my student will do the right thing. Your case will be re-opened, and you'll be free of all this.'

'And Roland Fenderby will still be dead,' said Mina.

There wasn't really any response to that, and the cousins parted with a hug. The sky was dark by then, but the street was lit and busy. If anything, it was too busy. Dulcie felt a little claustrophobic as she jostled her way on to the Number

One bus. Rush hour wasn't something she usually had to contend with, and she found herself thinking of the business types at Alyson's apartment as she swayed among her fellow straphangers. Was this what life was like after graduation? Would she be able to stay in academia, or would she become part of this suited mass, following a regimented schedule five days a week?

'Coming through.' A strained voice – somehow familiar, if out of place in that busy, urban setting – called from the other end of the bus.

'Excuse me.' Another voice, directly behind Dulcie, made her turn, and she squeezed back as the speaker pushed by. Only after the woman had exited and the bus started moving again did Dulcie glance outside – in time to see the blue light of police headquarters pass by. She'd missed her stop.

'Excuse me!' She pushed between two other straphangers to hit the call signal. Another two blocks and the bus came to a lurching halt. 'Coming through!'

It took all her strength to fight her way through the crowd, which seemed to have grown in both height and density since she had boarded. Finally on the sidewalk, she caught her breath just as the bus departed in a blast of exhaust. The ensuing coughing fit left her feeling weak. If she had been closer to home, she would have packed it in. But since she had come this far, she steeled herself. One last task and then she could go home. Maybe, she promised herself, she'd even take a cab.

'Detective Rogovoy, please?' She was grateful that she didn't recognize any of the officers mulling around the station. It would be easier not to have to deal with one of the cops who had questioned her after Fenderby's death.

'He's with someone right now,' the woman she had gravitated to responded. 'Is there something I can help you with?'

'No.' Dulcie hesitated. There was something kindly about the woman, her broad face and wild hair reminding her of Lucy. Still, Rogovoy knew the history. 'I'll wait.'

'Suit yourself.' The woman turned without another word, leaving Dulcie leaning on the wooden counter.

Ten minutes later, Dulcie had begun to give up. She'd been

leaning back on the wooden bench, her eyes closed, when the booming voice woke her.

'If it isn't Dulcie Schwartz,' said Rogovoy. He was standing right before her. 'Let me guess. You've got some new information for me.'

'I wish I didn't,' said Dulcie, rising to greet him. 'Believe me. This is all just too sad.'

'Well, since you're here.' Dulcie saw the look the detective exchanged with the woman behind the counter. It had to be simple acknowledgment, she told herself. After all, she was doing her civic duty.

'I want to make clear from the start that he thought he was doing the right thing,' she said. 'I'm sure of it. He's a very gentle soul, actually.'

'He being?' Rogovoy's eyebrows shot up, waiting.

'The person I think may have killed Roland Fenderby,' said Dulcie.

'Ah, of course.' The detective put down his pencil. 'And you undoubtedly know this because of something you found in the library?'

'Well, no.' Sometimes the detective could be so dense. 'Though the Mildon collection does play into it, in a way. In fact, there's something I learned tonight that makes Fenderby's murder even more . . .' She stumbled, looking for the right word. 'Well, not inevitable. But he was not a nice man.'

'I'll keep that in mind,' Rogovoy grumbled. 'Because it's not like we're any good at our jobs.'

Dulcie ignored the self-deprecating slight – the detective really shouldn't be talking like that – and forged ahead. 'You should know, I think he was protecting her. Or he thought he was,' she continued. 'He knew she was being taken advantage of, and he knew she was hurting, and, well, I guess things just got out of hand.'

He looked at her, waiting.

This was it. The moment of truth. 'Tom Walls,' she said, with a heavy sigh. 'He's an undergraduate. And I believe he may have murdered Professor Roland Fenderby.' She closed her eyes, the relief leaving her exhausted.

'Well, isn't that interesting,' said Rogovoy. Something about

his voice made her sit up and look at him. 'Because Mr Walls
was just in here, and he was telling me a very different story.'

'Excuse me?' Dulcie stared at the detective. 'That's not
possible.'

The oversized shoulders shrugged. 'I wouldn't have told
you if I didn't know you, Ms Schwartz. And if I didn't know
how dogged you can be when you have a theory.'

'I don't—' Dulcie sputtered. 'I'm not dogged.'

'Stubborn, then,' the detective replied as he pushed himself
back from the desk.

'Wait.' Dulcie held up her hands. 'Maybe he figured out
that I'd come here. Maybe this is all to counter what I have
to tell you.'

Rogovoy didn't comment. He didn't stand up, either, though
one of his eyebrows rose inquisitively.

'He basically confessed,' Dulcie continued. 'He said, "I did
it for you." I mean, not to me but to this other student. She's,
well . . .'

'She was involved with the late professor.' Rogovoy finished
the thought. 'Yes, we know. In case you hadn't figured it out,
yet, I've been leading the task force on sexual harassment on
campus. We've been investigating even before the late professor's demise. We take crime seriously, Ms Schwartz, all crime,
and that poor girl was a victim, too, which I'm sure will be
considered.'

'Then you know?' Her mind reeled. Task force? Rogovoy?
'I mean, about Alyson – about Tom?'

'That he removed evidence? That he altered the scene?
Yes.' Rogovoy shook his big head sadly. 'Poor kid. He saw
her leave and went after her. Then, when he went back . . .
well . . . He thought he was helping her. He thought that
because of his disability—'

'Disability?'

He looked up, as if startled. 'Yeah, the kid's hard of hearing.
Didn't you know? That's why we didn't totally trust his
testimony about the Love girl. I mean, he says he saw her
come into the library when it opened and that she usually
worked on his floor. But a marching band could have come

through behind him, and all he would have heard was a dull roar.'

Dulcie left soon after that, her head spinning. Tom's hearing . . . it all made sense. His intense focus, the time he walked away. Even his plaintive cry – *I did it for you.* He hadn't wanted to say anything. Hadn't, perhaps, trusted his own limited perception. And, maybe, hadn't thought he was worthy of love.

No, she shook that one off. She had suspected Alyson Beaumont, too. Only – what had changed her mind? The cat. The fact that her student had a cat. Somehow, she couldn't see a cat lover killing a person. But, she remembered, Alyson's cat had been a gift – a gift Alyson hadn't even thought of, at first, when she'd been hospitalized.

Dulcie knew there were people – some of her own friends – who would wonder at her priorities, but she couldn't help but feel bad for that little marmalade cat. She – what was her name, Penny? – was the only true innocent in all this. The only one who hadn't acted out of selfishness or greed.

'*Now, now, little one.*' Dulcie stopped short, the voice in her ear startling her out of her musings. '*Who we choose to love and why are not always in our control.*'

'Who?' Dulcie stared up at the streetlight, its blue-white glow haloed by the damp air. 'Do you mean the kitten or Alyson?'

But the only response was the wind.

FORTY-THREE

*D*eep *in the shadow'd Gloom, a single candle flickered and did smoke. The wind that howled did naught to dispel the darkness that clouded o'er her thoughts e'en as it filled the room, and yet its icy touch made onslaught against the fragile flame, which guttered nearly out. And yet she wrote, the urgent scratch of her fevered pen quick and desperate against the paper. Too quick – for in the moment,* *she must pause, must make to shave off the errant ink – and hurry on, lest thought be carried off by storm and time. 'Not by choice,' she wrote, mouthing the words. Her voice, as tired and pale as that weak illumination, might be carried off, but the words she penned would last as long as ink could stain its paper.*

Dulcie woke feeling groggy, as if she had been working through the night rather than simply dreaming it.

'Chris?' she called out. 'Are you still there?'

'Of course,' he called back, popping in a moment later with a mug of coffee. 'I wanted to let you sleep. You were tossing and turning last night.'

'I'm sorry.' She took the proffered mug gratefully. 'I was dreaming, but I guess I kept you up.'

'Not a problem. I wanted to keep an eye on you anyway.' He stood, appraising her. 'I still think you should have gone to the health services yesterday.'

'Maybe.' She sat up. Her head was throbbing. 'But I had so much going on.'

'I thought . . .' Chris stopped, then shook his head. 'You should have some breakfast.'

He left the room, and Dulcie rose to get dressed, a little chastened. Chris had been worried when she'd been so late yesterday, particularly given how ill she'd been the night before. And her explanation – about visiting Alyson and then going to the cops – had only bothered him more. They'd had words about it, and only avoided a full-on fight when Dulcie had pleaded fatigue. No wonder she'd slept badly.

Walking into the kitchen, she came up behind her boyfriend to surprise him with a hug. The smile he turned toward her was sad, though, and she knew he was holding back words.

'I'm going to get back to work today,' she promised, as Esmé twined around her ankles in what she could only interpret as encouragement. 'I'll go straight to my office, and I won't leave until the next chapter is at least hashed out.'

'Good girl.' His smile was looking more natural, as Dulcie stepped carefully over the tuxedo cat to check her phone.

'Well, maybe not straight to my office,' she corrected herself.

'Urgent departmental meeting,' she read and then looked up. 'Well, if I'm getting departmental messages, maybe that means I'm reinstated.'

'I hope so,' said Chris, looking like he was trying to hold that smile as he took Dulcie's coffee and poured it into her travel mug.

'Thanks, hon.' With another kiss and a quick pet for Esmé, Dulcie took off, bustling down the stairs and out to the street. Despite the chipper tone she had assumed with Chris, she was worried. An urgent meeting could mean many things – maybe the plumbing had finally gone in the old clapboard. Maybe their emails had been hacked. But Dulcie couldn't dodge the suspicion that if the urgency had to do with something good – say, an announcement that Renée Showalter was joining the faculty in a more permanent position – the message would have been phrased differently. No, this had to be—

She stopped cold. Alyson. It had to be about Alyson Beaumont, of course. Following Tom's visit to the police the night before, the young woman had probably been taken into custody. And as sad as that was, it was probably a good thing. A resolution that would set the stage for a return to normalcy.

As she began walking again, Dulcie felt a strange buzz in her bag and heard a muffled mew. Of course, she hadn't changed the settings since yesterday – and she reached in to see another text was waiting. A text, she saw with a start, from Alyson Beaumont.

Unable to contain her curiosity, she opened it – and found it blank. Well, that had to be an error. Maybe, she thought, that cute little cat had stepped on the phone.

Dulcie pictured the cat's white paws landing on a phone keyboard as it began to buzz again.

Not by choice.

The phrase caught her eye, and for a moment she wondered. Was that what she had dreamed? Or was she superimposing those three words on her dream? And what had it meant anyway? Whatever, she knew it wasn't the work of even the most talented cat, and so she typed back.

Hello? She walked on, staring at the phone, but there was no other response. At the corner – after a nervous pedestrian had alerted her to the oncoming traffic – she made up her mind. She would have to turn off the phone when she went into the meeting – a meeting she'd be lucky to make at this rate. She would. Only it was just too frustrating. She had to find out what that abbreviated message meant. This wasn't really breaking her promise to Chris. It was just . . .

She hit 'dial'.

'Hello?' Her call was answered right away, but by silence. 'It's Dulcie,' she said, to the void. 'You texted me?'

Nothing. Or – no voice, anyway. Dulcie heard a beeping in the distance, too high-pitched to be a truck backing up. And voices in conversation just out of earshot.

'Hello?'

Silence.

'Hello?' A shushing sound, like fabric sliding over the receiver. Then suddenly, a voice.

'I'm sorry,' said a woman. But not, Dulcie thought, a woman she knew. 'Phones aren't allowed here.' And the line went dead.

Staring at her phone, Dulcie saw that the departmental meeting was about to start and she was still a few minutes away. The voice, she figured, had to belong to someone down at the police station. Or maybe Alyson had been taken into custody, already, her possessions not yet catalogued.

Not by choice.

The phrase could be meaningless. Perhaps Alyson was interrupted while talking to her lawyer or her mother – her phone's voice recognition software translating a snippet of dialogue into a meaningless text. Dulcie knew she should put it from her mind and keep on. If there had been time, Nancy might even have gotten donuts.

She scrolled through her contacts and hit dial.

'Good morning, Ms Schwartz.' Detective Rogovoy did not sound surprised to hear from her. 'To what do I owe the pleasure?'

'Detective,' Dulcie bit her lip, unsure of how to proceed. 'I just got a text from Alyson Beaumont,' she said at last. The burly policeman could figure out what she should do.

'Well, that's a relief.' His words came out in a rush, like he'd been holding his breath.

'Detective?' None of this was making sense. 'I thought you were – I thought Alyson Beaumont was going to be questioned?'

'What's that saying about mice and men?' The detective didn't wait for her to answer. 'Though it all turned out for the good. When my people got there, the girl's neighbor was calling for an ambulance and they were able to expedite. If it hadn't been for the neighbor, and for that young man who came in to speak with me, that young girl might be dead.'

FORTY-FOUR

Rogovoy wouldn't give her any details. 'If she's texting you, then she's doing better than I had feared,' was all he'd say. About Alyson, at any rate.

'The neighbor said she'd found the girl's cat roaming the hallway,' he had been willing to share. 'Went to bring it back in and saw her lying there. We see this kind of thing more than you'd think. Guilt, fear. Depression.'

In other words, thought Dulcie as she speeded toward her meeting, Alyson had tried to kill herself. She remembered when Alyson had first gotten ill. Then people had been murmuring about suicide, but she had dismissed it. Now, well, by some light it must have seemed sensible, especially after one added in heartbreak and betrayal. At least she'd been found in time. Another plus of having a—

Wait. Dulcie stopped again, to muttered cursing from the pedestrian behind her. The cat. With all the hubbub of the police and the EMTs, where was the little marmalade now? Surely, the neighbor would have taken her into her own unit. Though with the shock of finding Alyson – and then the police and the ambulance . . . It was too easy to imagine the kitten being overlooked and forgotten in all the brouhaha. And now? Might she be wandering the halls? Or, worse, have managed to get out of the building and on to that busy street?

The bells marking the hour began to chime, each toll driving home Dulcie's promise to be responsible. To focus on work. To do what she should. She ducked her head, as if she could avoid thoughts of that kitten, and dug her hands into her pocket – where they hit something hard. Alyson's key. She didn't need more than that.

'You think I'm doing the right thing. Don't you, Mr Grey?' she whispered to the air as she turned and trotted back down toward the river, the honking of a startled driver the only response.

Fighting off the horrible suspicion that his silence meant he disapproved, Dulcie hurried toward Alyson's building, all the while running through possible scenarios in her mind. If the kitten were nowhere to be found, she would knock on doors. Alert the neighbors. If none of them were around – it seemed like the kind of building where the tenants had office jobs – she could probably use the key to check out the basement and any utility rooms. If she had to, she'd start searching outside. House cats tended to hide when they got out, she knew, and that bode well. Better to think of that little marmalade huddled under a shrub than racing into traffic. Unless she was spooked by the noise of ambulances and police pulling up, sirens wailing.

'Please, Mr Grey,' Dulcie whispered. 'Watch out for the kitten.' Again, she got no response, but she felt better for having asked.

She was nearly at the building when her phone buzzed again, and Dulcie decided to ignore it. If it were Thorpe, she had no good excuse. She was blowing off a departmental meeting on what he would consider a wild goose chase. If it were one of her friends, sharing whatever news had been broken in the last ten minutes, well, she would deal with it later. As she pulled open the lobby door, she felt the buzzing begin again. But there was nobody in the lobby to turn toward her and ask why her bag was humming like an angry bee. And so, using Alyson's key, she unlocked the main door and strode toward the elevator, doing her best not to think about what might be going on in the little clapboard and focusing instead on what she might find up on the tenth floor.

'Hello?' Dulcie knocked, wondering if perhaps that helpful neighbor might still be there. The door to Alyson's apartment was closed but unlocked when she got there, and simply walking in seemed presumptuous. 'Anyone there?' she called, after opening the door a crack.

'Mew.'

Dulcie looked down to see a white paw reaching around the door, one blue eye peering upward.

'Oh, thank God!' Dulcie sank to her knees and scooped up the kitten. 'I'm so glad.'

The kitten purred and kneaded Dulcie's shoulder as she carried her through the living room, past an overturned chair. The sofa she had comforted Alyson on had been shoved out of the way, as was the coffee table, its fashion magazines spilled on the floor and trampled. Dulcie averted her eyes from the mess – that large boot print had to be from an EMT – and continued on to the kitchen. At least there had been no blood or vomit. At least, she recalled, Alyson had been found in time.

'Let's get you fixed up,' she said to the kitten, as much to calm herself as to communicate with the little beast. 'I'm glad someone made sure you were safe inside, but I bet you haven't been fed.'

She looked around. No, the dish on the floor was empty except for a dry crust that looked particularly unappetizing. The counter was empty, too, except for a plate of cookies. Oatmeal raisin, by the look of them, and one already broken into pieces.

'You first, kitten,' said Dulcie, as she opened the cabinet and located both an appropriate dish and a can of food. 'Here, this is better.'

She replaced the dirty dish with a full one, taking the crusty one to the sink to wash. It was the work of moments, and the least she could do. But if she was going to help clean up, surely no one would blame her if . . . She propped the wet dish up to dry as her fingers strayed over to those cookies.

'Good, huh? Looks like you were a hungry girl.' Dulcie had turned to watch the kitten eat, but as she spoke, she savored the subtle spice of the cookie. Cinnamon and allspice, she thought, the classic pumpkin pie mixture playing up the fruitiness of the raisins. Maybe something more. She broke off another piece, curious to see if she could identify the flavor and, instead, found a note tucked under the plate: *Sorry for your loss*, it read in tight, even cursive.

How odd, Dulcie thought, as she nibbled another fragment. The cookies must have come from a close friend, someone who knew Alyson's secret. And yet that note looked so formal, its neat script was so familiar.

'*Dulcie . . .*' A sound like a growl made her stand up straight, dropping the cookie back on to the plate.

'Was that you?' Dulcie looked down at the kitten, who paused to glance up, but then returned to eating. 'Mr Grey?' She scanned the room before catching herself. She should know better than to try to see her feline visitor while he spoke. But as she did, she became aware of another sound – a soft presence, like the shuffling of paper in the next room.

'Hello?' She stepped carefully by the kitten, aware as she did so that she had left the door unlocked behind her. 'Is anyone there?'

Following the noise, Dulcie stepped back into the living room. From here she could see into the bedroom, where a woman was crouched over a waste basket, pouring out its contents into a larger garbage bag.

'Oh, you scared me.' Dulcie exhaled. It had to be a maid, going about her rounds and probably unaware of the emergency that had removed the tenant. None of her friends had a cleaning service. Then again, none of her friends lived in a place like this. 'I didn't hear you in there,' she said. 'You must have been in the bathroom when I came in.'

'No, I heard you.' The woman stood, bag in hand. 'I was wondering when you'd show up.'

She turned, and Dulcie found herself face to face with Polly Fenderby.

FORTY-FIVE

'Mrs Fenderby!' Dulcie stepped back in surprise, bumping into the door frame.

'Dulcie, isn't it?' The widow stood, still holding the trash bag.

'Yes.' Dulcie stepped back to let the other woman pass. 'Dulcie Schwartz. I'm tutoring Alyson.'

'I bet you are,' said the widow. At least, that's what Dulcie thought she heard. The other woman had gone into the kitchen and was busying herself emptying the kitchen waste basket into her bag.

'Excuse me?' Dulcie tagged along. The widow appeared to be poking through the trash, even as she shook it into her bag. 'May I help you?'

'I believe you already have,' she said.

'Oh, you mean cleaning the dish? That was nothing.' Dulcie shifted awkwardly from one foot to the other. 'I just came to check on Alyson's cat, and so I fed her.'

'Her cat?' The woman asked, her voice sounding strangely flat.

'Yes.' Dulcie felt a chill and began to look around. Something about the woman's tone – though, surely, the little marmalade was still on the premises. 'You didn't see her when you came in. Did you?'

'Why no.' The voice cool.

'She can't have gotten out.' Dulcie turned back toward the living room. 'Penny! Penny!'

'Why are you calling her that?' Dulcie stood and turned, in time to see the widow dump the plate of cookies in her trash bag.

'Wait.' Dulcie reached out, not understanding. 'Those were good cookies.'

'You tasted them?' The widow paused.

'Well, yes.' Dulcie admitted. 'Just a bit.'

'I made them,' said the widow turning back to her task. The plate followed the cookies into the bag. Only when the widow began to spray cleanser on the counter did Dulcie realize that she was wearing plastic gloves.

'You made the cookies?' Dulcie knew she sounded like an idiot. Only, none of this was making sense. 'And you're here cleaning? You and Alyson were friends?'

'Oh, I wouldn't say that.' The widow turned and fixed her with a piercing glare. 'Not at all.'

'But why . . .' Dulcie stopped, a horrible suspicion beginning to emerge. 'What are you looking for, Mrs Fenderby?'

'Why did you call that cat Penny?' the widow countered. 'I let her out on the balcony, by the way.'

'You – what?' Dulcie turned and raced toward the balcony. The sliding glass door was ajar, and she pushed it open. The kitten was nowhere to be seen. 'Penny!' Dulcie called, desperate. Steeling herself, she looked down – and saw nothing. Nothing but the dark green of shrubbery. Surely, if the kitten had tumbled from the edge, those bushes would have broken her fall. 'Penny!' she called again, heart racing.

'Feeling a little woozy?' The widow was behind her, and she whirled around. A mistake. The wave of dizziness that hit her made her grab at the railing.

'I've been— I was ill,' she explained. 'And the height.' Dulcie took a deep breath, hoping to dismiss the queasiness. 'You didn't leave her out here. Did you?'

The woman standing in the opened doorway simply smiled.

'Penny?' Dulcie turned and had to close her eyes as another wave of nausea swept over her.

'Pretty Penny.' The voice behind her took on a sing-song quality. 'She was his latest, but I was the original.'

'Penny.' Dulcie made herself turn. Made herself open her eyes. 'That's you – Polly, Penelope. Penny. I forgot you were one of his students originally.'

'I was his *wife*.' She spit out the last word, and Dulcie stepped back against the railing. That's when she saw the knife in Polly Fenderby's gloved hand.

FORTY-SIX

If she weren't so dizzy, it would all make sense. The knife – and the poppy-seed lemon loaf Dulcie had sliced with it only two days before. The woman – a wife, a former student. The sickness that made her grab the low railing at her back.

'The cake . . .' The nausea subsided, only to be followed by a cold sweat as Dulcie realized what was happening. 'You poisoned it. That's why I got sick. Why Alyson fainted.'

Polly Fenderby was smiling again as she took a step forward. 'That will teach both of you to help yourselves to others' treats.'

'Others?' It must be the sickness. Dulcie couldn't make sense of any of this.

'That wasn't for her. That was never for her.' Another step, the knife raised. '*She* took it. I gave him everything.'

Dulcie closed her eyes again. Fenderby's history of sickness. The devoted wife who cared for him. It was – no, it was worse than any novel she had read. And then it hit her: Polly Fenderby had signed her work. 'The note,' she said, her voice a croak. 'In the foil wrapper. That's why I thought . . . the kitten.'

'He was done with her, you know.' Polly Fenderby sounded so sure. So sane. 'I could tell I was his little flower, his Penny again. His pretty Penny, only they wouldn't let up. She and that other girl – the redhead – she wanted it all.'

'No.' Dulcie was sweating. She was sick, but the certainty steadied her more than the railing cold against her back. 'No, Alyson didn't take your cake. Fenderby gave it to her. He didn't want it. Maybe he figured it out – all the treats, all the illness. Maybe he thought that his paunch was holding him back, stopping him from getting . . .' She broke off to catch her breath.

'Only he didn't want anything from you. Not any more.'

She tried to swallow. Her mouth was filling with saliva, but her throat felt swollen. Numb. 'He told you. That was the yelling Tom heard, even if he couldn't hear well enough to make out the words. You were the guest visitor Thomas Griddlehaus didn't see. But how . . .'

She paused, her breathing labored, still stymied by one question.

'You saw her leave that morning. She must have been upset. Crying. You knew he was done with her.' Dulcie pieced it together, her voice barely a whisper. 'And nobody thought . . . the guard must have waved you in, just like he waved me . . .' Dulcie looked up at the widow. The former student. The familiar face fading with time. 'The cops will figure it out, you know. They won't just look at the card reader. They're talking to the guards. They'll find out you were there. They might have already.'

'Why should they when they have a confession?' Polly Fenderby's voice had sunk to a hiss. 'When the murderer has already OD'd out of guilt?'

'But she's alive.' Dulcie had to force her eyes open. She leaned back on the railing, doing her best to fight the dizziness. The fatigue. 'The neighbor found her in time. And I'll tell them the truth.'

'You're another drug-addled student.' The widow's voice sounded like it was coming from very far away. 'On academic probation, unable to complete her dissertation. Another suicide.'

'The cookies.' Dulcie fought to stay awake.

'What cookies?' That voice, right in her ear. 'There are no cookies.' The clammy feel of a yellow plastic glove on her shoulder. The blade at her throat. The railing cold through her shirt. She was so dizzy.

'*Dulcie!*' Mr Grey calling her. The prick of claws like a slap on her face. Urging her to wake. To rouse. To move.

She couldn't.

'Look what I found!' A voice from the past. She had been calling to Suze, fishing out a wet, bedraggled stray. His long grey fur plastered to his shivering body. 'Look at this little girl.'

No, that was wrong. Not a female . . .

'What's going on?' Polly Fenderby stepped away, and Dulcie fell forward – nearly colliding with the grey-haired neighbor who stood at the sliding door. Holding the marmalade kitten. 'Are you all right?'

'She's fine.' Polly Fenderby already had her arms up to urge the neighbor off the deck – out of the apartment.

'Mrow!' With a panicked howl, the kitten pulled herself free, climbing up the neighbor's shoulder and leaping back into the apartment only to come to a skittering halt as the door opened inward to reveal a large, lumpy figure.

'Detective Rogovoy!' Dulcie wasn't sure if she said the words or only thought them, as she fell forward on to her knees. What she did know was that the hands reaching for her, helping her into the apartment and on to the couch, were not gloved.

'Call for an ambulance.' The detective's ordinarily gruff voice was high-pitched and tight.

'Ma'am.' Another man speaking somewhere behind him. 'You'll have to come with me, ma'am.'

'Dulcie, hang in there.' The voice was gruff, but comforting, and Dulcie smiled as she drifted off, the warm purr of the kitten by her side.

FORTY-SEVEN

'**H**is wife was poisoning him?' Chris was having trouble taking it all in. 'She had been poisoning him all along?'

'Yes, Chris.' Dulcie lay back and closed her eyes. She'd been over this several times already, and still Chris found it hard to accept.

Mina hadn't been as incredulous. She'd come by as soon as visitors were allowed, joining Chris at Dulcie's bedside. But she and Dulcie had quickly moved on from the Fenderbys' saga to what Dulcie called her 'real news' – her find in the Mildon. The altered page and all that it implied.

'*My daughter,*' Mina had breathed the words back to her.
'Yes,' she had said. 'That was what I thought I saw, too. So,
she was writing about her own life – about a child of her own.'
They had clasped hands then, both excited about the possibility
of finally tracing the lineage of the author they both loved.

Mina had left with the promise that she'd wait. The two of
them would go back to the Mildon as soon as Dulcie was
released – as soon as she'd confirmed Professor Showalter on
her committee. This was a project they would work on together,
a work that concerned all three.

Chris, however, was still caught up in the more recent affair.
That Fenderby had been murdered by his wife after years of
slow poisoning wasn't something his logical mind could easily
encompass.

Dulcie had had time to figure it all out, lying here in the
health services. 'I think she would poison him,' she explained.
'She used the plants from her garden, and then nursed him
back to health. Maybe that kept him dependent and grateful,
or maybe it was simply a way for her to express her anger
over all his affairs. About all the money he spent, and the risks
he took with his livelihood – their livelihood.'

'You'd think he'd have suspected.' Chris sounded doubtful,
but Dulcie shook her head. She'd slept most of yesterday and
had spent this morning puzzling out what had happened. Her
own blood tests had showed the presence of scillitoxin and
lycorine, found in daffodil bulbs.

'I don't think so. I don't think he thought much about her
at all any more,' she said, struggling to sit up. 'I don't think
he'd have given the poppy-seed cake to Alyson if he had any
qualms.' She leaned over to address Chris, who had jumped
up to examine the controls for adjusting the bed. 'He was
simply discarding it, like he discarded her affection. Only, she
found out.'

'And if she wouldn't play along . . .' Chris didn't have to
finish the thought. His tone said it all, even facing away from
her as he fetched the extra pillows from the closet.

In that moment, a terrible thought came to Dulcie. 'Chris,
it was my fault,' she said.

He turned, but before he could argue, she explained. 'I went to talk to him. I saw Polly. She thought that I was the student who had sued him – the reason the university had Rogovoy put a task force together. I bet that's why she went back to confront him after Alyson and Griddlehaus left. I bet that's why she killed him.'

'You can't know that, Dulce.' Her boyfriend's voice was sad.

'The horrible part is that he probably was ending his affair with Alyson.' Dulcie leaned forward to allow him to fit the pillow behind her, as she thought about the tragedy of it all. 'Especially with Rogovoy's team investigating him. With the threat of censure or even being put on leave, it was all more motivation for him to move on. Or move back, really. He would have gone back to Polly.'

'Yeah, but there would have been someone else. If not here, then at some other college. Someplace would've taken him, and he'd have kept on preying on his students. There'd be another victim.' Something in Chris's voice made Dulcie look up at him. 'There always is with guys like that.'

'Maybe.' She took his hand. 'I'm afraid I wouldn't know.'

When Trista came by a little later, Chris excused himself to seek out some breakfast.

'Now that nobody's worried about her, they're just kind of ignoring her,' he said to their friend, as he ceded the guest chair. 'I'll see if I can find anyone to talk about releasing her. Might take me a while, though.'

'He's a sweetheart.' Trista watched him go, her voice uncharacteristically soft. 'He knows. Doesn't he?'

'Some of it,' acknowledged Dulcie as the slight blonde pulled her chair closer. 'Not all.'

The two sat in silence for a moment, while Trista looked at everything but her friend's face. Finally, Dulcie reached for her hand. 'Tris, why didn't you tell me? You could have, you know.'

'Yeah, I know.' Trista shook her head without raising it. Even her nose ring looked more subdued today. 'I just felt so stupid.'

'You aren't,' said her friend with emphasis, holding her

hand tightly. 'You weren't. You were vulnerable, and he was an experienced predator.'

'Experienced manipulator, that's for sure.' Trista didn't pull back, not much. But her eyes were still lowered, as if the hem of the bed sheet were the most fascinating thing in the world. Sensing that her friend was gathering her courage, Dulcie waited, and the two sat in silence for another minute.

'At first, you know, I was flattered.' Trista let out an exhalation that was half laugh, half sigh. 'Can you believe it? God, I was stupid. It was the beginning of the year – last fall. I'd been struggling. Things with Jerry were strained, and it's so weird to not be a degree candidate any more. I have the post doc, but that ends next year and if I don't find . . .' Her voice trailed off.

'Anyway, I'd been looking. Talking to people who could recommend me. Pull some strings. You know, and Fenderby had been out for a few weeks – one of those "attacks" he had – and then when he came back, he seemed to really take an interest. Actually gave me some work, helping him catch up, drawing some connections between his area – the political writings – and the fiction of the time. I mean, I know that's your area, Dulce, but, well, I was grateful for the work. Of course, he suggested that I not tell you. That I not tell anyone exactly what I was doing for him.' Another sigh. 'I was so gullible.'

'He played up the sickness, too.' She shook her head, remembering. 'He told me how he'd felt so weak and vulnerable. How his spirits were so low, and how he really looked forward to our meetings as proof that he was still competent.' Another laugh.

'He saw right through me. If he'd come on tough or smooth or . . . I don't know, if he'd tried to wow me, I'd have kicked him to the curb. I'm used to guys like that. But here he was, telling me how low he felt. How he relied on me to cheer him up, at the same time, isolating me. The next thing I knew, he was telling me that I helped him more than his wife ever had. That he loved me. He said our meetings were the one bright spot in his day.'

'You were his bright, shiny penny.' Dulcie kept her voice soft.

Still, Trista heard her. 'Yeah, that's what he said. And then he tried to kiss me. And I—' She broke off and shook her head.

'You don't have to go on,' Dulcie reassured her.

'No, I do.' Trista's voice was sounding stronger. 'I was just so shocked. I guess I shouldn't have been, but at the time . . . I felt guilty. I let him.'

She fell silent. 'Afterward, I felt sick. And I got angry. I told him I was going to report him. I was gathering my papers, my books, and he started yelling at me. I was the one who had come on to him. I was trying to use him to get a position, a recommendation. *I* had manipulated *him*.'

She looked Dulcie squarely in the eye now. 'I believed him, Dulcie. I blamed myself, and I kept quiet. I stopped working for him, but that was it. And by the time I realized how he'd set me up, I vowed I'd never let that happen to anyone else. I was so furious! That's when I started going to the counseling center. And then Mina came in for a support group, and I found out what he'd tried with her.

'And so when Mina told me what she'd found – her discovery in the Mildon – I was so proud of her. She wasn't scared of him. She wasn't going to be chased out of the library. Only, I ran into him the next day, and I–I couldn't resist.'

Trista's voice dropped down again. 'I told him. Not in detail, but that she had found something in the Mildon. That no matter what he thought, he couldn't break her. Couldn't break any of us. I guess I envied her. She said no. She refused him, and she was on her way to doing better work than he ever would – in his field, too. I wanted to hurt him, but I ended up hurting her – and you too.

'You know Mina came to see me that morning. She left the library because I was having a panic attack.' Trista looked up at Dulcie, who could only nod. 'She's a peer counselor with the center. That's why she wouldn't tell anybody, though I'd have come forward if things got serious. But we worried you, I know, and I'm sorry. If she had been there – at her carrel . . . Who knows? Maybe his wife wouldn't have gone back.'

Dulcie shook her head. 'Or maybe she'd have attacked Mina,' she said. 'But Fenderby's career was over. The task force was on to him. The evidence was piling up. He might have negotiated with the university to keep things quiet – that's how the university prefers it too – but they were maneuvering him out. I bet that's why he wanted to be on my committee.' She laughed, a rather humorless chuckle. 'That's what it was, I think – the fear of losing the job, the status, and the money – that finally pushed his wife over the edge. I wonder what will happen to her?'

Dulcie thought back to that morning, only two days before. She'd been so sick, the memory was hazy. Still, she shivered.

'I kind of feel bad for her,' Trista admitted. 'The affairs, and all the money he was spending on Alyson.'

Dulcie nodded, remembering. The little garden had been so beautiful and lush. And so much smaller than the ones in the photos. 'Still . . .'

The friends fell silent at that, but it was a companionable quiet. And when Chris reappeared – with a paper bag imprinted with a familiar logo – Trista popped up with an alacrity she'd been lacking before.

'You went to La Patisserie?' She reached for the bag. 'Here, you can sit.'

'No, really.' Chris motioned her back and handed over the goodies. 'I'll get another chair.' He handed her the bag while he went to hunt one down.

'They're still warm.' Trista poked around. 'Dulcie, you up for a sweet?'

'As long as it's not oatmeal raisin,' her friend said with a smile.

'I guess I should have brought coffee.' Dulcie looked up at the familiar voice. Nancy Pruitt was standing in the doorway, closely flanked by Martin Thorpe.

'Nancy!' Dulcie beamed – and then caught herself. 'And, uh, Mr Thorpe.'

'Ms Schwartz.' He ducked his head in acknowledgment and followed the secretary into the room. Trista had bounced up to offer Nancy her seat, but the secretary ushered her back down as Thorpe cleared his throat. 'I come bearing good tidings,' he said.

'Oh?' Dulcie chewed her pastry. She was curious, but a fresh raspberry Danish was not to be wasted.

'You are officially off academic probation,' Thorpe said. 'I would have come by to tell you yesterday, but we were all quite busy.'

'I bet.' Dulcie took another bite. The way her adviser was standing there made her suspect he had more to say.

'Martin.' Nancy gave her colleague a pointed look. Dulcie, who had never heard the secretary address the acting department head so informally, stopped eating.

'Yes, well, what with all the brouhaha, it came to our attention that you had missed the departmental meeting,' said Thorpe. 'And therefore you missed a major announcement.'

Dulcie swallowed, the last bit of pastry dry in her throat. 'Yes?'

'I should begin with an apology,' he said. 'I never should have let Roland Fenderby join your committee so late in the game.'

He looked over at Nancy, who nodded encouragement. 'You see,' he continued. 'Roland was threatening me. My standing in the department.' He cleared his throat. 'He had become aware of a certain impropriety – an irregularity in departmental relations . . .'

'Martin and I have been dating.' Nancy rescued him. 'And while we are certainly both adults, I am, strictly speaking, a member of the support staff.'

'Making me liable for censure under the university harassment rules,' finished Thorpe. He had dropped his gaze and colored faintly, and Dulcie was seized by a horrible thought. Everybody in the department knew of the relationship, and it was so far from what Fenderby himself had been guilty of. If because of that man, the department lost Thorpe, or, worse, Nancy . . .

'Oh no,' she burst out. 'Don't say it!'

'Now, Dulcie.' Nancy's voice was gentle but stern. 'This is a good thing.'

Dulcie looked up at her, and then turned to Trista, who was beaming. 'It is?' she asked, her voice trembling.

'It is for me,' Thorpe piped up. 'Once Ms Pruitt – I mean,

Nancy – found out what was going on, she spoke up right away.'

'I knew Martin would never consciously sabotage you, Dulcie,' said the motherly secretary. 'And therefore I knew there was something else at work. Some pressure being applied.'

She turned to Thorpe and waited.

'Nancy has done me the honor of saying she will be my wife,' said Thorpe, coloring further. 'She spoke with her colleagues in human resources, and there are no sanctions against married couples working together.'

'Problem solved,' said Nancy, with a grin.

'Wow.' Dulcie forgot all about her pastry. 'Congratulations, you two.' She turned to Trista. 'You knew?'

'Yeah, they announced it at the meeting.' Her friend was beaming. 'We all cheered. I'm sorry, I forgot you didn't know.'

'We had other things to talk about.'

'Did I miss anything?' Chris reappeared, with a chair. 'Oh,' he said, looking around. 'I should have gotten more Danish.'

Nancy and her fiancé – it was going to take Dulcie a while to get used to thinking of him like that – left soon after, and Trista not long after that.

'Did you two get a chance to talk?' Chris asked, his voice soft.

'Yeah.' Dulcie nodded. 'Did you know?'

'I knew something was up,' he said. 'I figured you two needed some time.'

'You're a good man, Chris Sorenson,' said Dulcie taking his hand. 'I hope she and Jerry . . .'

He nodded. 'They've been together forever. He's trying to help her.'

'We will, too,' she said, and looked around. 'When do you think they'll spring me?'

'Soon, I hope. Esmé misses you. Oh!' He jumped up. 'I was supposed to tell the doctor when your visitors had left. Give me a minute to find her.'

Dulcie watched him go, marveling at all the changes. Thorpe and Nancy getting married. Trista coming to terms with her vulnerability. Dulcie herself nearing the end of her dissertation. They were all growing up, she realized, as she lay back on the elevated bed. All moving on. She took in the empty room, the faint sounds of people and machines, off in the distance. The rare moment of quiet, of solitude. Did this mean . . . she didn't dare voice the question.

'*Growing up doesn't mean losing those you love.*' The whirr of machinery gave way to a soft voice, as the room filled with a rumble like a purr. '*Even when we pass,*' said the voice, as warm as fur. '*The love remains.*'

ACKNOWLEDGMENTS

As always, there are so many who deserve my thanks: the eagle-eyed Karen Schlosberg, Lisa Susser, Brett Milano, Colleen Mohyde, and Jon S. Garelick all read multiple versions, and John McDonough kept me free of illegal searches. All errors are despite their care. Heartfelt thanks as well to Frank Garelick, Lisa Jones, and Sophie Garelick, who have encouraged and supported me. All at Severn House, who have been an author's dream. Thanks, as well, to Linda Grulke, for your generosity, and, as always, to my dear Jon, without whom . . .